Crypt & Claw

Drechenaux

Table of Contents

Chapter One

The Mayor's Party

An intoxicating breeze laden with soft poetic notes carried the traces of a soothing symphony throughout the grounds in front of the major. The sky was cloudless - with the crescent moon shining radiantly alongside the stars like a queen surrounded by her handmaidens.

"Good thing it's not a full moon tonight," Raphael murmured as he and his father, Abraham, made their way down the cobblestone steps leading to the manor.

"If it were a full moon," Abraham answered, his voice low but clear as day, "they wouldn't have dared hold this event on this night. This isn't like the old days, back when they thought us little better than wild dogs. A new era is upon us."

Raphael had to consciously smooth over the expression on his face so that it was more neutral. He had heard this speech from his father many times, yet the words still sent a thrill of excitement through him. But he couldn't walk into the party grinning like a slackjawed idiot.

"Now, it's our era," Abraham continued, lowering his voice further. "The old guard is going to vanish, and soon we will take over. They know it. They may turn up their noses at us, pretending they are still untouchable in their high castles and ivory towers. But mark my words, deep down, they know their time is up."

Abraham spoke the last words so softly only a Lycan standing right next to him like Raphael would've heard, a necessary precaution. Even if that was how he felt deep in his heart, Abraham knew better than to trumpet it throughout the land.

"It's not like we're at war with them anymore, Father," Raphael said.

"That may be, and trust me, I don't want fighting either," Abraham replied. "But only a fool puts away their weapons when they're no longer needed. The point I was trying to make is that they know we are important. That's why they couldn't have this on the night of a full moon."

Raphael nodded. His father always referred to the vampires as 'them.'. The dinner party tonight was to celebrate the appointment of the new mayor.

Necropolis had a long history spanning over ten thousand years and had transitioned from an autocracy to a representative republic around three thousand years ago. The shifting political winds were made all the more evident by this occasion - for the first time, a human had been elected mayor.

The mayor's manor was almost as radiant as the moon; standing five stories tall. It is said that money talks, in which case this manor was screaming to the high heavens about the deep pockets of its owner.

Raphael had grown up in a rather run-down house before his father had catapulted their way up the social ladder. He always felt slightly disconcerted walking into any place he thought was "too fancy" which lately described most of the places he accompanied his father to.

Raphael shrunk as they walked inside. Something deep within him screamed that he didn't belong. His heart began to pound as if he was constantly worried someone would suddenly point a finger and cry out, "What is this street urchin doing here?" He felt far more at ease in the warehouses where he and his friends hung out. Here, he felt like a prey animal caught in a strange and bizarre trap.

Unconsciously, Raphael stepped closer to his father, a childish instinct to hide behind the man almost overcoming him.

This did not escape Abraham's notice. He put a reassuring hand on his son's shoulder. "Don't worry. Remember, you're *my* son. There is nothing they can do to touch you. We're just here to smile, shake a few hands, and let the mayor know we congratulate him regarding his victory. No need to be so uptight or worried."

Raphael swallowed and nodded. Even if he felt uncomfortable, he knew that it was important for his father's image that he stand beside him. His father had sacrificed much to better their family's standing. To don this stuffy suit and attend an even stuffier party was insignificant by comparison.

The interior of the manor was like how he'd imagined a king's palace to be like during his younger days. It only made the disconcerting feeling all the stronger. Still, he did exactly as his father asked, wandering around and offering the practiced smile he had worked on to the crowd at the party. He knew his genuine, toothy grin often unnerved people; making them feel he was about to jump out and pounce upon them. That was why he had spent hours in front of a mirror perfecting this fake but far more affable one.

"So pleased to meet you," he said in a soft tone what felt like a thousand times over, conducting himself exactly as he should.

They soon found Mayor Corvin, an elderly human in his fifties with a corona of gray hair surrounding a shiny bald spot that reflected the light from the crystal chandeliers above. He smelled of old furniture and sweat even on this cool night - he might be putting on a brave front but there were very few things that could fool a werewolf's nose.

It did make Raphael feel slightly better knowing that he wasn't the only

5

person who was stressed out by the party.

"Mayor Corvin, quite a party you've decided to host here," Abraham said, shaking the man's hand. "We must thank you again for your invitation."

"No, no, the pleasure is all mine to have you here," Mayor Corvin replied. Though he looked unassuming, he possessed a commanding presence, a charisma that put people at ease so long as they couldn't read him too deeply and notice the subtle ticks that gave his anxiety away.

"And I assume this is your son?" Mayor Corvin asked, turning towards Raphael.

"Indeed, it's a pleasure to meet you, sir," Raphael said, giving the man a quick, non-threatening smile.

"The pleasure is all mine. Why, you look exactly like your father!"

Raphael noticed Mayor Corvin had an ability to make you feel important, as if he was hanging on to your every word while you were speaking to him.

"He's a chip off the old block," Abraham chuckled, slapping Raphael gently on the shoulder. Gentle by werewolf standards, that is. It carried enough force to dislocate a human collarbone. Then again, humans were quite fragile by the standards of both werewolves and vampires. Raphael had learned that the hard way after breaking three human children's arms while playing around when he had been younger.

His father and Mayor Corvin began talking about finance and trade - dry topics that Raphael struggled to follow for more than two minutes, despite their relevance to his future. He nodded appropriately at various intervals, figuring that he could at least try to look deeply interested.

It was easy enough to lose track of the conversation because something far more enthralling soon caught his eye. A sudden commotion spread among the partygoers as they all turned toward the front door. Whoever was entering was clearly important.

A throng of guests surrounded them, though they also weirdly kept their distance from the people in question as if they wanted to be close but not too close. They obscured his line of sight, but the guests parted soon enough.

Raphael's breath caught in his chest as he caught a glimpse of her.

She was absolutely *gorgeous*.

Her hair was like spun silver, shining in the candlelight, a tiara studded with rubies crowning her head. Raphael instinctively knew the tiara was made of silver as glancing at it made something deep within him shudder in fear, yet he had to admit that it blended perfectly with her hair with the way it shined like a halo atop her head under the warm candlelight. The rubies matched the deep crimson color of her eyes and earrings. Her face was delicate and smooth, like that of a porcelain doll, and her skin was as pale as freshly fallen snow. When she unleashed her own practiced smile, her fangs flashed, confirming what manner of creature she was. Her deep blue dress, the color of sapphires, contrasted sharply with the red of her accessories and the softness of her pale skin, only enhancing her beauty. Even from this distance, Raphael caught the

6

delicate scent of crushed pine needles.

He realized he had seen her before when he turned his gaze to the lady beside her. He recognized Victoria Carpathia, the head of a powerful vampire family. She greatly resembled the first girl in question although she wore a flowing golden gown instead. Raphael quickly put two and two together: the lady must be Victoria's daughter, Liliana.

***

Liliana's eyes scanned the party as she stayed close to her mother. She valued her personal space, and tonight, the humans present were a bit too accustomed to breaking bread with vampires to instinctively keep their distance as many normal humans did. She began to miss the times when they recoiled at her presence.

These people wanted to stay away from them, but they were masking their unease. The signs were more subtle, but present nonetheless - a trembling hand while holding a glass of wine, a slight increase in their heart rhythm, or a bead of sweat sliding down their neck gave their unease away. But they still pushed on forward despite their instinctual apprehension.

Liliana had not been looking forward to this night, but her mother insisted it was crucial for the Carpathian family. The mayor could not be ignored, and they could not afford the whispers that the vampires had lost their authority and were not invited to this party.

Liliana personally thought that it was more likely that people would think they thought they were too high-class to be there in case they didn't show up, but her mother had a point. The time during which they could be considered the city's unchallenged rulers had long since passed. A new age had dawned on Necropolis, an age in which humans were no longer livestock but actual citizens.

Liliana did not underestimate them; they may have been weak individually but they were a potent force when united. She vividly remembered the screams, the shouting, and seeing the line of torches moving down the street from glancing out the castle window *that night* while trembling in fear...

These memories were thankfully interrupted as her mother led her to the mayor.

"Mayor Corvin, what a lovely party you've arranged for," Victoria said.

Liliana thought the party was a bit too ostentatious - the elegance was forced, speaking of someone trying too hard to compensate for their lack of a proper heritage in the city. No wonder Mayor Corvin was so eager to court the favor of the Carpathian family. He had the money, but he needed the backing of history and the approval of the city's elites to maintain power.

"The pleasure is all mine to see you and your lovely daughter tonight," Mayor Corvin said, beaming.

Victoria almost completely disregarded the compliment, her eyes locking instead onto a man nearby: Abraham Cain.

7

When her mother's and Abraham's eyes locked, silence dropped like a hammer atop the party. The intensity of their gazes spoke of an animosity that could not be expressed through mere words. Alone in some forest, they would undoubtedly be at each other's throats if they were to cross paths. But the days of open warfare were long gone, things could no longer be decided through brute strength.

The tension was palpable enough that many of the humans stopped what they were doing to turn and stare at the two of them. Some of them began inching away.. Then, as abruptly as it began, the pressure vanished.

"How lovely to see that you are in good health, Lady Victoria," Abraham said with a small, toothy smile.

"And how good to see that you are well," Victoria answered, her gentle tone matching his. The silent war was over - at least for tonight.

Raphael noticed that his father's left fist was clenched behind his back, the only sign of his repressed rage. Liliana, likewise, noticed the way her mother tapped her right foot rhythmically on the ground a bit too fast.

It was only when the mood relaxed that Liliana turned her attention to the man beside Abraham. She had definitely seen him before, though it had only been a passing glimpse. She did not know his name.

He was not as imposing as she would have imagined a werewolf to be. When one spoke of werewolves, the thought of a hulking monster towering like a mountain came to mind. This man was clearly strong - her eyes could easily make out his toned muscles beneath his tuxedo so there was no doubt about that - but there was an awkwardness about him, a subtle hint that he didn't quite belong in the fine suit. It was almost endearing, like seeing a child trying to wear their parent's clothes.

His hair was neatly combed, a pale blonde that reminded her of the grain fields lit up by the sunrise at her uncle's estate. His eyes were a soft shade of brown, almost like freshly tilled soil. If she had been asked before this moment, she would have said that she thought that brown eyes were the most boring color of all. Up until this moment that is; when she felt like she was sinking into brown irises, which beckoned to her the earth's soft embrace. He smelled like an open field during springtime.

While Raphael's father and Liliana's mother stared at each other with barely concealed ferocity, even now; he stared at Liliana with an expression of innocence and confusion. For a moment, the practiced mask on her face fell as their eyes locked.

Both momentarily forgot about their parents.

To Raphael, her eyes were two deep pools of blood that invited him for a swim. His werewolf heart, which ordinarily beat at three times the rate of an ordinary human's, skipped a beat entirely.

To Liliana, his hair felt like a welcoming field, awaiting her embrace. Her vampiric heart, dead and silent most of the time, beat twice.

The two of them didn't know what they were feeling, only that they both wished to approach the other. To understand the strange feelings that

8

were bubbling inside of them.

The world seemed to stand still for a moment; a bubble forming where it was just the two of them. And then, the bubble popped, snapping both of them back to reality.

"This is my son, Raphael," Abraham said, his voice flat and devoid of emotion or tone.

"And this is my daughter, Liliana," Victoria replied in much the same manner.

With a few more strained greetings from the mayor, Liliana and Raphael were separated, taken towards their respective camps within the party alongside their parents.

Mayor Corvin, turning away, took out a handkerchief and wiped the beads of sweat, which were now quite visible, from his brow. He was balancing on the precipice of a ledge - one wrong move, and he would go tumbling into the abyss.

It's almost more work than it's worth, he thought. But as he glanced around the room, he reminded himself why he was doing this yet again. He was the first human mayor of Necropolis and as such needed as many allies as he could find. To pacify both the werewolves and the vampires at once was to try to get a lion and sheep to get along together in the same room. He had been somewhat successful so far, but he knew that tough choices lay ahead.

Raphael went towards the other werewolves, many of whom like him were more at home leaping through the woods than attending a party. Raphael was like them, in all honesty, but had to present himself a certain way before the humans.

Abraham, noticing Raphael's frantic glances toward the other side of the room, misinterpreted the meaning behind his son's gazes directed at Liliana. "No need to be intimidated by them," he whispered. "That hag's evil eye is only for coping with her loss of influence."

Liliana, likewise, was led to a few low-ranking vampires and their supporters among the humans, who occupied the opposite end of the room. She was forced to courtesy to many who kissed her hand in reverence. She, too, tried to steal glances back at Raphael.

"No need to fear them, dear," her mother whispered. "They look rough, but I know their kind. A few bites of a silver whip, and they're fleeing with their tails between their legs like the dogs they are."

Liliana unconsciously nudged the silver tiara atop her head ever so slightly. Each of its prongs had been sharpened to the point that they were as good as daggers - an unconventional choice for a piece of jewelry, but a welcome one for an implement that could be used as a weapon of last resort.

The party continued well into the night, featuring dancing, a large feast, and dedicated menus for all present: Blood Lilies for the vampires, roasted meats for the werewolves, and everything in between for the humans.

It was well past midnight by the time things finally wrapped up.

Raphael and Abraham Cain exited the party along with eight other werewolves - a mix of Abraham's business contacts and close friends. Their pack set out on foot..

"Dad, everyone else is leaving via carriage. Do you really think we should be walking down the streets like this?" Raphael asked.

"Why are you still afraid of the dark?" Abraham asked, chuckling.

"I'm not afraid of anything. I could run all day if you asked me to," Raphael replied, meaning it sincerely. Running was one of his favorite pastimes. His only objection would be that these restrictive clothes chafed at his powerful body. It would have been even more freeing to run around in their Lycanthrope forms, but that could not be allowed within the confines of the city. It would cause far too much panic.

"I mean, aren't people going to look down on us if we're walking? It makes it look like we can't afford carriages." They cared intensely about their image lately, hence the fine and restrictive suits. But leaving on foot seemed to contradict that image of wealth and power.

"Maybe they will," his father conceded, "but I can't stand being cramped in one of those things. Most of them don't even have windows. No, I'd much rather walk like this. Heck, you can even think of it as a sign of strength. Unlike humans, we don't need six legs to walk around." There was some shared laughter among the werewolves at the common joke that humans (with their horses) needed six legs to get anywhere.

"Alright," Raphael said, loosening the collar on his shirt, the maximum adjustment he was willing to risk. He didn't want to damage the fabric.

On the upside, the night air was cool and fresh.

His rapid metabolism meant the wine's effect wore off quickly. He couldn't help but see Liliana's delicate face before his eyes even after it had worn off. *She's not nearly as fragile as you think*, he reminded himself. She could probably punch through a stone wall; her strength not far beneath his own. *And she probably doesn't like you very much*, he told himself.

His mother had told him that she and Abraham had nearly fallen in love the instant their eyes locked, but that had to be an exaggeration even if it made for a lovely love story. And it could not possibly be what was happening here.

The disdain between vampires and werewolves was, after all, mutual. He thought that she was looking at him with curiosity and even a hint of admiration, but that more likely than not had been him projecting his own feelings onto her he figured.

It was better that he not entertain any such further thoughts as they could only lead to further pain down the road. *Even if she seems kind, she's a monster underneath that fragile facade. She has to be.*

The werewolves had been a part of Necropolis for over five thousand years, yet the vampires still maintained that the Lycans were newcomers and immigrants who should be thankful they were allowed to live there. Essentially the vampires thought of them as not being 'true' residents of Necropolis.

Originally, the werewolves were permitted entry into the city because

10

the empire needed creatures of supernatural strength to work during the daytime - moving stone for castles, hauling large shipments of goods, defending their human livestock from other werewolves, and other assorted tasks. The Lycans functioned as simple muscle-for-hire under the vampire boot.

Several factors had improved their social standing over the centuries: their faster breeding rate compared to vampires, the devastating vampire civil war three thousand years ago which crippled the vampire's numbers, and most importantly the proliferation of humans. The human population exploded after the vampire's numbers dwindled, becoming the majority faction within the city. To survive, they developed their own defenses: garlic, silver coins, and, most effective of all, political organization. The werewolves, having no inherent need for human blood, were considered the 'lesser evil' by most humans and quickly became their allies in this political game.

The math was simple: a victory for the humans was a victory for the werewolves.

Abraham had leveraged his immense strength at the docks along with his own business acumen, moving cargo before eventually forming his own shipping company. Now, he controlled over a fourth of the goods flowing into the city via the docks, amassing a massive fortune that bestowed upon him considerable political influence and made him the de facto face of the werewolf faction.

Everything Abraham did politically was to advance the Lycan's interests - or, failing that, the human's. Raphael sometimes felt it wasn't that his father wanted the werewolves to win so much as he simply wanted the vampires to lose; though if told this Abraham would maintain that the two things were essentially one in the same.

The Lycans were not really going anywhere so much as they were wandering around, swapping stories and enjoying the cool night air.

As the sky above lightened the pack separated. Raphael and Abraham returned to their house near the docks.

Although Abraham had the means to buy a mansion in the wealthier parts of the city, he had instead chosen to live in a more modest home near the docks. Modest was relative though; the house cost more than a human worker would make in a hundred years. Abraham had chosen this location partly to remind himself of his roots and partly to be closer to his business operations. Raphael, rubbing his eyes, followed Abraham into his office.

"I can tell you want to sleep, I know it's late," his father said apologetically.

"It's not a problem," Raphael replied. "It must be important if you want to talk about it after the party, I can tell. And I'm all ears then."

While Raphael's views were not as extreme as his father's, he shared many of his father's concerns. Raphael also wanted to make his father proud and make his own mark on the world. The pressure of filling his father's immense shoes sometimes was enough to make him queasy just thinking about it.

There were times Raphael thought about asking his father for a chance to strike out on his own, to show the world he could earn things without relying on his father's name, but he had a duty to his family. He had to prioritize that above his own desires. He also was aware that striking out on one's own, despite how nice and poetic it might sound, was anything but in practice.

"For now, I just wanted to go over the state of the city with you," Abraham answered. "There are going to be far-reaching changes now with a human as mayor. The humans will be clamoring for a bigger share of the pie. Up until now, they have been dependent upon us for protection, but as they grow, this reliance will diminish."

Raphael nodded affirmatively. "You don't want us to be pushed to the sidelines, right?"

Abraham gave a curt nod. "Humans are fickle creatures with short lifespans and even shorter memories. Once they are in power, they will quickly forget most of what we did for them when they were weak."

"Are you sure father? That sounds rather… cynical," Raphael said. "I couldn't imagine some of my human friends suddenly turning on me… even if they do, what could they do against our strength and speed?"

"I know not all humans think like that," Abraham said, "however, enough will that it could be a problem for us. Our strength can only do so much. And do not underestimate our weakness to silver. I saw a weapons shop owner five streets down from us selling silver-tipped blow darts. How long do you think it will be before they think of silver-tipped crossbows or something even more advanced? The time may soon come where our physical strength will not be able to carry us against them. We will have to rely on our wits to survive." The idea that not everything could be decided through simple contests of brute strength was a concept that the werewolves were often maligned for struggling to understand, even those who lived within the city. His father, though, understood far more than most. Which is why he had succeeded where many others had failed.

"So, you want us to ingratiate ourselves with the humans a bit more?" Raphael asked.

"That is correct, to some extent," Abraham said. "Remember, son: when a blind man regains his eyesight, the first thing he discards is the walking stick that guided him all his life."

"I understand. I already have some ideas regarding what we can do," Raphael said.

"That's a good lad," Abraham said, flashing a smile. "But I need you to remember that we can't be *too* subservient. It's one thing to be friendly with someone, and it's another to be a dog licking their boots clean. We don't want to be the latter."

"I don't think that will be a problem," Raphael said. "I think I have an idea that can show that we are still with the humans, celebrating the prosperity they've gained, and at the same time, also showing our strength."

"Good, but that's enough of that now," Abraham said. "Go get some

12

rest, you've earned it."

Raphael then made the long journey from his father's office back to his bedroom. In their old shack, this trip would have been nothing more than a few strides long. Their new house was so large however, that even though he wasn't fatigued, it still felt like quite an effort to go from one end to the other. The entire place was built with practicality in mind - most walls were bare and only the essentials when it came to furniture were present. His father really wasn't much for pomp and decoration within his own house.

Raphael walked into his room, arguably the most well-decorated room in the house. There were several portraits of him and his late mother lining the walls, and several rows of books - mostly regarding business, but a good chunk dedicated to fiction and world history - beneath the portraits.

Raphael usually looked through his small rock collection before falling asleep as he found it comforting, but this time he simply allowed himself to collapse into bed. His mattress creaked a little; it had been heavily reinforced to bear his weight. It was very easy to tear through one's clothes as a werewolf, and to break furniture as well if one did not mind one's strength. Beds were usually the most unfortunate victims of this, as Lycans would often break them in their sleep. Most Lycans avoided beds entirely for this very reason, opting to sleep atop haystacks, but Raphael had gotten used to this kind of bed.

Despite telling himself that dwelling on such a thing would only end badly - Liliana's face, in all its beautiful glory, floated before his vision before he entered the land of dreams.

***

Liliana and Victoria exited the mayor's manor and entered the pitch-black carriage marked with four crimson lilies, the coat of arms of their branch of the Carpathian family. Liliana cast a glance at the pack of werewolves walking away, her eyes seeing clear as day even in the darkness which would've clouded the vision of mortal men.

"Something on your mind?" Victoria asked.

"I was just wondering; it looks like they're going home on foot," Liliana said, curious. "But that can't be right, can it mother?"

"Oh, don't mind them," Victoria said, ushering her into the carriage before the door closed behind her. "They're all like that - more animal than man. More likely than not, they're just going to walk all the way home, maybe even spend the night in a park howling at the moon along with the rest of the stray dogs." She laughed lightly at that.

Liliana chuckled uncomfortably. Her mother's words sometimes put her on edge. "It's just... we could also run back home. That wouldn't be an issue, but we don't."

"Of course we don't," Victoria answered. "Those who live in high society need to take care of such things. But then again, I don't think you can expect those mutts to understand that."

The carriage was notably different from the others lined near the manor in one way; its driver was a vampire. The Carpathians were one of the few families wealthy enough to exclusively employ vampire servants, a fact Victoria took great pride in even though it ate into their budget. Because of this, Liliana had very few interactions with humans, and even less exposure to werewolves. Vampires staunchly refused to sell their houses to those parties in the area she lived in, keeping that location werewolf-free.

Due to this lack of exposure, she had developed unflattering ideas about humans but especially werewolves in particular simply through cultural osmosis. Those ideas were challenged the moment she had seen Raphael. Even as their carriage sped down the streets, she couldn't get the sight of him out of her mind. *You should stop thinking about him,* she told herself. Her mother probably had good reason for her prejudice, she figured. He could very well have been planning how to tear out her throat for all she knew even if he appeared quite gentle during the party. All she had gotten was a simple glance at him, after all, and her warm feelings could very well just be nothing more than projection.

"So, what did you make of the mayor's party?" Victoria asked.

"He seems a bit too concerned about appearances," Liliana said.

"It's not a problem to be concerned about appearances," Victoria answered. "The problem is that he can't do it properly. He's dressed up and behaving like someone who's only ever heard of how a high society person should. Not someone who really knows what that means."

"And he's indecisive," Liliana added, a flicker of insight in her crimson eyes. "He seems to want to toe the line between us and the werewolves, and he isn't sure how to do it. But-"

Liliana hesitated, about to say something before thinking better of it. "But what? Go on. It looks like you had an idea on the tip of your tongue. I would like to hear it. The worst that can happen is I'll tell you it's not a good idea. You're at a young age, but you'll need to learn how to navigate the political waters of the city sooner or later, my dear."

"I mean, the werewolves are trying to do more to appease the humans," Liliana said cautiously. "Because they know the political tide is shifting. I think we should do something regarding the same. Be more friendly to them, I mean?"

"You want us to start courting the human's favor, Liliana?" Victoria asked, raising an eyebrow. "It has only ever worked the other way around. *That* is the natural order of things."

"No, nothing like that, but we can be more friendly to the ordinary humans," she replied, still unsure if she was saying the right thing. "At least we can try reaching out to them as well."

Victoria sighed. "One thing you must remember, child, is that humans are our prey. No matter what we try to do, there will always be friction between the two of us. A horse cannot become friends with the grass it eats now, can it?"

"I understand that, Mother," Liliana conceded. "But maybe if you give me a chance to go and meet with a few more ordinary humans, I might be able to think of something else."

Victoria considered her statement. "All right. Let me see if there is another opportunity to meet with a few of them coming up - people who aren't already devoted to us, that is."

"Thank you, Mother," Liliana said, smiling.

Blackwood Castle rose out of the side of a mountain, casting shadows upon the land as it blocked their view of the moon. It was designed as one of the original fortresses erected by King Alistair in order to keep threats outside of Necropolis at bay. The estate in and of itself was larger than half of the docks. Liliana's family had lived there ever since it had been built during the dawn of Necropolis.

Liliana and her mother exited the carriage. Victoria's insistence on only hiring vampires meant that most of the castle was empty. While the castle had been built to be easy to defend, the lack of staff meant that it was not nearly as secure as it might first appear.

A massive garden led up to the front door. There was a hedge maze on the right side, and a field of Blood Lilies on the right. Blood Lilies were magically engineered lilies that could absorb blood that seeped into the ground, processing it into a digestible form for vampiric consumption. They had first been pioneered by Liliana's late father, which is why they were sometimes called 'Lucian's Lillies' after him.

"Though, the most precious lily in my garden is you, my dear," her father would tell her many times when the two of them walked around the garden together.

The field was used as a butchering ground for animals, their blood raining down onto the soil to enrich it. The invention of the Blood Lilies was revolutionary, allowing vampires to subsist on something other than fresh human blood. The rampant slaughter of humans for food greatly slowed down after this.

Near the entrance, a twenty-foot-tall statue of a vampire clad in armor stood proud, holding a spear in one hand and the head of a werewolf in the other. There was not a single pair of eyes in the city which would be unable to recognize who the statue depicted: Alistair, the founder and first king of the city, who had protected his coven from werewolves and fortified himself within the mountains which would eventually become the foundation of what would come to be called Necropolis. He had taken three wives - Queens Carpathia, Montefalco, and Volkov. The three 'great families' among vampires traced their origins from these bloodlines. The Montefalcos had been annihilated during the Vampire Civil War, leaving only the Carpathians and the Volkovs with the prestige of being descendants of the city's first king.

The interior of the castle was extraordinarily dark by human standards as one of its defensive measures. Even undying eyes took a moment to adjust to the dark ambience. Victoria led Liliana to a small room which functioned as her office. Numerous books lined the shelves, a bronze dragon head glared at them atop the empty fireplace, and the faint smell of old parchment permeated through the room.

"It is time you started learning about matters regarding the estate," Victoria said. "I will show you how to manage the accounts of this castle in the coming days. It would not do if I left you in charge and someone managed to rob us blind." She shook her head slightly as she picked up a document.

"Is there something wrong?" Liliana asked.

"Nothing major to be concerned about," Victoria said, anger evident in her voice. "But with the Lycan encroaching upon our territory, our finances are not doing as they once did."

Liliana understood. The vampiric aristocracy, being long-lived, had accumulated massive wealth, but they were also slow to change and were often tempted by excessive grandeur, buying massive estates far too big for them. They were too confident in their position, and were prone to squabbling amongst themselves as it had been a long time since the last major threat to the city.

The humans and werewolves, being in a disadvantaged position, had to band together for survival, making their societal structures more coherent. Because of this, the vampires found their old businesses undermined by these upstarts.

The two were interrupted by a sudden knock at the door.

"Who could that be?" Liliana wondered. None of the servants would dare intrude upon them unless there was something urgent.

"Come in," Victoria said.

A moment later, a man in a green coat embroidered with gold walked in, his silver hair tied into a small ponytail, a fashion choice popular among vampire men roughly four centuries ago.

"Uncle Athelstan," Liliana said, jumping up from her chair to embrace him. "How are you?"

"I'm doing well. I'm sorry for dropping in on the two of you unannounced," he said.

"It's never a problem when you visit, brother,." Victoria said. "But this is quite the pleasant surprise. Did anything specific bring you in?"

"Nothing wrong. I simply came upon seeing the changing situation within the city, dear sister," Athelstan said. "Sooner or later, we were going to have to make a bold move, and now with a human mayor, the winds truly are shifting. I think we should've acted sooner."

"Well, then I'm sure we would appreciate your wisdom in these trying times," Victoria said. "And I'm sure that Liliana would also like to learn a thing or two from you. She has to grow up one day, doesn't she?"

"Indeed, she does," Athelstan said, smiling warmly while patting Liliana's on the head. "We will have much to discuss in the coming days. If you don't mind though, I'm having my coffin moved into my usual room and just want to make sure they don't damage it..."

"Of course not." A proper coffin was essential to any vampire regardless of station - and what constituted a 'proper' one was often up to personal preference. Liliana, for example, had hers lined with fox fur and would hate to spend a day in anything that was not personalized for her. If she went anywhere she absolutely had to take hers with her even if she had no other piece of luggage accompanying her. Likewise, Athelstan had brought his coffin with him from his estate to ensure that he could get a proper rest.

"Well then, Liliana," Victoria said. "I think we can continue this conversation tomorrow night."

"As you wish, mother," Liliana said.

Chapter Two

Winds of Change

Necropolis was surrounded by dangerous wastelands, and so overland trade was an impossibility even if they could find someone willing to barter with them. As such, all trade in the city that was not internal flowed over the sea.

The city had two major trading partners. The first were the dwarves, expert craftsmen who dwelled in the depths of mountains far away.

The other was the human nation of Solaris. In the olden days, the only thing Solaris exported to Necropolis were human slaves. During the times when vampires were the unquestioned rulers of the city, all humans were considered property and had no rights. During those dark days, vampires could stroll the streets, find any human they wished to consume, and do so. If a human so much as annoyed them, a vampire was fully within their legal rights to sever that human's head from their body.

There were, however, limits imposed over time. The city occasionally entered periods where the human population was not sufficient to sustain the vampire clans before the invention of the Blood Lillies. Humans, realizing they were raising their children only to be food for their overlords, simply refused to breed, oftentimes starving themselves to death as their final - and only means of protest. Some would even cut the throats of their friends and family, draining them of blood before turning their blades to themselves as a way of denying the vampires sustenance in a desperate last act of defiance.

During these times, Solaris - then at war with several rival human states that neighbored it - found itself in dire need of funds in order to keep up its war efforts. Selling their human captives to Necropolis had been profitable for a while until the discovery of the Blood Lilies.

The Blood Lilies were initially considered the salvation of the vampire race. This breakthrough immediately relaxed the constant culling of the human population, which the vampires initially allowed, figuring a backup food supply was always welcome.

This invention, however, had unforeseen consequences. Humans exploded in terms of numbers, far exceeding anything the vampires had expected. Before the vampires knew it, their dominant position was threatened. The hunters had become the hunted. It was only the fact that the vampires could retreat into their nearly impenetrable castles that prevented them from being completely wiped out in the riots that followed. A stalemate soon followed and a truce was formed, restricting the authority of the vampires and guaranteeing rights to the humans.

Solaris had long since conquered any nation capable of rivalling it and no longer had slaves to sell even if Necropolis would buy them. Instead, all manner of other goods flowed from that country to Necropolis.

A huge shipment from the Sutherland Shipping Company, one of the largest shipping companies in Solaris, was going to arrive this afternoon and Raphael awaited their arrival alongside some of his trusted crew.

There was Vincent, the burly son of a tanner whom Raphael had grown up with. When Raphael's mother had passed away, he spent a summer alongside Vincent and his family while his father got matters in order – practically living with them for the majority of that time. Vincent was far closer to a brother than to a friend to Raphael, and he also enjoyed collecting rocks.

Then there was Edward, whose father was an accountant and ran most of the books for his father. He loved swimming the most out of all of them and would oftentimes be seen diving into the sea at the crack of dawn.

Last but not least was a dark-haired werewolf by the name of Carlton, whose parents owned a spice store that was heavily reliant on imports from Solaris.

In one way or another, Raphael's motley crew all worked under his father. This was not by design, it had simply happened to be so. Raphael knew that werewolves in the wild organized themselves in packs and had a strict hierarchy, though such mannerisms had died out for the most part after centuries of living in the city.

That wasn't to say that remnants of it didn't persist. Perhaps it was hard-coded into the blood that flowed through their veins. Raphael's father was the head of their parents so to speak, and so his friends looked to him as 'pack head' as well.

Not that Raphael would ever say so out loud. He did not see himself as a leader or his friends as subordinates. He had once complained about this to his father who had simply said, "Some men are born great, others have greatness thrust upon them. It's only natural for people to seek out a leader – since they fall in line behind you, it means that you have the qualities to be one. Rather than shirking this responsibility, you should go ahead and accept it. Find the qualities of being a leader within yourself, and refine them."

Raphael was put off by that kind of talk, though less so recently. He had been walking around with his father for the last year, and had gradually begun to understand the full weight of the influence that his father commanded. Many of the werewolves had their hopes pinned upon his father, and by proxy, eventually him.

19

Raphael did not want to let them down.

"-and the sun never sets there."

"Impossible."

Raphael had been so engrossed in these thoughts that he had zoned out of his friend's conversation, only coming back down to earth during what felt like the middle of a heated conversation.

"Sorry, what was that?"

"Ed was saying that Solaris is called that because the sun never sets on their capital city."

"I heard that from somebody."

Raphael frowned. "The place is really sunny most of the year round, even in winter, but the sun does go down eventually. Whoever said otherwise was just telling you some tall tales."

"Ha - told ya!"

"Still, must be nice when it's always sunny out, right? None of them *leeches* around to annoy you." It was a derogatory term for their former employers. Not only did leeches drain blood, but they also parasitized without contributing anything - a fitting description, many felt, for their undying overlords.

Raphael put a finger to his lip before turning around.

"Oh, come on now, there's no one here that's going to hear that and be offended. None of the humans or werewolves are fond of 'em."

"What if *they* hear you?" Raphael asked.

"Right now? In the middle of the day?"

"Some of them have these trinkets that let them come out into sunlight," Raphael said. "I've seen them walking around with them. They're these strange amulets that absorb daylight or whatever. But point being is, we're trying to show these merchants that we mean business, alright? They probably also trade with the vampires as well. I just don't want something odd to happen and ruin our image."

"Who is this guy anyway? I thought he was just some merchant – but you're talking about him like he's nobility."

"He might just be a merchant – but his family owns over fifty ships and the second largest shipping company in Solaris," Raphael said. "So 'just a merchant' doesn't do him much justice."

There was an edge to Raphael's voice that did not go unnoticed by his friends. This meeting was typically something his father would take care of, but Abraham had entrusted it to Raphael to see how he could handle the business. Raphael knew the consequences of messing this up would not be minor; they stood to lose a significant portion of their trade.

Calm down, he told himself, trying to slow his heartbeat. If it started palpitating any faster, his Lycan friends would be able to hear it thrumming in his chest. *We need them, but they also need us. We are one of the biggest buyers of their goods, aren't we?* His father had taught him that a good leader must always keep a brave face, regardless of how dire the situation was.

His friend, Edward, commented, "I think I'd love to actually see Solaris. A place where it's sunny most of the time sounds nice. And I heard that the Solaris Empire is massive. Probably lots of stuff to see."

"Of course, it's massive," Raphael replied, welcoming the distraction. "They spent several centuries conquering the nearby kingdoms. They probably would have subjugated the dwarves too if they weren't fortified within their mountains."

Raphael looked out at the vast sea, a constant source of wonder for those who lived by the docks. He longed to see the wider world away from Necropolis - to verify if the Solaris Empire's capital's roads were truly paved with gold, or to witness the dwarves' massive architectural feats. But he was his father's only son, and the reality of sea travel - long, miserable voyages full of storms, whirlpools, and monsters - was far less romantic than the dreams he'd had as a young boy.

"They're here," Carlton announced, being the first to spot the specks approaching on the horizon.

"All right," Raphael said, snapping back to the present. "Get ready. Smooth your hair, Edward. Carlton, there's a stain on your shirt - see if you can get a different one. We want to look our best, don't we?"

"Aye, aye, Captain," his friends joked, as Raphael rolled his eyes.

A ship from Solaris could be told apart from one from Necropolis at a glance. Most Necropolis vessels were small, hastily constructed, wood-based fishing vessels or longer-haul ships reliant on oars and manpower. Solaris ships, however, were far more elegant. While Necropolis ships seemed to be built entirely for function, Solaris ships looked like works of art, often featuring three sails, both square and lateen, that utilized the wind efficiently, and bows carved with decorative shapes, like the favored dragon head.

Four Solaris ships arrived in total. The lead vessel, named the *Dragonfly*, was a true beauty - probably one of the finest products of their expert shipbuilders. The vessels came to port, and Raphael and his pack could hear the shouts of the crew as they dropped anchor.

Raphael did not have to wait long before four guards, clad head-to-toe in chainmail inscribed with the Solaris coat of arms - a rising sun cresting a hill - marched out onto the docks. Raphael noted, but did not speak out loud, the fact that their heavy armor would be worse than useless if they fell into the water, but he understood the need to maintain appearances.

"Mr. Dunn Sutherland. It's been too long," Raphael said with a practiced smile as the head of the fleet disembarked right after the guards.

Dunn Sutherland was a slim man who looked far more at home in a library than as the captain of a ship. His skin was lightly tanned despite most of his work taking place indoors as a consequence of Solaris's environment. He smelled of the salty sea, as was expected, but also a strange kind of citrus fruit - no doubt some kind of perfume from Solaris.

"I hope you had a pleasant journey," Raphael added.

"As pleasant as it can be when you're at sea for three months,"

Sutherland said, stretching his arms. "Thankfully, we didn't run into any major issues. A few smashed crates and some damage along the way, some cargo overboard, but nothing major. Nothing out of the ordinary, at least."

"Glad to hear that," Raphael said. His friends then introduced themselves.

"Your company has been doing well, it seems."

"To be more accurate, my father's company," Raphael clarified, "but yes, things have thankfully been going well for us. You might be interested to know that Necropolis has elected a human mayor for the first time in its history."

"Is that so?" Dunn asked, an eyebrow raised. "Well, that is quite a bit of interesting news. I was wondering, though, if I could speak to your father?"

"My father? Why would-" Raphael said, speaking too quickly as several thoughts bounced around his head like lightning. Why does he want Father? Did I do something wrong? No - it probably is just something only Father can talk about. He quickly composed himself. "Certainly. You can meet with him. He was working earlier this morning, but I am sure he'd be happy to make time to see you."

The cargo, mostly grain and other produce hard to come by in the less-fertile fields of Necropolis, was offloaded. But there were also things that were more expensive - a good portion of the dwarves's trade came through their company as well as other works of craftsmanship only the rich would be interested in.

"Will you be staying at the *Misty Marionette* like last time?" Raphael asked, referring to one of the most prestigious inns near the docks.

"Why, yes."

"Well, then, I'll be sure to arrange for a meeting. My father and I will send over a messenger," Raphael said.

"I thank you kindly."

As was custom, they then exchanged gifts. Raphael and his friends gifted several pieces of furniture in the distinctive Necropolis style, easily demonstrating their strength by heaving heavy dressers with a single arm. In return, Sutherland gave them several grain wines brewed by the dwarves, known for their potency and a mark of high status, even if the taste was muted for vampires and Lycans.

"That one went better than expected," one of his friends remarked as they wrapped things up and left. Raphael relaxed a little. It was not easy, but also not as dauntingly impossible as he'd been building up in his mind.

***

Later, Dunn Sutherland, Abraham, and Raphael sat in Abraham's main office. The reason Dunn wanted to meet with the father, not the son, was quickly revealed: he was looking for an investor.

The office at the Cain Company's headquarters, though more decorated than Abraham's private one at home, was still quite sparse compared to what one might expect. Raphael noticed a strange contraption of twisted iron in the corner of the room which had been placed there by Dunn and his workers.

"I apologize, but the nature of what we're doing needs to be kept somewhat of a secret," Dunn said. "There is also a slight chance it might go wrong, so if you have anything delicate here that you wouldn't want damaged, it would be wise to take it out before we begin."

Abraham raised an eyebrow. "Just… how dangerous is what you're going to show us?"

"I don't expect anything to happen," Dunn reassured with a small smile. "I just prefer to be cautious. We could have tried to do this out in the open, but again, I didn't want information on this to leak out."

Raphael noticed several buckets of water kept at the side of the room, suggesting they were expecting some kind of fire. "Is this something related to that little machine of yours?" Abraham asked.

"Yes. This is a smaller model of what we're proposing, but well - I think it'll be easier to show you rather than trying to describe it."

Abraham easily pushed the heavy table aside with a casual movement. Raphael and Abraham approached the machine, which consisted of a small furnace at the bottom, a large cylinder, and pistons on the side.

"So, this is what we are calling a 'steam engine' back in Solaris," Dunn explained. "The idea is that it uses steam as a source of energy."

Several workers lit a fire near the bottom of the furnace and poured a small amount of coal into it. "There's a water reservoir in here," Dunn said, as water was added. "The fire heats the water, creating steam that is funneled to move the piston." The piston began pushing a plunger back and forth. Initially, the movement was minuscule, but then it picked up speed to the point where even Raphael's enhanced eyesight had trouble keeping up with it. The machine worked, albeit making strange, alarming noises all the while it operated.

"I think that's enough for a demonstration," Dunn said, quickly cooling off the machine.

"So, what is the use of this?" Abraham asked, looking amused. Aside from the noise, the miniature machine didn't seem to do much.

"This machine converts fire into energy that can be used to move things," Dunn explained. "We found coal to be far better than wood, although both could be used. The main point is it can be harnessed for many things. In Solaris, we've been using trains pulled by horses, and we've tried replacing them with one using a steam engine with moderate success. Unlike a horse, this thing does not tire, so long as you have the fuel, it can continue running."

He paused before getting to the meat of the matter. "The reason I come to you is because I intend to use the steam engine for a different purpose: for sailing."

"For sailing?"

"Yes, for sailing," Dunn said. "If we incorporate this engine into our ships, we could potentially cut the journey to Necropolis to just one month."

"A month? That would greatly shorten the journey," Abraham mused. From his facial expression, he seemed to think it was too good to be true.

"Indeed. Of course, there are many things to consider," Draco continued. "The ships have to be designed differently, and the actual engine might end up being nearly as large as an ordinary house. But the potential payoffs are immense. We would no longer be as dependent upon the wind and currents. We could potentially do voyages all year round."

"Or potentially, this could end up producing nothing," Abraham countered.

"I understand your skepticism," Dunn said with a strained smile. "And I'm not expecting you to put anything substantial into the project right now. I simply wanted to show you it because I am planning to have a working ship model made by the end of next year. I hope that when I can show you that, and we have some more results, it might change your mind. I really just wanted to put the concept out before you."

"Well, then we'll look forward to seeing how far you manage to get," Abraham said. "My company will certainly buy a stake if it happens to produce something useful."

"Thank you for your time. If I could just ask one favor: could you keep knowledge of this to yourselves? I would prefer that news of this not leak," Dunn said.

"Don't worry, our lips are sealed," Abraham said.

Once Dunn and his company had left, Raphael asked, "Do you think anything will come out of it?"

"Oh, you're still a young boy," Abraham said. "Humans are innovative, yes, but they'll often promise you the world whenever they stumble upon something new. If he actually manages to turn that thing into something which could propel a ship by the end of the year, I'll eat my hat."

Abraham laughed. Raphael found the idea incredulous as well, but a part of him didn't want to completely dismiss the concept completely. If travel by ship could be made more efficient and easy, his dream of sailing to Solaris might indeed be fulfilled one day.

"Putting all that nonsense aside," Abraham said, waving his hand, "there's something that you wanted to do for the humans near the docks, wasn't there? What is it?"

"Yes," Raphael said. "I'm sure this will help improve our relationship with them."

***

"Is there another reason why we're here, Uncle?" Liliana asked Athelstan the next night as they walked through the garden.

Athelstan had claimed he wanted to observe the Blood Lilies and asked her to accompany him, a rather weak excuse given he knew exactly where they were and that their location hadn't moved in hundreds of years.

24

"Sharp little thing, aren't you? Just like your mother," he said, smiling. "Yes, there is actually something that has been bothering me."

Athelstan did not elaborate immediately, instead plucking a Blood Lily. The extraordinary flowers, a vibrant sea of crimson in the moonlight, had come to symbolize their clan. He put the flower in his mouth and chewed it, savoring the faint, tickling fragrance of blood. "Not bad, if I must be honest, but nothing can be as good as the real thing." Athelstan turned towards Liliana. "Tell me, child, have you ever tasted real human blood before?"

Liliana tried to remember. "Sometime once, back when I was little, Mother tried feeding me some. It tasted... too strong. I couldn't really stomach it."

Athelstan shook his head with a pitying look. "Those who are raised on Blood Lilies since birth are like that. It wasn't that the blood was too strong, Liliana. It was just far too overwhelming for you but it is exactly what we drink. I'm sure if you had tried it a bit more, you would have started to not only like it but crave it." He put another flower into his mouth. "These flowers, they quell the hunger, but they can't completely suppress it."

"Well, it's hard to find fresh human blood now," Liliana said. Ever since humans started to gain rights, things were highly regulated. Any loopholes - like taking the blood of criminals or going through underground markets - had mostly been closed. "Uncle... does that mean you've been able to get fresh human blood somehow?"

He looked past her, towards the west - the direction of his own estate beyond the mountain range. "Things are a bit different near the fringes, Liliana. Different from how things are in the main city. Do you know what lies beyond the outskirts?"

"Wastelands, right?"

"Not just wastelands," Athelstan corrected. "You and I may consider them to be wastelands, but in truth, many call it their home. The wild werewolves used that area before a good portion of them came to work with us. And that is where we vampires emerged, after all, before King Alistair founded the city. Not all our humans came from Solaris, you know. There are still those who live out there in the uncivilized wilderness."

Liliana was hearing of this for the first time. "Mother always told me there was nothing of importance outside the outskirts."

"Well, there might not be anything of importance to you and her, that is correct," Athelstan said. "But that doesn't mean that there is nothing there. There are many werewolves and other such animals out there, as well as unaffiliated vampires. They have always been kept at bay by our unity and strength. They would be hard-pressed to attack Necropolis, but the people on the outskirts don't always have such protection."

Athelstan reached down to pick up a handful of soil, tinted the color of clay. "The soil here is bloody, but it is also fertile. The only way it could be made like this is from the blood of animals. But the soil on the outskirts is not nearly as plentiful. For the humans out there, survival is difficult."

"About the humans…" Liliana asked, curious. "Is working with them difficult?"

"They have more than enough matters on their own hands to bother us," Athelstan said. "It isn't just that farming is hard - but there are other dangers lurking near the boundaries as well. That is actually why I came towards the city. Some of the farmers near my estate have been mauled. At first, we thought it was just a wild wolf or bear, but the speed and ferocity of these attacks are too great to be that of a common wild animal."

Liliana's breath caught in her chest. "Do you think there's a wild werewolf pack attacking your farmers?"

"I can think of no other explanation," Athelstan said. "I doubt it was an entire pack, otherwise we'd see even more carnage. More likely than not this is a single werewolf. Regardless, I would like help in dealing with the problem. I hope the new mayor isn't too opposed to that."

"He shouldn't be," Liliana said. "We helped him get elected. Well, so did the werewolves inside the city.. but if this is about wild werewolves, that's different from the werewolves living in the city, isn't it?"

Athelstan chuckled and rubbed her hair. "You have a lot to learn about how this world works, my dear. Whether they are wild or living in the city, they are still wild animals. They cannot get rid of their instincts."

"But there's a difference between vampires outside and those in the city," she pointed out.

"Without a doubt, I would trust a city vampire over one of those brutes who live out there," he said, waving his hand. "We at least had the good sense to realize that living under King Alistair's rule was far preferable to staying out there. The werewolves didn't join the city completely out of choice you know, but rather because circumstances had forced them to. Most of them arrived under the leadership of a werewolf named Balthazar who had been kicked out of his own tribe and offered his services in exchange for a place to live."

"I didn't know about that last bit," Liliana admitted.

"I doubt your mother would bother wasting her time teaching you such esoteric history," Athelstan said. "She's often told me, much like your father did, that the only good werewolf is a dead one."

Liliana patted the part of her dress wherein a silver dagger was hidden. "Yes, I've learned a lot about their weaknesses."

"But I'm not just here on business," he said, flashing a smile. "I did want to see my adorable niece one more time. And, if possible, I think now would be a good time to introduce you to the Council of Elders."

"Are you sure? Mother says I should still wait about five or ten years before that."

"I would normally agree," Athelstan admitted. "I was not introduced to them until I was twenty winters beyond your age. However, the times are changing. We need fresh blood among our ranks. I don't want to put too much pressure upon you, Liliana, but you are our future. A lot of these Elders still think of themselves as aristocrats, not seeing the writing on the wall that they should have started responding to changes centuries ago."

"But before we do so, you should probably ask my mother," Liliana said.

"Oh, don't worry, I'll go and have a word with her. I doubt that she'll say no."

Later that night, Athelstan did indeed go to Victoria, asking to introduce Liliana to the Council of Elders during the next full moon.

"I will think about it," Victoria said, which Liliana knew was usually code for 'no.' So she had little hopes riding on that eventual decision.

However, her mother had a different surprise for her. "Liliana, you wanted to spend some more time with the humans, to get to know them better, didn't you? There is someone who sought an audience with us regarding a certain investment near the docks. This is a rather large shipping company from a reputed Solaris merchant. Why don't you go have a look at it and let me know what's going on?"

It sounded to Liliana like Victoria was simply sending her on a silly errand to get her out of the way while she and her uncle got down to actual business. But Liliana would take the opportunity anyway. When else would an opportunity like this present itself?

***

"So, do you think this is a good place to set up?" Vincent asked Raphael as the two walked around the docks. The area near the ocean, though collectively called 'the docks,' was a vast expanse of greatly fluctuating quality when it came to wealth and architecture.

"I don't know. I don't think many people can come here. Also, it seems kind of dirty, don't you think?" Raphael said, noting the garbage piled up on the street corners.

"The places where we used to live were even dirtier," Vincent pointed out.

"Yes, but we're trying to serve food, aren't we? It's not exactly appetizing if there's rubbish everywhere near the entry. Not to mention the alley over there is way too narrow. If we had too many people here it'd cause a traffic jam," Raphael said.

Raphael's idea to improve Lycan relations was simple but practical. The recent economic downturn in Necropolis was hitting the already struggling human population hard. The most common complaint they were hearing was that the Lycans were hunting all the easy prey at the city's fringes and catching too much fish in the ocean, ruining the haul for common fishermen.

Raphael knew there was little basis for this in reality - a werewolf needed to consume more, but there were far fewer werewolves than humans.

Unfortunately, the lie that werewolves were over-hunting was repeated so many times by the human masses that it was considered fact by many. Raphael was still surprised how many humans did not realize what his heightened senses could pick up, often whispering things to each other that he could hear quite loudly anyway. Things they would most definitely not say to his face.

Given the rising tensions, Raphael wanted to create something long-term to alleviate the situation. Not just a one-off food distribution, but a structured soup kitchen that would provide aid and by extension gain goodwill. They had been scouting the docks for a while in search of an ideal location for such a place.

As they wandered, the destitution of the common citizenry became more and more apparent. While werewolves could usually hunt or fish their way out of an empty stomach, that was not an option for most humans. He saw children whose bones were clearly visible, dressed in rags, and men walking around with placards advertising their willingness to do any kind of work.

He tried hard not to think about the latest rumors from the black market- that desperate families would sometimes sell their dead or near-dying relatives to vampires or werewolves for... *consumption.*

He knew that things weren't exactly going well for the common citizenry, but he also didn't think that they were this bad. Had he become so out of touch given his recent elevation in social status that he was so disconnected from the plight of the average Joe? How had he not seen all of these signs earlier?

"All right, I think this might be a good spot," Raphael said, pointing to a shoe store on the corner of a moderately busy street. It was far enough from the ocean that the worst of the docks' stench wouldn't reach them.

"Only one thing to see: is the guy going to actually sell it to us?" Vincent muttered.

"There's only one way to find out," Raphael said.

The store was run by an old man in his eighties who looked up with a warm smile before realizing what they were. "Good afternoon, sirs. Thank you for dropping by my shop, but..."

"You sell shoes here?"

"Yes, and I make them myself as well," he said, avoiding direct eye contact with them. Raphael could hear the man's heart quicken. "But as I said, I usually make footwear for humans. I'm afraid I would not be able to make something up to your standards."

Werewolves went through furniture and clothes rather easily. Most preferred to wander around barefoot as they would just tear through any shoes they happened to put on anyway. Raphael could not do so in public because of the image he wanted to maintain, but many of the others did.

"We actually were not here to buy shoes, but for another reason entirely," Raphael said. "Is this building - I mean, your shop - possibly for sale?"

"My shop... for sale?" the man trailed off.

"To be more direct, my friend and I would be interested in purchasing it," Vincent clarified.

"Thank you for your interest, but I'm afraid I must refuse," the man

28

said.

Raphael had been expecting this. "Before you say no, how about we tell you our price first? We could pay you far more than what this building would otherwise be worth."

"Once again, thank you for your offer," the man said more firmly, "but I'm afraid that I must refuse."

"All right then. Thank you very much for your time," Raphael said, giving Vincent a short shake of the head when he saw that the latter was going to try and argue.

"I'm sure if you talked to him a bit more, he would have agreed," Vincent said once they were outside. "You didn't even name your price. Why don't we drop a bag full of coins in front of his face? I'm sure that would change his mind."

"And what if it didn't?" Raphael countered. "The entire point of doing this is to improve our relations with humans. We can't go around looking like we're trying to bully them into selling us stuff like some kind of racketeering gang. Plus, this isn't the only spot in the city."

There were several possible reasons for the shoemaker to refuse. Maybe he just didn't like werewolves. Maybe he had a deep connection to the shop. Maybe he just wanted to keep working. Regardless, he had been very staunch in his refusal, which is why Raphael had figured it was a lost cause and walked out of there. There were many fish in the sea, and many other locations for them to check out.

As it turned out, Raphael was not wrong in thinking they could find another venue easily. Two blocks away from the shoe shop was a bakery that was the perfect size for what they were envisioning. It also got a reasonable amount of traffic near it. It was a bit further from the sea than he would've liked, and the building was older, but Raphael felt they could make it work.

The interior of the bakery lacked the fragrances that Raphael would've ordinarily associated with such a place, and there were no goods out for display. It looked like it was a slow afternoon. Or more likely everyone was feeling the pinch of the economic downturn. The woman running the shop, however, greeted them warmly unlike the shoemaker. "Good afternoon, sirs. What can I get for you?"

"We actually weren't here to buy bread or sweets," Vincent said. "We have a business offer for you. Are you the owner of this building?"

"Well, my husband and I run this shop together. What… what kind of business offer?"

"We wanted to purchase this building," Raphael said. "I know that that's a bit out of the blue, but we can provide you with more than an adequate price if you would be willing to part with it."

"Well, that's quite a big decision," the woman answered after a pause. "I mean, we've worked here for a long time. But for the right price…"

Raphael placed a bag of coins on the counter, partially open so the glint of gold within was visible.

Werewolves invariably did business with gold or copper – silver coins were a big hassle to deal with, as you can imagine, and had caused certain issues while conducting business in the past. In modern times though, most people understood this, and where silver coins could not be completely disposed of there were ways around them - such as tokens issued by banks to be representative of silver coins but made of wood; or the paper money used in Solaris – though the easiest method was to just get a human attendant to help you handle the coins.

"Oh my," the woman breathed, seeing the bag full of gold coins. "Are those... real?"

"Yes, they're real," Raphael assured her.

"Might you be considering it?" Vincent asked.

"Oh, I am, yes. But I'll have to speak with my husband first. He's out getting a delivery right now. Could you gentlemen back within an hour, please?"

"Certainly," Raphael said.

As they walked out, Vincent asked, "Do you think she's just stalling, really thinking about it, or that she doesn't want to sell to us?"

"Her heartbeat went up, but not as much as the shoemaker's. She likely has no problem selling to Lycans, but the money certainly excites her. I think she's definitely tantalized by the price. We have an hour; let's quickly scout some other places, just in case this doesn't work out."

They found two other spots that were not nearly as suitable as both had some major drawbacks - one was too close to the red light district, the other was near an iron factory, meaning there was a miasma wafting in the air.

When they returned to the bakery after a quick lunch of dried beef they saw the couple waiting for them. The husband tried to hurry along a customer buying bread once he saw them, but Raphael insisted they were fine with waiting.

The man dusted off the counter and gave them a warm smile. "Hello, sirs. I was speaking to my wife, and I just wanted to confirm if the offer is still available. You two are interested in buying our shop?"

"Why, yes, we are," Raphael said.

"To be fair, I've run this bakery for the last five years, and I have quite a number of fond memories of it," the man said. "However, it's not like it's my ancestral home or anything. For the right price, we would certainly be willing to part with it."

The baker closed the door to the entrance of the shop, flipped the sign to 'Closed', and the four of them sat down to discuss the deal. Although the Lycans' pockets were not as deep as the vampires', who had been hoarding wealth for millennia, they could certainly pay a price that would entice them.

"If you don't mind me asking," the wife, Elena, asked, "precisely what do you want to use this bakery for?"

"It's not a problem if you want to ask," Raphael said. "I wanted to basically turn this place into something of a charity house, to feed the poor and those who can't afford food. As a matter of fact, you already have something of a kitchen set up in the back, which saves us time."

"Charity? But…" Elena began. "I thought you could hunt as much as you wanted. I didn't know werewolves were going hungry too."

"No, no. The charity is mainly for humans," Raphael clarified, though he added quickly, "I mean, if a fellow werewolf came by, we certainly wouldn't refuse them. But it is mainly for the humans, yes."

"And what do you intend to gain out of this?" the husband asked, slightly suspicious.

"Gain? This is not done with any sort of profit in mind, in case that's what you're wondering," Raphael said. "It is only that my father's company - Cain Shipping - has flourished thanks to the cooperation and work of both humans and werewolves. This is simply our way of giving back and showing appreciation towards the people of the docks."

He delivered his rehearsed answer flawlessly, much like a politician. He wasn't sure if the couple believed him, but they did not voice any disbelief.

They agreed on a generous sum of three thousand gold pieces, two times the property's actual worth. Raphael paid half upfront, taking their signatures on a receipt. The next day, he would return with an attorney to draw up the formal paperwork. The couple requested about five days to clean up and move out, during which Raphael would handle other logistical aspects.

I won't let you down, Dad! Raphael thought as they walked away, barely able to contain his excitement. The first step in his plan was now complete!

Chapter Three

Trial by Fire

"Mother, if you don't mind, I'm going out to visit Beatrice tonight," Liliana called out before leaving.

Beatrice was Liliana's cousin; all aristocratic vampires in the city were related to each other to some degree. The journey to her house, which could have been covered in a flash if Liliana had simply run (as she occasionally did when she was a little girl, much to her mother's horror), instead took twenty minutes by carriage.

Beatrice's staff, much like her own, was exclusively composed of vampires. Word was sent ahead the moment that Liliana arrived, and Liliana was led into a dining room decorated with artworks dedicated to King Alistair. Food was on display for her but this was more of a formality than anything. Vampires had dull taste buds and usually could not savor the taste of anything unless it was extremely intense to the point of being nearly unpalatable to a human; and ordinary food held no nutritional value for them.

Liliana took a single, intensely sweet candy from a tray, noticing its light citrus fragrance as it melted on her tongue. Why did vampires even bother with eating when it wasn't necessary? It was because it was something to do.

Given that vampires lacked many of the basic human needs like eating or drinking, they often struggled to find ways to pass the time. This ennui explained their vanity - when one had nothing else to accomplish, one focused entirely on appearance, clothes, and collections. Older vampires often complained that life was becoming increasingly boring as the centuries dragged on by; hence, the popularity of things like cigars amongst them which provided a harmless distraction for them. It was something to do while whiling away the time, even though the tobacco and nicotine had no effect on them. Liliana, however, intensely disliked the smell.

Beatrice joined her shortly. She was half a head shorter than Liliana with wider shoulders, but otherwise, they looked so similar they could easily pass as sisters.

"Oh, Liliana, I'm so glad you came here today! I wanted to show you this new little piece I was working on," Beatrice gushed.

"I certainly don't mind listening in," Liliana said, beaming. "However, I was also here for some other reason."

"Oh, were you here for business or just to see me?" Beatrice asked.

"I am here for business, yes, but it can wait for after you've shown me your newest piece." Liliana added.

"Your uncle was visiting, wasn't he?"

"Yes, he arrived a few days ago."

Beatrice was handed her violin by one of her servants. "I composed this melody, and I call it 'The Song of Moonlight.' Are you ready?"

"Of course," Liliana said.

Beatrice began her melody. Liliana had to admit that her cousin's skills had truly improved over the last two years. The piece, which lasted four minutes, was mainly melancholic though there were hints of joy woven into it.

When Beatrice finished, Liliana clapped. "That was wonderful. You've really got a hang of this."

"I still miss a note here and there," Beatrice said, sighing.

"I didn't notice at all. What inspired you to make the piece?"

"I saw a rabbit under the moonlight, and I put myself in its shoes, wondering what it might be thinking. It looked so lonely in that field, just all by itself, gazing at the moon. That's why the start of the song is sad. But when I saw it run away happily, I wanted to add bits of that as well. Did you really like it though?"

"I really liked it. Like I said, you've improved quite a lot," Liliana said.

"Then why don't you order a violin for yourself, and the two of us can practice together?" Beatrice suggested eagerly.

"Maybe," Liliana said, laughing. "But perhaps some other time. I'm focusing on some other things right now."

"Boo! You always say that whenever I suggest anything," Beatrice said, frowning.

"Oh, cheer up. There *is* something that we can do together, actually. Your song was so good, I almost forgot what the reason was that I'd come here in the first place. Will you accompany me to the docks?"

"The docks? Whatever for?" Beatrice asked.

"Well, there's something my mother wanted me to do. There is this human company - I don't know if you've heard of them - called the Sutherland Shipping Company. They come from Solaris."

"Solaris, that country from over the sea? Actually I've always wanted to go there myself one day," Beatrice admitted. "But with how they describe the place, I don't know if it's really suitable for people like us." Vampires could adjust to the sunlight thanks to talismans, but few actually wanted to. "My parents would never allow me to go there."

"I don't think mine would either, it's too far," Liliana said. "Anyway, someone from the company has this new invention, which he thinks can be quite helpful, and he needs money for an investment. He wanted to petition to come to our castle, but you know how Mother feels about allowing *humans* inside. But she did agree to listen to him, so I sort of volunteered for it, as I wanted to get to know humans better."

"Why do you want to get to know humans better?" Beatrice asked, laughing.

"Well, just, you know, there's a new human mayor and all. And I guess I was just curious."

"Do you really want to go to the docks, though? I've heard that place is filthy, and it certainly seemed like that whenever I passed by there," Beatrice complained.

"I know, I know," Liliana said. "But it *is* near the sea. Think about that! Also, I just didn't want to go on this alone, and I thought maybe you might appreciate seeing some things in the city. I've heard they have a new batch of dwarf-made goods available."

"Dwarf-made goods?" Beatrice now seemed far more interested. The work of dwarven craftsmen were highly prized especially amongst the aristocracy.

"We can even see if there's a necklace that catches your fancy. I remember you telling me that you wanted a new one."

"You know my weaknesses very well, don't you?" Beatrice said, laughing gently. "Oh, I can't say no to a night of shopping - especially not when it is with you."

"Well, it's not during the night, exclusively," Liliana said. "I do intend to go sometime in the morning."

"In the morning!? Why?"

"If we go at night, there's less that we're going to be able to see. You have your talismans, don't you? And we'll take parasols along with us. It should be fine just for a few hours."

Beatrice sighed. "All right, then. Sure, we can go."

"Thank you so much," Liliana said. "I wouldn't feel as confident if you weren't there with me."

"It's not a problem. After all, who else is going to support you?" Beatrice replied.

Beatrice was essentially Liliana's only friend, and the same was true in reverse. Given that Liliana was headed somewhere strange, there was no one else she would rather have by her side. And with that, the deal was sealed.

It was a cloudy day when the two of them set off for the docks.

"Would you look at that?" Liliana remarked. "It looks like even Sanguinus wishes for us to go outside."

Sanguinus, or the Great Blood Ancestor as he was also called, was fabled to have fathered the first vampires and was worshipped as a deity by the vampires both within and outside the city.

Despite the clouds, neither girl was taking chances with the sunlight. They came well protected. The talismans in question took the form of pieces of quartz, which had been specifically enchanted to absorb sunlight.

There were several inconvenient aspects about their usage. One was that they needed to be in contact with the user's skin to work and so they could not be kept in one's pockets or likewise hidden. That was why most vampires wore them as necklaces. Secondly, after extended use they would break and the quartz would need to be replaced. Eventually, after the quartz had broken enough times, one would need to buy another talisman entirely.

These talismans were a relatively recent invention, only about eight hundred years old, but they had fundamentally changed the lives of modern vampires. The human who had invented them in question had quickly become one of the richest people in the city from manufacturing them and being able to sell them over and over to vampires. Several people speculated that he knew how to make a talisman that would not break over time but had purposefully made them so that they had a limited number of uses in order to maximize profits - but until this date no one had managed to successfully advance their design to be more durable, so these were probably just rumors.

Even with them, however, it was not recommended that vampires stay out for more than two to three hours at a time in harsh sunlight. While Beatrice and Liliana would not burn up instantly, they would start feeling intense pain within minutes and develop an extremely painful rash if exposed directly to sunlight unprotected.

The two were taking a carriage together. This was technically the time during which they should be asleep, but times in Necropolis had changed; gone were the days that many human shops only opened during nighttime hours to cater to their mainly vampire patrons.

"Do you have any idea what this invention is?" Beatrice asked as the carriage rolled down the streets.

"Not really, only that it's apparently something very important," Liliana answered. "I guess it's a secret, which is why they're not telling us much."

"Oh, that sounds interesting!" Beatrice said, perking up. "What do you think it could be?"

"More likely than not, it probably won't be anything impressive," Liliana said. "I think a lot of the truly important things have already been invented and there's not much that can be made beyond that. Humans come up with new ideas all the time, but that doesn't mean they're all good. It would be nice if it was useful, though. Something like these amulets, or like the Blood Lilies."

Beatrice frowned. "I don't think they would make something that would help us specifically. I've heard the people in Solaris don't really like vampires."

Liliana sighed. "Can you truly blame them?"

"What? They shouldn't discriminate against us just because we're vampires,," Beatrice retorted. "They even have people who are dedicated vampire hunters in that country! Can you imagine humans who spend their entire lives studying how to kill us? The very thought gives me nightmares..."

35

"Well, just remember," Liliana said, "that they're more scared of you than you are of them."

"As they should be," Beatrice declared. Beatrice was the kind of girl who would start screaming and flailing uncontrollably if she found a spider in her hair, so Liliana was not sure where this sudden burst of confidence had come from. Sure, Beatrice had the strength to punch through a wall, but her disposition was far more inclined to running away than engaging in fisticuffs.

As they neared the docks, Beatrice kept glancing out the window with a concerned look on her face. "Don't worry about it," Liliana said. "My mother wouldn't let us go out like this if it wasn't safe."

Beatrice bit her lower lip. "I mean, you might say that. But do you remember what happened to your father?"

Liliana's face fell. "We're not sure it was humans who did that. It could have been someone else, right?"

"Oh, right. Liliana, I'm sorry," Beatrice said, embracing her. "I'm sorry for making you remember something so horrible.."

"It's okay," Liliana said. It had been some time since her father passed, and she had somewhat come to terms with it. From what she could find out, it was far more likely a rival faction of vampires had killed her father, rather than the humans. Her mother also suspected the same, but despite digging deep into the matter had no headway regarding who the culprit might be.

Still, Beatrice's words brought back the memory of shouts outside their castle, of mobs moving through the city, of torches blazing in the night - three nights of chaos during most of which she had been forced to hide in a cellar waiting for things to end.

"Nothing like that is happening now," Liliana insisted. "We will be all right."

"And you have some silver on you, don't you?" Beatrice asked.

"Yes, but you have too much silver on you," Liliana teased. Beatrice was wearing silver earrings, a silver bracelet, and four silver rings, on top of which Liliana was sure she probably had a silver dagger hidden in her bodice, much like she did.

"But you can't be too careful when walking into werewolf territory," Beatrice said.

"It's not exactly their territory," Liliana corrected. "It belongs to everyone."

"Yes, but it's where they usually live, isn't it? They're not used to seeing us out here, are they?"

"No, they aren't. But we're not going to meet the werewolves." The mention of werewolves brought the image of Raphael to her mind. She had tried to suppress any thoughts about him over the past few days, having convinced herself that her feelings were nothing more than a passing fancy with little success.

"Hello?" Beatrice said, waving her hand in front of Liliana's face. "What happened? You zoned out right there. What were you thinking about?"

"Oh, nothing. Just what might be waiting for us, and what we can do afterwards," Liliana said, deflecting the question.

The carriage came to a slow stop. "All right, this is it," Beatrice said, looking outside at the *Misty Marionette*. It looked like a decent enough place to stay, even by her standards. Beatrice seemed to have been worried that they were going to walk into some kind of slum house, but the *Misty Marionette* was a classy establishment. Its architecture was far more modern than the castles they were used to, painted a shiny coat of green with lovely arches depicting mermaids and seahorses.

The staff outside opened the door for them. The interior was a little too brightly lit for either girl, who did not need so much light, but their eyes adjusted quickly.

The human receptionist at the desk glanced towards them. Both girls could hear the way his heart raced in his chest as he saw them; he even drew back instinctively. Liliana felt a pang of annoyance. She felt like she was a child again, approaching a small group of children and asking them to play, only to be shunned immediately and running back into her father's arms, scowling. "Don't worry dear," he told her. "They're just afraid of you. Afraid of what they don't understand." She didn't remember what he told her next as she buried her face in his arms.

"Ah. Hello. You must be Lady Liliana and Lady Beatrice of House Carpathia, correct?"

"Yes, we are."

"Well. Your host, Mr. Sutherland, is in the meeting room right now. You can go there at once, or if you prefer, sit here while we prepare some refreshments," he added, his last words laced with hesitation, unsure whether the hotel could provide the kind of refreshments that would satisfy them.

"It's all right," Liliana said. "We will be making our way, but thank you for offering."

"It's my pleasure," the man said, bowing his head. A single bead of sweat traced a path down his forehead as they made their way past the desk and towards the room in question.

"With the way he looked at us," Beatrice said, whispering to Liliana. "You'd think that we were triple-headed monsters or something."

"Or about to jump him."

"Or were brandishing cannons behind ourselves."

"Or had blood dripping down our mouths."

"Or that he had heard Boscow's singing."

Boscow was Beatrice's gardener who had a habit of singing while he worked – it was said that all it would take for a war to break out between the werewolves and vampires was to send Boscow to go and sing a few lines for them. He was a sweet gentleman, but couldn't carry a tune to save his life.

The two of them lightly chuckled at the remark before entering the room in question.

***

Dunn Sutherland took a deep breath, glancing around the room. He needed everything to be perfect for this demonstration; it might very well be his last hope to get things started. He turned towards the mess of iron and steel: the prototype steam engine he had hauled all the way from Solaris. This was a backup - their first version had tragically been lost at sea - but to him, this ugly pile of scrap metal and noisy irritation was nearly as precious as his own child.

Dunn had taken several calculated risks in his life, but he did not think this was one of them. No, this was not a gamble - it was a certainty. If only others could see it that way. Back in Solaris, few took him seriously. His uncle owned the company, but that didn't mean that Dunn could do whatever he wanted. His ideas for steamships had been ignored time and time again. They were all blind, he told himself. The steam engine was the future. All he needed was a seed fund to begin things for larger production. His personal fortune was insufficient as it was tied up in other investments.

His dreams of having a fleet of steamships would never be realized unless he was able to secure another funding source. He had been hoping to rope in the Cain Shipping Company, but it was clear from his initial demonstration that they would not be swayed unless he could provide more tangible results.

With the werewolves crossed out and the humans of Necropolis also proving unwilling to invest, he had turned to the only other source of funding with deep enough pockets to aid him: the vampires.

Dunn knew the stories of what vampires had done to humans in the past. He was barely comfortable dealing with the werewolves, who - at least the tame ones living in the city, were forbidden from feasting on human meat. Vampires, however, were well-known to be eccentric, excessively vain, and usually uninterested in simple profit. Advice he had received on dealing with them recommended using deep flattery and avoiding overly complicated explanations.

This was a problem given the nature of his project. The vampires weren't interested in making their massive piles of gold even larger. They were interested in things that would make their lives easier or bring them prestige. He could not imagine the ugly, coal-fed engine doing either. The only thing left was to appeal to their ego, perhaps naming a ship or the engine after one of them, but they could just as easily commission their own.

As Beatrice and Liliana walked in, he tensed. His workers fidgeted at the presence of the two vampires. Their skin was deathly pale, and their crimson eyes were quite striking contrasting against the white of their eyes. Dunn felt his stomach lurch - a primal survival instinct screaming at him to move away. No matter how much he had steeled himself beforehand, dealing with these creatures of the night in practice was something else entirely.

They were beautiful, yes, but in the same way that one might find a colorful, poisonous snake to be beautiful - best admired by looking at a picture

38

or portrait, not up close.

Dunn was reminded of how, in the olden days, there had been a cult within the former kingdom of Bain which had neighbored Solaris. A cult which worshipped the vampires as deities, with many of its members considering it to be the highest honor to be transported to Necropolis to willingly become their food. Vampires were feared, but also objects of reverence for a long time - this cult had been stamped out when Solaris conquered Bain, but it was rumored that those who worshipped them still persisted in secret circles to this day within Solaris.

Dunn pushed these thoughts away as he focused on the task at hand. *Relax, they're not here to eat you. You simply need to convince them that your idea is worth investing in.*

"A pleasure to have the two of you here," Dunn said.

Beatrice and Liliana looked across the room, their eyes falling upon the contraption lying in the corner.

"Oh, is that what you wanted to show us?" Liliana asked.

Dunn hoped to get through a few more formalities before jumping to the meat of the matter, but if they were eager to start right away, he saw no reason to delay things. "Yes. This is the latest invention that some of the highest minds within Solaris have come up with. It is called a steam engine. It is something that can take something as ordinarily worthless as coal or wood and turn it into magic that can move objects. I could tell you more, but I think a demonstration would be far easier."

Beatrice and Liliana both sat down. Dunn was unnerved by how they seemed to disregard everyone in the room except for him, and even then, they barely paid any attention to him, as if the humans were less than furniture.

He began the demonstration, putting away his unease. The long table in the room was constructed of smaller tables put together, and two of them were removed to place the engine near the middle of the room.

"The heat generated causes steam to rise through this part of the machine," Dunn said, pointing to the respective parts. "And the steam cylinder converts it into power, which can be used to drive various things - either a windmill, or a ship, or something like a train."

"You could power a windmill or ship by the wind, though," Beatrice pointed out.

"Yes, but in case the wind is not there it can still work," Dunn countered. "And, for that matter, it moves faster with the engine."

He added wood to the base of the machine and ignited it. The machine began humming as the water boiled and the components started grinding against each other. Beatrice and Liliana winced slightly.

"I'm sorry, is something wrong?" Dunn asked.

"It's very loud and screechy," Beatrice complained. Having a sharper sense of hearing was not always a blessing.

Smoke was beginning to come out of the machine and stained the roof. Dunn frowned, knowing he'd have to explain that to the hotel owner, but hopefully, a few coins would settle the dispute. As the machine began acting faster and faster, it began making even more noise, shaking almost dangerously.

"Don't worry, this is perfectly normal," Dunn assured the two vampire ladies; seeing their alarmed expressions.

Just as he said that, the machine burst into flames. The lid of the boiler nearly flew off.

Liliana and Beatrice stared at him dumbfounded. "Is that supposed to happen?"

"No, no, no! Put it out!" Dunn yelled, losing his cool almost immediately. This backup prototype was not as carefully constructed as the original, and this had now backfired in the worst way possible. He had already failed to win the women over - he resigned himself within his heart to that fact, but if they didn't put the fire out, they were going to have a far bigger problem on their hands.

Liliana and Beatrice got up once they realized that this was not part of the presentation.

A burst of steam erupted from the engine, nearly hitting one of his men in the face. The man stumbled away with burns on his hands, yelling out in agony. Dunn was in full-blown panic mode now.

***

Raphael was walking down the street, enjoying a light jog by the harbor after finishing his duties, when he heard people screaming. This was different from the usual street shouting; this was the sound of panic, and it was coming from the *Misty Marionette*.

Intrigued, Raphael jogged closer. He realized his alarm was justified - the lower section of the *Misty Marionette* was on fire! He could smell the smoke before he saw the actual flames.

He recognized Dunn Sutherland amongst the crowd of onlookers gathered near the building.

"Are you all right?" Raphael asked, concerned for his safety.

"Yes, I'm fine," Dunn said, his face pale, hands trembling as he stared at the flames. "It wasn't... I didn't intend..." Dunn began rambling, unable to give a coherent answer.

"My son! My son is still in there!" a man yelled as he was led out of the building, trying to run back inside before two people restrained him. "He's still in the kitchen! I have to go back for him!"

"Calm down - someone will be in to get him or he might've already gotten out."

"No use running back inside and getting yourself killed as well!"

Raphael's first thought was to join the human chain currently attempting to douse the flames by passing several buckets of water around. He could carry far more water than an ordinary person, and given how tightly packed the buildings at the docks were, a fire could quickly become catastrophic.

Before he could join, however, he heard a soft, barely perceptible cry for help coming from inside the building. It had escaped everyone else's notice - because they were all human.

Raphael paused and weighed his options. He could hold his breath for a long time, so the smoke wasn't a problem. He could withstand the fire and burst out of the building easily with his strength. Making up his mind, he plunged into the smoke, much to the shock of the onlookers.

He quickly found the boy, who was unconscious in a corner of the kitchen where the flames had spread considerably. But as he went forward, he found something that gave him pause. "Silver," he hissed. An upscale establishment like this naturally used silver utensils, and they were scattered all over the kitchen floor. Just looking at the metal caused his skin and bones to ache. There was no way he could carry the boy back out without stepping on or scraping against the silver or being caught in the flames.

What should I do? Even with my strength I don't think I can do it on my own...

With a frustrated growl, he dashed out of the kitchen. He poked his head out of a window, scanning the crowd and seeing only humans. The smoke was getting thicker, and the fire blocked most regions of the building. He couldn't bring a human into the fire without them likely becoming an additional victim. It would take minutes to call for one of his packmates, and even then, it would just result in two werewolves staring at a pile of silver. That was hardly a great deal of help to anyone.

As he was about to lose hope, he found *them*.

There were two of them, standing apart from the crowd, their faces covered by parasols which shifted every so slightly so that he could get a glimpse of a face he didn't think he'd ever see again, but which he had seen countless times in his dreams.

He was perplexed; it was very rare to see a vampire out near the docks. What was she doing here?

He was almost so entranced by her sudden appearance that he momentarily forgot about the situation he was in.

And it was then that a strange, desperate idea came to mind.

He almost immediately dismissed it.

Why would she help him? She was a leech, a bloodsucker, one of the main reasons Necropolis had been a hellhole for humans and werewolves alike for thousands of years. And yet, what other option did he have?

He approached her quickly. Beatrice noticed him and backed away immediately, grabbing her silver ring, ready to try and ward him off. Liliana's hand went towards her bodice until she saw his face.

"I'm sorry, I didn't mean to alarm you," Raphael said. "But you're Liliana Carpathia, correct? We met at the mayor's party a few nights ago. I don't know if... do you remember me?"

"Yes," Liliana said. If anything, she had an infuriating amount of trouble forgetting him. When she lifted her parasol fully, Raphael once again

41

caught a glimpse of her dazzling face. She was wearing a crimson red dress fitted with black lace this time which complemented her eyes.

"Right. Um, I'm sorry to ask this of you so suddenly, but there's a boy trapped in the kitchen, and it's hard to get him out," Raphael explained quickly. "I could dive in and grab him, but there are silver utensils blocking the doorway. I know this is a lot to ask, but if you could just come in and clear the debris from the door in a way that I could get in, then I could save him."

There was a moment of silence as the two digested his words.

"Are you daft?!" Beatrice asked. "Why on earth would you dive into the flames like that? And why would we dive after you?"

"Beatrice, it's fine," Liliana said, interrupting her. She gave Raphael a scrutinizing look. "Why exactly do you want to save the boy?"

"Because he's a person whose life I want to save, nothing beyond that," Raphael said. He doubted she felt the same way; as someone who could potentially live for thousands of years would naturally be used to humans dying like flies. *Just you watch, she's going to say 'no.'*

"All right, I'll come with you," Liliana said.

"You can't be serious!" Beatrice whispered. "There's a fire inside!"

"The fire doesn't bother me," Liliana said. "I think you're forgetting just how strong and fast I can be when I want to. It's not a problem."

Raphael could hardly believe his ears. She took two steps forward, beckoning him to follow her.

"Why are you going in there?" several onlookers yelled at them as they walked inside, wondering why a lady was now also jumping headfirst into a burning building. Much like Raphael, however, she was hardly in danger from the flames.

"That's where the silverware is," Raphael said, crouching down. "If you could just push it to the side - I know it's hot, but just sweep it aside somehow - then I could get to him."

Liliana sniffed the air and recoiled. "Garlic," she said. Amidst the smoke, there was the pungent odor of garlic fumes from the kitchen. Of course in a place like this there would be things like garlic and clove oil.

"Is it bothering you too much?"

"It's not too strong here, but I'm going to have to leave soon," Liliana explained.

"No problem," Raphael said.

Liliana swept the silverware away with her foot, nearly causing one of them to land on Raphael, who leapt back, his pupils dilating.

"I'm sorry, I'm sorry," Liliana said.

"No problem. I think that's enough! Thank you so much! You've done a lot of help. You can go now," Raphael said rapidly before diving into the room. He grabbed the boy, who was almost unconscious, took him into his arms, and leaped out through the clearing that Liliana had made.

"Why didn't you leave yet?" Raphael asked. He had only been in the room for a second, but Liliana could move just as fast as him. He had expected her to be gone by the time he got back.

"I… wanted to make sure that you got out," Liliana said.

The flames had blocked the window they had used coming in, so Raphael simply kicked a portion of the wall down. "After you," he said to Liliana, who went out, with Raphael following, carrying the boy.

The boy's father, one of the chefs, rushed over and took his son. The boy was not badly burnt but had likely inhaled a large amount of smoke. Raphael quickly directed the father to a nearby hospital, aided by other Lycans who had arrived on the scene by that point.

Raphael turned towards Liliana. She looked fine at first glance; not a single strand of hair on her head or even a part of her dress had been burnt - a testament to her power. However, there were slight blemishes around her nose, which she clutched as if they were painful.

"I'm sorry, are you all right?" Raphael asked.

"It's the garlic. Don't worry, it'll wear off," Liliana said, asking Beatrice to get her parasol so she could cover her face. She seemed more concerned about looking disfigured in public than the actual harm done by the garlic, which was already starting to fade in the fresh air.

Beatrice walked up to Liliana. "Liliana! Why on earth would you do something like that, and look at that! What happened to your nose? Did you get burnt?"

"It's not a burn, relax," Liliana said. "You worry too much. It's just a bit of garlic fumes." Even as she was saying this, she could feel the skin around her nose regenerating.

"What if something happened to you? What if there was a jar of garlic oil and it fell on you by mistake? What would I possibly tell your mother?"

"Relax, Beatrice. Nothing will happen to me. I'm too smart for that," Liliana said. "And besides, I managed to succeed, didn't I?"

Beatrice glanced at the boy. "He looks kind of weak already," she said softly, noticing his irregular chest movements. "He may not survive even after all of that. Humans are rather fragile creatures, aren't they? Why bother doing all that for… something like him?"

Liliana frowned. Beatrice's words sounded cruel, but she had a point. Wouldn't all their effort go to waste if the boy didn't survive?

The boy's father blabbered words of thanks rapidly one after the other to the point where it was nearly incomprehensible.

"It wasn't just me who did this," Raphael said. "You should also be thanking that lady over there. She dove in with me, and if she hadn't cleared the way, I wouldn't have survived."

The chef walked over to Liliana and grabbed her hands. She was so shocked that she didn't even withdraw them - it was very odd for a human to touch her like that with little disregard for their own safety.

"Thank you so much, ma'am! Thank you so much!" His words choked up slightly as he noticed her crimson red eyes and his heart skipped a beat. He clearly hadn't thought that she was a vampire. Maybe he thought she was a

43

Lycan? He quickly bowed his head. "Ah, thank you very much, Madam Vampire! Thank you!"

"It was nothing," Liliana said, unsure of how to respond.

"What do you mean, it was nothing?" Beatrice whispered in her ear. "You could have gotten killed!"

"I wasn't going to get killed," Liliana said. "Stop exaggerating, maybe lightly injured at most."

"You talk as if that's any better!"

"Come on now, let's just go." Liliana said. The fire was quickly being brought under control by the werewolves who had arrived. They quickly formed another chain of people carrying buckets of water to douse the flames, their efficiency several multitudes greater that of the humans.

"I hope he survives," Liliana said under her breath. She turned her attention to the retreating figure of Raphael, who was already several blocks away, carrying the boy in his arms. Once again, she felt the heart within her chest thump once or twice.

"So many werewolves at once," Beatrice said, clutching the silver ring in her hands tightly. "Well anyway, Liliana, let's not waste more time here - let's go. I heard of this great new shop that sells dwarven handicrafts."

Liliana agreed. They had come here to appraise an investment offer, and it was clear that the steam engine had no future. The slight burning feeling in Liliana's nose was completely gone by this point.

"All right, then, lead the way," Liliana said.

***

Hospitals in Necropolis were, to say the least, quite primitive. They were not well developed compared to those in Solaris, as medicine was still mainly limited to basic magical spells, talismans, and herbs. In the "good old days" as the vampires remembered them, the sick and elderly were simply fed to the lower class of vampires. While humans were no longer slaughtered like cattle and more care was given to their ailments, the clinics that arose were often filthy, filled with contaminants, and offered treatments that usually did nothing - or sometimes made things worse.

Sterilization had not been perfected, anesthesia was limited to opioid drinks, and surgery resembled butchery more than any scientific art form.

Both vampires and werewolves could regenerate quickly and had little use for such things, as such, medicine was almost entirely the domain of humans.

As such, Raphael doubted there was much they could do for the young boy, but what else could he do?

The doctors applied a salve to the boy's burns around his nose and mouth, but otherwise, he was essentially left to lie there. One of the staff attempted some kind of healing ritual. Raphael wasn't sure if it was an actual spell or just human superstition, but he did not object.

Humans truly are fragile, Raphael reminded himself. Werewolf bones could regenerate within hours; very few things could harm a Lycan, and those that could - like silver entering the bloodstream - had no cure better than a swift, merciful end from a friend. Most hospitals, for that matter, were more of palliative units where people's suffering as they died was taken care of than places for actual treatment.

The boy's father arrived soon after and went to see him. The boy weakly opened his eyes in response to his father's voice but gave no other response.

"Burns sometimes don't show their effects immediately," the doctor explained to Raphael. "The smoke can travel down into their lungs and cause burns along the airway. We can't see that easily, and unfortunately, there's not much we can do. I can bandage the external burns, but for the smoke in his windpipe, we just have to wait for him to clear it out, if he does so."

This put Raphael in a foul mood. He kept second-guessing his actions. Was there another way into the kitchen? Going to fetch Liliana hadn't taken much time - barely a minute, given their speed - but in emergencies, even a few minutes could make a huge difference.

He wanted to stay longer, but the crowded, stifling atmosphere of the hospital made him antsy. It was claustrophobic, much like being in a carriage. He left behind a few coins for the boy's medical expenses and went to roam the streets of the city.

Raphael checked on the *Misty Marionette* during his excursion. The entire lower floor was badly damaged, and though the building was still standing right now, it looked like it might collapse like a stack of dominoes at any moment. The local magistrate had taken Dunn Sutherland into custody, looking to press arson charges, as it seemed his "weird contraption" had started the blaze.

Later that evening, when Raphael returned to check on the boy, he saw a familiar carriage standing near the hospital, bearing a coat of arms he recognized from the mayor's party.

Is she here? he thought. The idea both excited and worried him.

He pictured her - different from the ice sculpture of a vampire he'd always imagined in his mind. She had helped him save a child, an act she had no obligation to perform. She had even hurt herself in the process, which filled him with guilt. He wrestled with his feelings: she was beautiful and different, yet she was trouble. It was no secret that his father and her mother hated each other. Getting deeply involved would mean turning his back on many of the people whom he knew. At least, that is how pursuing her would be seen as by them.

As it was, he wasn't even sure if she was interested in him in that way.

He was about to turn away when a voice echoed in his head: *You're being silly. You've already imagined yourself in love with her and what would happen then but who says it will even get that far? Why not just see her? What harm can a meeting do?*

He paused, hesitantly turning around towards the entrance.

Inside, Liliana was saying goodbye to the chef. "I wish him luck," she

45

said, glancing toward the boy, who was weak and coughing constantly. The doctor suspected he would develop pneumonia in the coming few days. Liliana had come back hoping to see Raphael, though the reason she gave Beatrice was to check on the child she had helped save.

"We should go now," Beatrice whispered, insisting they had lingered for too long.

As they turned to leave, Liliana caught his scent. It was stronger than before, mixed with a trace of smoke and the harbor's stench, but it was undoubtedly him.

"Let's go down this way," Liliana said, subtly urging Beatrice towards the path Raphael was approaching. All day, she had been distracted, deflecting Beatrice's concerned questions at times by insisting she was merely engrossed by the day's events.

And then, she saw him.

Ba-dump. Ba-dump.

Her heart pounded twice. He was dressed in less elegant clothing than when she had seen him during the party, but these suited him well. It gave him a noble, rustic look, only accentuated by his prior actions that day.

"Oh, hello," Liliana said. "Fancy running into you here."

"Yeah, some coincidence, right?" Raphael replied, having taken this passageway specifically to find her, tracking her scent like a bloodhound.

The two stood there in the hallway, staring at each other for a good ten seconds, the passing people carefully navigating around them like a stream around a rock, unwilling to disturb the strange pair. Beatrice constantly glanced at their faces, thoroughly confused by the lack of expected hostility.

Raphael broke the silence. "I wanted to thank you for helping me. If it wasn't for what you did, I wouldn't have been able to save him."

"It was nothing," Liliana said. "You are the one who did most of the work. I just removed obstacles out of your way."

"Yes, but you ended up hurting yourself in the process," Raphael said. "I'm so sorry that happened to you. Are you okay now?"

"Indeed, I am," she said, touching her nose, where the slight blemishes had vanished completely. "Do you see? My skin's as perfect as always."

"Indeed, it is," Raphael said, smiling. "It's good to know that. Did you find out how the boy is doing?"

"He still seems to be doing poorly," Liliana said, her tone softening. "They suspect pneumonia."

"So, a lung infection," Raphael said, his face falling. "I thought he might develop that. It was still very brave of you, though, to go and save him."

"I could say the same," Liliana replied. "But it wasn't all that brave, not as much as it would be for a human."

"Yes, humans are easy to break, aren't they?" Raphael mused.

Their small talk faltered again. Raphael felt his heart quickening, the *bump-bump-bump* audible to both of them. Beatrice, briefly thinking he might be preparing to pounce, which was why his heart rate was spiking, unconsciously tightened her grip on her silver bracelet.

"Well, Liliana, we should be going," Beatrice finally interjected after the two of them had stared dumbly at each other for far too long.

"Oh, right, of course. We have to leave, please excuse us," Liliana said.

"You must be busy," Raphael said. "Well, I'm sorry to have kept you."

"No, no, it's not a problem at all," Liliana insisted.

The question - *Will I be able to see you again?* - hung in the air between them; desperately wanting for an answer but an answer which they both did not want to hear. Once they parted, who knew when they would cross paths again? More likely than not, such an occurrence would never happen. Despite Beatrice's insistence, neither of them felt like their legs would move until Beatrice put a hand on Liliana's shoulder, breaking whatever trance they were in.

As Beatrice led Liliana away, she had to ask. "Well, what was that about?"

"Oh, nothing. I was just thinking about the party. I had met him earlier. And, you know," Liliana said, "with his father and all."

"Yes, I've heard his father is a real brute," Beatrice whispered under her breath. "And your mother absolutely despises him, doesn't she?"

"Yes, she does," Liliana said.

Beatrice was gauging her reaction by questioning her. A truth had blossomed in Beatrice's mind on why Liliana might be behaving this way - but it was a truth Beatrice's mind refused to accept as plausible until it was fertilized with further evidence.

Raphael, for his part, made his way out of the hospital and returned home, finding his father waiting for him.

"I heard that you had an eventful day," his father said when he walked in.

"Oh, yeah," Raphael replied. "Um, the *Misty Marionette* nearly burned down."

"So I heard," Abraham said, sighing. "And it looks like Dunn Sutherland really was responsible for it. He, or rather one of his employees, sent me a letter asking me if I could find a way to get him out of his current legal predicament."

"And, are you going to?"

"We'll see - arson is a serious charge," Abraham said. "I doubt the mayor wants to harm trade with Solaris any more than we do. Of course, if enough people call for his head, Mayor Corvin will have little other recourse."

"Are they going to ask for his head?" Raphael asked.

"I'm not sure. It depends on the damage done," Abraham replied. "The damage to the *Misty Marionette*, I suppose his money can cover, or at least his company could pay that off. And if not, the mayor could seize some of it to pay for the repairs. I guess a lot of it depends on whether that boy lives or not," Abraham said. "If he dies, there might be enough of an uproar that they'll demand a life in return. If he lives, perhaps Dunn might be able to get off."

"I don't think he did it on purpose, you know," Raphael said. Granted, even if it had been entirely an accident, the damage to the building was significant, and several people had been injured, some of them Dunn's own workers.

"That won't matter much when they see just how extensive the damage was," Abraham said. "A fire is no laughing matter, especially on the docks. However, I don't think there's a problem in posting his bail, at least. We can extend that much consideration, though I haven't finalized it. How is the boy, by the way?"

"His life still seems to be in the balance. The doctors aren't sure whether he'll survive, given how much smoke he inhaled," Raphael explained. It had astounded Raphael; he had assumed that since the boy hadn't been badly burned, his life wasn't in danger. From what the physician said though, a lot of his injuries were internal.

"Well, humans are rather easy to break," Abraham said, echoing Raphael's earlier sentiment. "That's part of the reason why they fear us so much. Even if we don't mean to, we could end up hurting them." He seemed to be hinting at the times Raphael had broken a human child's bones while playing.

Raphael bobbed his head sheepishly. "Yes, Father. I'm sorry."

"What are you sorry for? Oh, you mean *that* incident? No, I'm not talking about that," Abraham said, waving his hand. "Just talking in general. But you definitely did good today, son. How are your preparations for that little charity project of yours?"

The events of the day had consumed so much of Raphael's attention that he had forgotten about his little project.

"Oh, that. Yes. Well, the original owners of the bakery have vacated. We're going to set up everything, and, uh, we just need a proper supplier for the ingredients to ensure that we have enough food for everyone. Then there are other things to look at - utensils, bowls, someone to actually go ahead and wash them and all that stuff. We're probably going to need a lot of human staff, and some of them balk a little knowing that they're going to be working for werewolves."

"Would you want me to lend you some workers?" Abraham asked. His company employed several humans, though their skills were not exactly suitable for running a kitchen, which is why Raphael shook his head. "What sort of things will you be serving?" Abraham asked.

"Well, our goal is to serve nutritious things that are cheap and easy to source," Raphael explained. "I was thinking of things like soup."

"Soup is not exactly very filling," Abraham pointed out.

"That's why I was thinking of adding a side of rice or some other kind of grain. Something packed with energy, you know," Raphael said. "Meat or fish could also be good, but there just isn't enough to go around."

Eating meat, even if it was just fish or fowl, was still a luxury that not many people could afford. It was considered a sign of great prosperity, especially among humans, to be able to eat meat with every meal. Lycans could easily do so through their hunting abilities, but it was one thing to hunt for oneself and one's family, and another thing to hunt on a massive scale to feed so many people. If Raphael did that, then he really would be over-hunting.

"Well, you can't give them everything," Abraham noted. "Many people, I think, will be happy just to have something going into their stomachs. How much do you intend to price this food at?"

"Price?" Raphael said. "I wasn't planning on pricing it at anything."

"You want to go ahead and give it away for free?" Abraham asked. "Are you entirely sure? I would ask for at least a copper from them. Or, even if they can't afford a copper, you can have them do some sort of menial task for their meals. The reason why I'm telling you this is, trust me when I say people do not value that which is given for free. You may give them meals, but that may only grow into entitlement on their behalf. If you want them to truly appreciate what they are being handed, you should charge them at least a nominal price. A copper is a steal for the kind of meal you would be giving."

"I know," Raphael said, "but I don't think there are enough jobs that we could give out that they would be able to somehow afford to work for a meal. I don't know if you've seen the streets outside, Father, but I have, and things are a lot worse than I remembered. There are a lot of people looking for work, and our goal through this is to improve our image. I don't think it would improve that much if we were giving it out for an extremely reduced fee, compared to giving it out for nothing, you know."

In response to this Abraham simply said, "The streets have always been like that, Raphael. Maybe you didn't notice because you were young and looking at it through the rose-tinted lenses of a child. But there's always been issues like vagrancy and disease. Those aren't new things."

Perhaps he was right. Raphael tended to stay to himself and near their house when he was little, usually only going out with his mother, and she certainly wouldn't have taken him anywhere dangerous or which looked that run-down.

Abraham took a long look at him. For a moment, Raphael froze – as if his father was suddenly going to berate him for his feelings towards Liliana. As if his father could somehow gaze right into his soul and extract that information right out of him. But, it wasn't regarding any of that. "I don't think that is a good idea - to give out things for free. But this is *your* project, and if you think this'll work, I'll give you free reign on it."

Raphael relaxed. Why was he acting like this though? He couldn't possibly be feeling anything that deep for her – or she for him, given how little they knew of each other.

And yet, that night, he tossed and turned in bed, his mind unable to let go of the image of her face floating before her eyes as his heart raced even while relaxing in bed.

Unlike before, his attempts to dissuade his own mind – to lead the raft of his thoughts away from the rocks they would surely crash against, were futile. He couldn't get her out of his head and was already thinking of ways that they might be able to meet up again.

His thoughts went to the boy; not regarding his welfare, but as an excuse for the two of them to run into each other. Would she go and visit the boy again? It might be worth it to spend some time around the hospital just in case she did – but the odds of them happening at the same time were low. Especially given how busy he would become setting up his little food house...

That thought made something deep in his stomach ache. The land of dreams proved to be ever elusive as he stared at the ceiling, his mind clouded by thoughts of her and thoughts of his other duties clashing against each other in tumultuous waves.

Chapter Four

The Painting

Beatrice and Liliana were making their way back home in their carriage. "Oh, today was so exhausting," Beatrice whined. Liliana had to use quite an effort not to roll her eyes; the only real muscles Beatrice had managed to exercise were those controlling her vocal cords.

"It was an interesting day out, though, don't you think? You wouldn't have had this much fun staying back in the castle, now then would you?" Liliana pointed out.

"Yes, I guess seeing a place catch on fire is kind of interesting," Beatrice said, speaking of the disaster - which caused massive property damage and injured several people - as if it was some kind of street performance.

To them, that was all it was for the most part. Even Liliana, who tried to care for human lives and see them as more than fleeting existence, knew that humans dying was a daily occurrence; their lives as brief and fleeting as the morning dew.

During the ride, Beatrice showed off many of her purchases, even though Liliana had already seen them. The most prized catch was a heavy stone goblet.

"Look at this!" she said, handing it to Liliana. "The moment the shopkeeper told me it was dwarven-made, I just knew I had to have it!"

The goblet was sculpted entirely out of stone, but molded and decorated as easily as if it had been made of clay. Liliana noted gentle patterns etched into the rim and dwarvish runes carved into the bottom, perhaps the name of the artisan. It looked surprisingly delicate yet was extremely dense. The depiction of a dragon along the exterior was flawless, and the interior was smooth to the touch.

"It's just wonderful, isn't it?" Beatrice gushed. "Nothing is as good as dwarven art pieces. They say they spend all their time in their mountains, working in their forges. That's why everything they make is so neat! And they're supposed to be very tiny, with long beards, making these masterpieces. They

51

sound so adorable!" Beatrice spoke of them almost like they were fluffy rabbits hopping around her garden.

Liliana, however, pictured burly craftsmen who spent most of their time drinking - excellent workers and engineers, but hardly *adorable* like Beatrice described them.

"It's strange, you know," Liliana muttered. "I've never actually seen a dwarf in person, nor has my mother or uncle, despite how long they've lived."

"Oh, you don't know?" Beatrice asked. "Dwarves can't sail on the ships that come over here. They're very strong, but their bones are too dense. They sink very easily and don't like swimming."

That can't possibly be true, Liliana thought, knowing Beatrice had a habit of confidently presenting gossip as fact. "I thought they just didn't like going on ships because they prefer to live underground?" All of the dwarven trade with Necropolis occurred indirectly through third parties - with most of it passing through Solaris.

"Well, yes, but they're also definitely afraid of water because they can't swim," Beatrice insisted. She then paused. "Look at me, going off on the goblet! I should be asking you how you're doing. Does the garlic still sting?"

"No, I've been fine for the past couple of hours, like I told you," Liliana said.

"I still don't think you should have run in there," Beatrice sighed. "Why didn't you just get someone else? Don't do anything like that again, ever!"

"Alright, I'll be more careful in the future," Liliana promised.

Beatrice hesitated, then held her tongue on the subject of Raphael. She wanted to voice her suspicions about the strange... *interaction* she had witnessed but didn't want to give shape to the implausible thought in the back of her mind. Surely what she was thinking couldn't be true?

"Ah, I wanted to ask you something about that Raphael fellow," Beatrice finally said, slowly getting the words out of her mouth.

"Raphael?" Liliana stuttered slightly.

"Yes. You met him just a few days back at the mayor's party, correct?" Beatrice asked. "From the way you two acted, it didn't seem like it was the first time you had met."

"I guess I might have seen him at some public event before that too," Liliana admitted. "It would be strange if we hadn't. However, I never really talked with him."

"Right. So," Beatrice said, calculating inwardly on how to proceed, "don't you think it was a bit... cowardly of him to have asked us for help like that? What kind of man goes running toward a woman to run into a burning building?" She chose her words carefully, wanting to test Liliana's reaction.

"I don't think he was being a coward. He was just trying to help someone, you know." Liliana did not say anything further, and Beatrice's line of inquiry ended there as she couldn't wring out anything further from her.

Eventually, they arrived back home. Beatrice went back to her estate, and Liliana went to hers. It was past nightfall, so Victoria, Liliana's mother, was wide awake.

"Liliana, you and Beatrice seem to have been gone for quite some time. I thought you would be home a few hours earlier," Victoria said.

"Yes, we got a bit sidetracked. You know how Beatrice can be," Liliana said.

"I was so worried I was almost about to send someone out for you," Victoria said. "How was everything?"

Liliana had meticulously planned how much to describe regarding the fire and the rescue attempt during the trip back home - she needed to control how much she said to prevent her mother from flying off the handle. She left out Raphael's name entirely. Despite her best attempts, the moment she finished the story regarding the fire, her mother immediately exclaimed, "Liliana, what on earth were you thinking?! Why would you dive into a burning building like that?"

"It was to help a human…"

"Who cares about a human!" Victoria snarled, causing Liliana to flinch. "Is their life worth one of yours? I'd gladly see a hundred thousand of them burned before even a scratch came upon you!"

"Mother, I knew what I was doing," Liliana said. "If it was dangerous, I wouldn't have gone."

"But you don't know what could have been dangerous inside!" Victoria countered. "What if there was more potent garlic somewhere? Or a piece of wood broke off, injuring you?" She then sniffed the air. "I can still smell the smoke and ash on your clothes. Honestly, Liliana, what were you thinking? If you keep on doing things like this, I might have you confined to the castle for the rest of your days! And Beatrice - I'd think that she'd have more sense than to let you do something like such! Why on earth did she bother going with you if it wasn't to look after you?"

"Mother, don't drag Beatrice into any of this. Please don't blame her; this is entirely on me," Liliana pleaded.

"She should know better still," Victoria said, though she had settled down somewhat by this point, having let out quite a bit of steam.

"Mother, it doesn't sound nearly as bad as what you think. I was fine, really."

"And you're trying to tell me that a werewolf put you up to this?" Victoria railed. "What else could one expect from those dogs? Just because they have no problem rolling around in the mud doesn't mean that you should join them!"

"I understand, Mother," Liliana said, exasperated. "But like I said, it isn't as big a deal as you think. Nothing really happened." She avoided mentioning the garlic entirely.

Victoria went on another tirade, raging about the stupidity of humans who caused problems like the fire. "Humans - they think they're so smart, and yet they were the ones responsible for the fire in the first place! Always getting themselves into situations they can't fix on their own! I should have just rejected this request in the first place! I only took it because of the name of the company and because they were from Solaris."

Even the vampiric aristocracy somewhat respected Solaris to a small extent.

Half an hour later, finally granted a break from her mother's monologue, Liliana went out to the garden, hoping the fresh air would wash off the lingering scent of smoke that still clung to her. Her thoughts drifted to Raphael when she heard footsteps approaching. It was Athelstan, her uncle.

"Liliana, are you all right?" he asked, looking quite concerned.

"Yes, I'm fine. Why are you so worried?" she responded.

"Your mother said you had been injured, so I came around as quickly as I could to check on you."

"Mother was just overreacting a little. I'm not injured at all. You can see that I'm fine."

Athelstan listened to a short summary of the day's events, shaking his head midway through. "You never should have done something like that. What if you had gotten hurt? I can understand wanting a bit of adventure, but you can find it in other ways, you know?"

"Yes, I know, I'm sorry. I probably should have thought things through a bit more. I guess that means I won't get to meet the Council of Elders, then?"

"That might still be on the table, actually," Athelstan said. "However, I'll have to talk to her later when her mood is a bit better. In the meantime, I figured you might be bored sitting here, which is why you might have done something so reckless. Would you want to come to my estate? You remember it, don't you? Near the outskirts of Necropolis, beyond the foothills of the mountains."

"Your estate?" Liliana asked. It had been nearly a decade since her last visit.

"Exactly. I don't think your mother would object to that if you want an excuse to get away from here," Athelstan said gently. "No need to thank me. I know your mother can be a bit overprotective. You are her only remaining close family other than myself, you know. Knowing her, I'm amazed she hasn't kept you inside a glass box like a doll deep within her castle, actually."

"She probably would do so if it were possible," Liliana said, agreeing wholeheartedly. She knew Victoria would likely become even more overprotective in the coming days, meaning she would have even fewer chances to go outside. A visit to her uncle's estate would be a welcome excuse to leave.

As it was, her mother soon found something else to be angry about and had nearly forgotten about the incident at the *Misty Marionette*. A pack of werewolves had attempted to buy a castle near their area - nearly an hour away measured by a human's walking speed. Up until now, this area had been maintained as an entirely vampire district. It seemed the current owner, belonging to the Volkov family, did not mind selling it, regardless of who the buyer was so long as they received an appropriate price.

"Brother, you must help me try to talk sense into them!" Victoria railed

54

to Athelstan. "How can they possibly give up a piece of their heritage to one of *them?*"

"Well, we can certainly pay them a visit," Athelstan replied. "They may have reasons beyond their control, however, why they are selling this."

Victoria shook her head. "This is the vanguard of their invasion. First one home will go to them, and then another castle, and another mansion. Before you know it, we'll be surrounded by them!"

"Where did they even get enough funds for one? It is a bit of an oddity, no?"

"Probably one of the new ones who have popped up, like that man Abraham," Victoria said, spitting the name from her mouth like it was a piece of rotten fruit she had accidentally bit into.

"On that note, we can maybe even speak with the Council of Elders first," Athelstan suggested. "Although they don't have the power to stop the Volkovs from selling their estate, perhaps they could put more pressure upon them."

Victoria's eyes widened slightly. "Ah, that is an excellent idea, Brother! Why didn't I think of that?"

"And in the meantime, we can introduce Liliana to them."

"I don't know about that," Victoria said, hesitating. "I still think that it is too early for her to put her nose into political matters." She then turned toward Liliana who had been seated in a corner of the room. "But... would you like to meet with them?"

Liliana was shocked that her mother was actually asking for her opinion. Perhaps her recent actions had told her mother that she really was growing up, or perhaps her mother feared further disobedience if she didn't give Liliana some freedom? Regardless, she found herself tongue-tied and wasn't sure what to say until she finally managed to get out: "Certainly, I would love to."

"The next meeting is going to be hosted at Castle Blackthorne during the Walpurgisnacht," Athelstan said.

"All right then, Liliana, you need to start studying and make sure everything is proper before you go there. Why don't you speak to Beatrice? The two of you can study and then present yourselves together. You wouldn't want to embarrass yourselves in front of them."

"Of course not," Liliana said. She also made a note to keep a low profile from here on out. Her mother had granted her a bit of freedom, and she did not want to see it yanked away because of something she did carelessly.

Despite telling herself to keep a low profile, before the week ended, something would happen that would thrust Liliana into the limelight no matter how much she didn't want it - though she was not initially aware of it. Since she rarely ventured outside the castle, and her mother had little use for news outside their tiny bubble, she was unaware that she was gaining quite the reputation among the general human populace.

Raphael, as a werewolf, was already somewhat widely known and a werewolf coming to help humans, while significant, was not entirely unprecedented. Werewolves and humans had basically been in the same boat for a long time.

However, for a vampire - one of their former masters, akin to eldritch horrors which many of them little understood - to descend from their castle to help a mortal human was almost unheard of.

The official report on the fire, detailing Sutherland's machine malfunctioning, was confirmed by many witness accounts. Although most onlookers had only caught a passing glimpse of Liliana and Beatrice due to their parasols, some had indeed seen Liliana in action. And news of this spread faster than the fire did throughout the *Misty Marionette* - she had quickly gained the moniker 'Lady Liliana of the Light.'

One afternoon, a servant approached Liliana at her estate. "My apologies for interrupting you, I would normally not bother you with something like this. But there is a human near the gate. He said he would like to speak with you."

Liliana found this very odd. No ordinary human willingly sought out a vampire's home without serious reason. Even those in their upper class who pandered to the vampires kept their distance.

"He also said that he's traveled some way, milady, and though I tried to chase him off he insisted I relay the message to you."

"Alright, I'll go see what he wants," Liliana said, accompanied by the servant.

"Lady Liliana," the man called from beyond the iron gate. "My apologies for bothering you. I don't know if you remember me?"

"Pardon but… have we met before?"

"Not entirely. I was there near the *Misty Marionette* when it caught fire. I happened to see you and your little act of heroism."

Liliana nodded. "That is correct. I was there."

"Well, your actions greatly inspired me, and that's why I ended up making this," the man said. "I'm a painter, you see. I was by the docks that day, actually, just looking for inspiration for my next work. Usually, I paint scenes of the sea, but you inspired me to create something different. I just wanted to give it to you as a… token of appreciation, you could say."

"Are you related to the boy in question?" Liliana asked.

"No, I'm not. This is something I made more for myself, and I didn't know whether or not you would like it. But here it is, if you would take it."

Liliana glanced at the painting. Ordinarily, portraits of vampires depicted them in a dark, gritty light - a bias that had become a tradition among human artists. This portrait, however, was different. It did not depict the scene accurately at all, but instead showed Liliana standing over a young boy (who looked nothing like the one she rescued) at her feet, with a crowd in the background. A ray of sunshine parted from a cloudy sky, illuminating her head like a halo, which although was probably meant to signify purity and kindness, would have been extremely painful if she wasn't wearing her talisman.

The man had gotten her dress correctly, and Beatrice was also depicted standing next to her, but the faces were clearly based only on a fleeting glimpse, having generic, gentle, angelic features not typically associated with vampiric portraits.

"This is very nice, really," Liliana said, not wanting to make any kind of negative remark. He had likely not seen their faces close enough to make something very accurate based on memory alone, explaining why it looked like so.

"Ah - it is for you. I didn't intend to keep it. I really do appreciate everything you did, and so does everyone else."

"Alright then," Liliana said, looking at the portrait. "Thank you very much." A part of her felt she should invite him into the major out of courtesy, but she knew what her mother would say. "I would invite you into the castle, but-"

"Oh, no, no, I'm fine," the man said, waving his hand. He seemed hesitant to step inside the castle proper. To come to the gates was one thing - but to go inside the castle? That seemed to be out of the question for him.

As the man turned to walk away, Liliana quickly called out, "Excuse me! I have a question! Did the boy survive?"

"He did. I've heard he's a bit sickly, but yes, he did." A look of relief flashed across Liliana's face as she took another glance at the painting in her hands as he wandered off.

Liliana took the portrait back with her. She immediately decided to show it to Beatrice.

"Oh, it's great that you dropped by," Beatrice said, pulling out her violin. "I managed to think of another piece."

"Great. I have something I wanted to show you, too."

"Oh, a painting!" Beatrice said. "That's wonderful! Why, Liliana, this is amazing for a first try!"

"No, it's not something I made," Liliana said. "Do you remember the incident near the *Misty Marionette*?"

"Oh, yes, that. You won't know how much of an earful my parents gave me for letting you walk in there."

"They really shouldn't have; it was entirely my decision," Liliana protested.

"Yes, but they said, 'Oh, you're older than her, you should know better!'"

"You're only two months older than me!" Liliana said. "You can hardly count that in any terms of maturity."

Beatrice stuck her tongue out while mocking her. "No, actually, I think that they're right. Younger sisters should listen to their elders, shouldn't they? Anyway, this painting isn't bad," Beatrice said, examining the work more closely before voicing her complaints. "Why does he have us being struck by sunlight? Does the human want to see us hurt?"

Ordinarily, humans who were used to making artwork and the like for vampires knew what they wanted - it was an integral part of living within Necropolis for millennia, after all. If you were even tangentially useful to the vampires, you had a far higher chance of survival. Not only would it mean more money, but also a lower chance of you or your loved ones becoming their next meal. This aspect had carried forward in Necropolis's culture since its founding days.

"No, that's just a way of making us look heroic, I think."

Beatrice took a closer look at her own image. "That doesn't look like me at all! He's gotten my cheekbones all wrong, and my nose is too small! I'd like to give this human a good talking to!"

"Well, he's already left, and I didn't really get his name," Liliana pointed out.

"Well, he really needs to work on his painting skills."

"It isn't that, I just don't think he ever saw your face clearly," Liliana said.

In response to this, Beatrice fetched some of her other portraits - depicting her in a dark, moody light, smiling a sinister, scheming smile. She looked far less angelic in these, which was exactly how she, and most vampires, preferred their portraits. "See? This is what I actually look like."

"Apparently, people are talking about us," Liliana said.

"Oh, what kind of people?" Beatrice asked, quite interested.

"Well, the humans."

"Oh, you mean the humans," Beatrice said, losing interest. "I thought our own folk were talking about us."

"You're not the slightest bit curious as to what they're saying?"

" No, I don't really care what they think."

"What do you think I should do with the portrait? Do you want to keep it?"

"Not really. You can keep it," Beatrice said. "Though, if you see the artist again, do give him a piece of my mind and remind him to do better."

"Sure thing," Liliana said, very willing to make that promise as she assumed she would never meet the person again.

"Now, I call this one - 'The Blood Sea'," Beatrice said, reaching for her violin.

This was not the end of Liliana's newfound reputation having unforeseen consequences, however.

***

Raphael wandered through the streets of the city. He was clutching the deed to the bakery shop in his hand - soon to become the site of his new venture.

If this went well, it would prove to his father that he really could do something on his own. While the meeting with Dunn Sutherland had technically been successful, it was also true that it had ended up in flames later on.

Even if that hadn't been what he intended, nor his fault really, it still left a bad taste in his mouth. It was something that he felt that he had to make up for.

Raphael paid the boy he had rescued alongside Liliana, named Chester, one last visit. The fire at the *Misty Marionette* proved somewhat fortuitous for his plans. Chester's father, a chef, was going to be out of work given the time it would take for the building to be reconstructed. The fact that several unemployed chefs were looking for work after the tragedy was a blessing in disguise for Raphael.

Raphael felt a bit bad that he was benefitting from such an incident, but then again, it wasn't like he had caused it.

When Raphael went to check on Chester, the boy was still pale and coughing, but the doctors were hopeful he would eventually recover enough to walk and care for himself, though his long-term prognosis was still unclear.

The boy's mother cried while holding Raphael's hands, thanking him over and over. When Raphael asked the boy's father if he would consider working for the new charity, he replied that he needed to take time off to care for his son.

"I'm not really that desperate for money yet. I can go live with one of my brothers for the time being. My apologies about that, sir."

"No, no, please relax, that wasn't a demand," Raphael clarified. "I was just looking for people for this little venture of mine."

Raphael described the soup kitchen project in more detail. The man estimated Raphael would need about twenty people - chefs and ancillary crew - to cook for the anticipated traffic of one hundred and fifty people a day.

"Twenty - that many?" Raphael asked, surprised.

"I'm afraid so. But if you want, I can tell you the names of some people who I used to work with. They're probably going to be out of work as well, so you can reach out to them."

Many of the cleaning staff and kitchen crew, though trained for finer work, were eager for anything they could get after the fire. Raphael therefore found the entire hiring process far simpler than he had imagined.

There was far less reticence regarding working for him, a werewolf, than he'd initially thought from them - as the stories of his heroism had spread like wildfire. He almost felt for a moment like this venture might be pointless, given how much his earlier act had already accomplished. However, he knew the fame from the rescue would be short-lived, while the fame from his project could last for decades.

When it came to wage negotiations, he was forced to play hardball now that the costs of running the place were going to be higher than initially anticipated. "I'm sorry, I know that you used to get paid more back at the *Misty Marionette*," Raphael would usually tell them. "However, for the work that we're asking for, we really can't give you any more than this."

"Come now, surely the Cain Shipping Company can afford a bit more than this," was the usual response to this.

"This is going to be a net loss for the company," Raphael explained. "We're doing this for the good of the people of Necropolis, not for profit, and because of that, we really can't offer to pay you any more."

The negotiations usually ended there. Not everyone agreed to his terms, of course, but enough of them did to the point where he had all the staff he needed.

One thing that surprised Raphael was the extent to which people were now talking about Liliana. He didn't mind that she was getting recognition, but the issue was that, for whatever reason, people assumed the two of them were related in some way - and since they clearly weren't related by blood, talk went in other directions. This speculation was something that would cause him significant problems if it reached the wrong ears, namely his father's.

The evening before his soup kitchen project was finalized, it turned out that unfortunately, the rumor had indeed reached Abraham.

"What is this about you and the Liliana girl?" Abraham asked casually over dinner. "Some people have been asking me about it."

Raphael, normally good at reading his father, could not discern his feelings. Was he angry? Curious? Irritated?

"Boy, I asked you a question," Abraham repeated when Raphael had not responded.

"Right, right, right," Raphael said, struggling not to become tongue-tied. "I just happened to see her on the street, and I needed someone to help with rescuing the kid, and then she offered."

"Of all the people you could've asked, why did you ask her instead of one of your friends?" Abraham pressed.

"They wouldn't have come there in time, and I wasn't really sure what to do. I just went with whoever I could find," Raphael explained. "If we would have been late, we wouldn't have been able to save the boy, and even if we had, he may not have survived like he did now."

Abraham paused. "Why was she there anyway? That's not vampire territory, and it's rare for one of them to come out, especially in the middle of the day."

"I don't know," Raphael admitted.

Dunn did not want his dealings to be known to the Cains - that would be "breaking bread with the enemy" and so had not revealed that fact during his communications with Abraham.

"Well, you had to do so this time," Abraham conceded. "However, be careful about our reputation moving forward. No one will forget about it that easily. The other werewolves - they may start looking at you differently if you begin to associate too closely with them." The Cain family was rich, but it was far from the richest family of werewolves in the city. Abraham happened to be more politically astute than most of his other counterparts, which is why he was the face of the werewolf faction, but that was a tenuous position that could very easily collapse.

"Father, where do you think our relationship with the vampires is going to go?" Raphael asked.

"What's that supposed to mean?"

"I mean, I know we're enemies, and for a good reason bu-"

"Well, not *enemies*. I would not go to describe them using such extreme terms," Abraham said, chuckling. "It's been a long time since the last war, but we are still political adversaries. Both of us want diametrically opposite things, son. And it's not just that. Vampires are different," he said, his voice void of emotion, as if he were a scientist describing a strange venomous organism. "They feast on human blood. They live for practically forever. They don't have the same emotions as we do. It would be for the best if we had our own city away from them, but this is the best spot on the continent, and we've already made a home for ourselves here. I can't see us going out now."

"What I meant to say was," Raphael began, "the humans have more and more political power day by day. It's soon going to basically become their city, with the two of us just living here. Both the vampires and we have to adapt somewhat to that."

"I don't think the vampires will," Abraham said. "There are far too many of them who are too old, who still remember the days when they were the uncontested kings of the city. To go from that to being under the human's boot is something they're not ready to admit. Not until it's far too late."

"And what do you think will happen after that?" Raphael pressed.

"I think there's going to be another war," Abraham said, sighing. "I don't want one, but that's likely what's going to happen. Some of them won't be able to deal with reality until there's a stake driven through their hearts. By then, those who are smart enough to adapt will, and the others will simply be wiped out. But I can't see that happening for another few hundred years."

"It just seems pointless to keep fighting with each other," Raphael muttered. "It looks like the humans are going to be the ultimate winners."

"Maybe, but I don't think there's anything that you can really do to change their minds. They're too stubborn for that, especially the older ones. They still look at us as vassals who they hired centuries ago. And some of them, I know, are just downright evil." Whenever there was a murder which was not easily solved, or someone had disappeared without a trace, there was always the talk that it had been a vampire responsible. Raphael knew it would be easy for a vampire to take down some of the less fortunate members of society, like beggars and tramps, who wouldn't be missed.

Still, the memory of Liliana's eyes carried a strange kind of warmth. Surely she would never do that?

He had been asking his father these questions simply to understand how feasible it might be for the two sides to come to some kind of compromise. The only real thing that worked in his favor, now that he thought about it - was that neither Victoria nor Abraham had any personal grudges against one another. They vehemently opposed each other because of their ideologies and political stances, but neither family had ever struck against the other specifically.

61

It was a very small shred of hope, but it was still something, Raphael supposed - even if what the rest of what his father said did not fill him with confidence.

***

It was a gray, cold, and cloudy day, as most days were in Necropolis, but the inside of what used to be a bakery, now titled Cain Soup Kitchen, was bursting with warmth and the aroma of cooking. It was a welcome reprieve for many from the dark and dreary environment around the docks. Raphael had gone with his father's advice regarding what they were going to serve: rice with a side of vegetable soup - a bit more watery than expected, but certainly better than nothing.

Five cooks, a head chef, and ten other staff members were needed for miscellaneous tasks like cleaning, distributing utensils, and serving. Raphael wanted to rely on paid staff initially to showcase the resources of the Cain Shipping Company and ensure consistency rather than relying on volunteers.

The soup kitchen had advertised its opening through local shops and the hospital, but there was no better advertisement than the smell that was slowly wafting through the streets. Soon, about twenty people had lined up for the first batch of meals.

Raphael, overseeing the distribution himself, noted that a lot of ordinary people had joined the line, not just the destitute, but others interested in a free meal. He briefly considered intentionally making the food less tasty to deter those who didn't truly need it, but dismissed it as self-defeating.

Complaints quickly arose.

"The soup is kind of watery, isn't it?"

"The rice is slightly burnt."

"Is there a rock in my bowl?"

With the sheer volume of food they were making, it was difficult to maintain quality. Raphael realized he needed a system for quality control, since the chef couldn't sample all of it.

The "real" customers came in about two hours later - as in people wearing torn coats, lacking proper shoes, and smelling of destitution. These people did not complain about anything. Utensils were already piling up near the side of the building, a sign that they would quickly need more cleaning staff and an adequate supply of water. The first day was fraught with issues, but Raphael welcomed them rearing their heads sooner rather than later; he could now identify and smooth out these problems so the kitchen could eventually run without him.

Later that evening, after closing, Raphael reviewed the costs that they were occurring. It was far more than he had anticipated. He could have asked his father for more funds, but Abraham had agreed to the project because it was relatively cheap for the potential positive results. Raphael would either need to adjust the budget or look for other sources of funding.

He glanced at the number of people they had fed that day: two hundred and eleven. That filled him with pride, but he knew that compared to the population of the city, it was a drop in the ocean.

Over the next few days, the kitchen became more popular, serving an average of around three hundred people daily, but with greater success came greater problems: more staff and ingredients were needed, and the location turned out to be too small.

Furthermore, the crowds were rougher. Fights broke out, and it was only Raphael's presence as a werewolf that convinced people to let things go easily without a full-blown brawl breaking out on the street. There were also concerns about the quality of ingredients after someone vomited a while after eating from the soup kitchen, which could harm their reputation.

Raphael could deal with many of these issues, but there was one that emerged that he was not prepared for, nor was he able to deal with on his own.

***

Ten days later, Raphael apprehensively brought up the need for additional funds to his father. He had tried to find a way to cut corners, but there was no dancing around the problem and he had to address the elephant in the room. Abraham, instead of responding immediately, said, "Why don't you come with me on a walk? There's something I need to show you."

Abraham led Raphael quite a distance away from the docks to an unfamiliar location. A strange scent began to reach Raphael - the smell of garbage and something else. Something that was rotting. Something that had died recently.

"All right, we're here," Abraham said.

Raphael looked around and saw the aftermath of what looked like an animal sacrifice in a corner of a cemetery. Candles had been lit, and though the wax was cold, they were arranged around a glade purposefully. Letters were inscribed into the dirt.

Raphael read the letters aloud: "The Mother of Compassion, Lady Liliana of the Light. We give this bounty-" it was followed by a lot of fanciful language that made little sense to him.

"'Lady Liliana of the Light'," Abraham pointed out. "That's what they're calling her now, after she saved a human. It's amazing, really. Vampires have been oppressing and slaughtering them for millennia, and all it takes is one act of kindness, and she becomes a saintess overnight."

"So, this is some kind of offering to her?" Raphael asked.

"Not just an offering. This sort of practice used to be very popular at one point. These are from the Bloodborne."

"Bloodborne?"

"They are a group of cultists here in Necropolis - a group of humans who worshiped the vampires," Abraham said.

"Worshiped them?" Raphael asked incredulously.

63

"Yes, I'm as shocked as you are. They're not exactly numerous, but they've always existed as far as I can tell. In the millennia when vampires could do whatever they pleased, some of them would willingly sacrifice themselves to their overlords."

"That sounds borderline insane!"

"My point being," Abraham continued, "is they haven't really had an actual cause with regard to supporting the vampires up until now. But this little trick by Liliana has somehow worked on some of them. The fact that vampires mainly stay in their own quarters helps them a little bit. Because they can't see them for the monsters they are. You see where the problem lies, don't you?"

Raphael tried to think of it from his father's perspective. "So, you're afraid that the humans will start worshiping the vampires again? In large numbers I mean?"

"Perhaps," Abraham answered. "And we do need to stop that. Your little idea of creating the soup kitchen was actually very nice, and I think we should go ahead and continue supporting it."

Raphael relaxed a little. "Okay, that's good."

"But," Abraham said, "we're running into a major issue. I've gotten complaints from two different guilds, the Weaver's Guild as well as the Butcher's Guild, who are complaining about your shop."

"Complaining? I don't understand. I haven't done anything to them."

"*You* haven't done anything. It's because of your customers," Abraham said. "The kind of people that you're attracting to that area don't just get their meals and leave; they camp around it. And because of that, ordinary people don't want to stick around the place. Nor do they want to visit the shops there. Basically, you've been hurting their businesses. It isn't just the two guilds - the other shop owners around the area are also complaining."

"Oh."

"You're still young, so it's understandable how you made this mistake," Abraham reprimanded, "but you shouldn't have chosen such an upscale area for this. You need to move the location of the shop to some place which is more suitable for the kind of people you're serving."

"I've already spent quite a bit on the bakery shop," Raphael sighed.

"Don't worry about that. We can find another use for it or sell it later on. As a matter of fact, I happen to know this human noblewoman by the name of Cecilia who is also interested in doing such acts of charity. If you speak with her, you may be able to find a better spot."

"Do we really want to bring in someone else?" The point of this was that it was supposed to be the Cain family's project.

"No, but let's be practical here," Abraham said. "There's a limit to how much we can do on our own, and we don't want problems arising if we can't do it properly. A human who is experienced with this will be able to give us a large amount of help, even if she ends up picking up part of the credit. What does it matter? Our name will still be associated with it."

Raphael resigned himself to spending the next few days looking for a new location and moving the entire operation. "You've done great work, excellent work, as a matter of fact, but we need to make some changes," Abraham concluded. Raphael nodded, disappointed but not so pig-headed as to proceed with a plan that was actively hurting the businesses of his father's human allies.

Chapter Five
Walpurgisnacht

"Mother, do you think that this is appropriate for the Walpurgisnacht?" Liliana asked Victoria, showing off the same dress she had worn to the mayor's party.

"You've worn that before, haven't you?" Victoria asked.

"Yes, but there's a reason for that. It's quite good."

"Change it to something new. Something you haven't worn before," Victoria commanded. "Otherwise, people might gossip that our coffers are lacking. Ask your cousin Beatrice. She probably has a better idea of what to wear."

As Liliana was accompanying her mother and uncle to the event, Beatrice was also tagging along. Beatrice initially thought about wearing a dress she had recently acquired from Solaris. The design featured deep colors, far too much lace, and exposed a bit too much for the generally conservative tastes of the Council of Elders.

"You don't think it's too much, do you?" Beatrice asked Liliana.

"I think you might want to go with something else," Liliana said gently. Her mother might have thought that Beatrice had better judgment when it came to fashion, but she would've likely also disagreed with Beatrice's current choice. "It's not that it doesn't look good on you, but we're meeting with all of the old-fashioned Elders, aren't we? They probably won't take kindly to someone dressed up in the fashion of a different country."

"Oh, boo. But I think you might be right," Beatrice said. Vampire fashion changed very little over the centuries. Beatrice had been eager to show it off as it was a recent purchase, but this was the wrong time and place for that. Unlike Liliana, her parents did not go to as many social events and so opportunities in the future would be rare, but not entirely absent. She would just have to wait for one.

Liliana went with a dull blue dress with thin frills and a bonnet, while Beatrice chose something similar but dull green. Neither wore silver to the event, as it was a werewolf-free occasion.

Castle Blackthorne was elegantly decorated. A cloudy sky obscured the moon and the stars, but vampiric eyes did not mind in the slightest. If anything, the general gloomy air and fog that surrounded the area only added to the kind of ambience that they preferred.

The permanent members of the Council of Elders numbered only about a dozen, but they had served for millennia. No major points of discourse were anticipated. This gathering was simply a chance for Liliana and Beatrice to get to know them.

Liliana felt this party was far classier than the one the mayor had thrown. It did not reek of tackiness or of someone attempting to throw money around to make up for a lack of tradition or heritage. This place was made by those with genuine power and standing - they were not trying to prove anything to anyone. The dark hallways were lit up with candles, the decorations dignified, the paintings depicting various ancestors, and the sculpture of King Alistair and his three wives as the centerpiece - all of it perfect for the kind of ambience Liliana had come to expect.

Walpurgisnacht was originally a festival during which the vampires would offer yearly sacrifices - sometimes hundreds or thousands of human slaves were ritually sacrificed to the altar of their great god Sanguinus back in the day. Though the old faith had greatly declined and very few genuinely believed in Sanguinus, the importance of the night continued to remain deeply inscribed in their hearts.

"This is boring," Beatrice muttered in Liliana's ear about two hours in. Liliana couldn't necessarily disagree with Beatrice. Although she had initially been excited for the event, it rapidly became clear that not much was going on. There weren't many vampires even close to their age, which was why the two of them had grown so close in the first place, and much of what the elder vampires wished to talk about were matters that had occurred long before either of them had been born.

The latest "gossip" that many of the guests were distributing was at least from a few decades ago, concerning political situations that had long since passed. The actual members of the Council of Elders were a bit more up to speed, yet even they seemed oblivious to just how much their authority had eroded and that the humans were now effectively in control of a large part of the city.

The ebb and flow of the conversation continued all around them as they watched people drift by. They felt more like two audience members watching a boring opera rather than attendants of a party.

"Has your mother started looking for a suitor for you yet, Liliana?" Beatrice asked.

Liliana was a bit taken aback by the question. "Um, no. Why do you ask?"

"I just thought that - or at least I had heard - this would be about the time when they would begin looking into such things."

"My mother hasn't. Have your parents started looking?" she asked.

"Not directly," Beatrice replied. "But they have begun dropping hints here and there."

The two ladies then looked around the party. Raphael's face flashed before Liliana's eyes for a moment before she suppressed the thought.

At the mention of the word *suitor*, both of them were reminded of how extraordinarily small the vampire community was. If one was looking for a suitor among the aristocratic class, as their parents would absolutely demand, there were few options - perhaps enough that Beatrice could count them on one hand.

There were the Effors, who thought of themselves as the "new third" of the great vampire families, given the elimination of the Montefalcos. They were the owners of Castle Blackthorn and the hosts of tonight's Walpurgisnacht festivities. However, very few people actually saw the Effors this way; the old class still considered them upstarts because they were not descended from one of King Alistair's wives. They had a son about a century older than Liliana - a difference that was not prohibitive or as stark a difference as it would be for humans. They were likely looking to move up in the world and would probably want to anchor themselves to a family like hers or Beatrice's so even if their parents didn't approach the Effors, the Effors would probably approach them at some point.

There was someone in the Malefactor family, which was technically one of the Carpathian's distant cousins - just distant enough that the marriage would not be considered consanguineous.

The Umbra had just had a newborn son, four months old by now, though it would be a wild before he would be old enough to be of marriageable age.

And finally, there were the Colters, who did not belong to any of the "Big Three" families but at the very least owned a large enough castle to have some influence.

Liliana went through all these options in her head, as did Beatrice. The people they were thinking about were not present at the current party, but they had seen these people at other events.

Gone were the days when powerful vampires had multiple wives, so neither of them needed to worry about that. However, whatever choices there were did not appear very enticing.

"Hmm, I don't really think anything's good, but maybe Lestrange Malefactor might be fine," Beatrice mused.

"Don't worry, it could take decades for them to finally decide on something," Liliana said, patting her shoulder reassuringly.

"I'm not worried," Beatrice said. "I'm just curious, is all. If we look at the hard facts, there's not much choice, unless you want to marry someone of a lower social status?" Liliana shook her head. Forget marrying Raphael, marrying even someone like that would be completely out of the question if she wanted to maintain her social standing.

"If only this had been during the old days, you know," Beatrice said, "back when there were a lot more options and there were far more vampires here."

Consanguinity and inbreeding were becoming a large problem among the current vampires particularly the aristocracy. There were two solutions. One was to marry beneath their station, but even that would only save them for a few generations. The second was to allow some of the "wild" vampires living outside the city to join their ranks. Most of them had been wiped out, but a few still existed. That had always been a controversial idea, mainly because it involved sharing the city's benefits with those who had not sided with King Alistair during the great war against the werewolves ten thousand years ago. The vampires, for the most part, still believed that the city belonged exclusively to those who had supported King Alistair. .

"Oh look, something's finally happening," Liliana said as some priests began arranging for something in the middle of the hall.

Since human sacrifices were no longer allowed, the vampires performed a few basic rituals to Sanguinus before the actual meeting of the Council of Elders started.

"The rituals grow shorter every Walpurgisnacht, it seems," someone mused.

Liliana noted there were probably only two people other than the priests who truly seemed to care about the worship of Sanguinus. Even her mother did not really bother other than put on the most superficial of shows regarding that matter.

Most religious acts among humans involved rituals of death, Liliana noted. Every single religion prepared them, in some way or another, for dying and for what lay beyond the great veil of death. Of course, there were things on how to live one's life, but to her, it seemed humans clung to religion as a way of dealing with the inevitable reality that they were going to die one day. Vampires were freed from this notion for the most part, and the shamans who had been said to be blessed with the power to wield black magic from worshiping Sanguinus were long dead.

The only use for religion was regarding their treatment of each other and for social cohesion. However, their devotion to the god dictated very little regarding such things. There was no mandated loyalty or charity towards one another, only the most basic rules on how one should behave and the importance of sacrifices to the elder god.

The sacrifices in the current day were animals rather than humans, though to many, there was not much difference. Liliana knew that her mother was certainly among those who thought that. However, Liliana's perception had changed ever since she had saved that child. She found that she was strangely invested in whether he had lived or not. Did she think like that simply because she had put in so much effort, however minuscule for her, that it felt like if he hadn't lived, she had wasted it? Or was it something deeper? Whenever she thought of the child, she also couldn't but help think of Raphael and the brief moments they had spent with each other.

"And this is my daughter, Liliana," Victoria said, introducing her to the Council of Elders, snapping Liliana out of her thoughts as she blurted out her self-introduction.

The council consisted of both permanent and temporary members. Its structure had changed since the days of King Alistair. Anyone over two thousand years old was automatically considered a temporary member, so long as there was no cause to remove them. The permanent members were appointed by each of the three (now two) great families. From the Carpathian side the main representative was Liliana's mother, Victoria.

It was because of this position of relative influence that she had gone to meet with Mayor Corvin when he was elected during that party. The collective gazes of the council washed over Liliana before Beatrice likewise introduced herself before the meeting began.

Liliana was not a permanent member and did not meet the requirements to be a temporary member. However, she was allowed to observe what was happening and at times could petition the council to speak. To her surprise, many of the members were relatively far more aware of what was going on in the human world than she had initially thought. The discourse revolved mostly around the new mayor, who had been elected, and what this would mean for their sphere of influence.

Some of them thought that nothing would really change, although most begrudgingly acknowledged that they would have to alter certain behaviors. Liliana had heard that some were very fond of drinking human blood, even during these times, and might have been responsible for certain deaths within the city or at the outskirts of Necropolis.

An adult human's blood could satiate a vampire's thirst for about a month. Even if they did feed exclusively on humans - which she doubted as many would still take Blood Lilies from time to time, there wouldn't be many deaths so as to be noticeable unless they were very careless. The human population of Necropolis had, of course, exploded to the point where they could have potentially hunted humans to their hearts' content without making a massive difference in population figures. Of course, they could not do this openly because of the negative publicity it would attract and the fact that humans would retaliate.

Things then went on to more mundane matters, which nearly put Beatrice to sleep beside her. Liliana also found herself zoning out, thinking of other things, before her mother spoke up.

"There is a law suggesting regulations regarding the selling of historic castles that I wish to put forth. I think we can all agree that many of our castles and homes, which have endured the test of time since King Alistair, are extraordinarily important to our culture and heritage. We must guard them with all of our effort. They are remarkably vital to our position within the city. These castles defended us not only from external invaders, but also were and remain a way of defending ourselves from the humans and werewolves to this day." The memory of torches going through the streets of the city was once again aroused in Liliana's mind before she suppressed it. "Given that, we need to enact laws in order to ensure that they continue to remain within our hands," Victoria concluded.

The proposal passed without much argument. For the vampires, the decisions of the council were considered to be binding far more than any human law would be.

Everyone knew who Victoria was talking about and why she had put this motion forward: a castle about to be sold to a werewolf. No one in particular seemed to want that.

Yet, at the same time, no one was ready to speak up against it. Grudges between vampires could easily last for centuries, and so by being the first to speak up, Victoria had placed a target upon herself. Many essential pieces of legislation were halted for centuries simply because no one had decided that it was worth rocking the boat for. It was Victoria's devotion to her ideals which made her disregard any potential consequences that she might incur and act with such swiftness.

With that matter settled, Athelstan spoke up regarding the matters of his estate. "There have been strange attacks upon the humans there, which I believe may originate from wild werewolves." This drew the attention of many. They were always on guard against the so-called 'tame' werewolves in the city but the 'wild' ones in particular were a constant source of apprehension for many. "I would therefore request a small committee of investigators in order to aid me in surveying what is going on." If there were werewolves, they would need specialists to hunt them - vampires armed with silver instruments, many of which were made by humans and adapted by vampires.

Eventually a decision was made to investigate further before setting up a team. From what Liliana had heard from her uncle, such matters tended to move with glacial speed unless he could provide conclusive evidence of there actually being a werewolf, which he couldn't.

The general conversation continued to ebb and flow afterwards until it was almost daybreak, and the council broke. If there were further matters to discuss, they would continue on the next night and the night after. However, there was little left to go over, and so their small introduction to the Council of Elders ended.

In case there was an emergency the permanent members could call a meeting at any time - though there hadn't been one since the Night of A Thousand Torches.

"Well, that was a whole lot of nothing," Beatrice said as they rode back to their estate.

And while that may have indeed been a whole lot of nothing, something of consequence soon reared its head regarding Liliana. The story of how she and Raphael had saved Chester had spread throughout the human world to the point that the mayor felt like he had to address the matter.

71

Chapter Six

Unanticipated Reunion

Mayor Corvin declared that both Raphael and Liliana were to be awarded the Medal of Valor. In olden times, this would usually only be given to those who had fought off werewolves or other major threats, though in times of relative peace like this, people who had done great, extraordinary acts for the public good were also candidates.

Raphael and Liliana heard this news as soon as it was announced through their respective networks.

The first thing that crossed their minds was that they could see each other again. The second was how their parents would respond.

Abraham was quite proud of Raphael. He did feel the need to warn him about Liliana and her mother though. "I don't think there's a need for me to tell you again about what she must be like. I think you already know how *they* tend to be. Just remember, she saved the human girl out of boredom more likely than not, and not from any genuine place of generosity," he'd said.

As for Victoria, she did not really want to let Liliana leave the estate after her little stunt at the *Misty Marionette*. She initially insisted that Athelstan should go and take the medal in her stead. However, Athelstan suggested that since it was important for their image it would be better for Liliana to go in person. Beatrice offered to accompany her, after Victoria had spoken with her at length about what she needed to prevent Liliana from doing.

The ceremony was rather simple. There would be a small crowd gathered in the City Square, where they would be given the medals in public. They would then have the opportunity to speak a few words, and while neither of them was really in the mood to give a speech, their parents thought it was the perfect opportunity to further their causes and so neither had any choice but to oblige.

"Dad, is it all right if I go there a few hours early? I just want to see what the place is like and maybe practice my speech there to ensure that everything goes smoothly," Raphael said. Abraham thought nothing of the

72

request.

Liliana asked her mother, "Mother, the event is early in the evening, but I just want to get there a bit early so that I can have my dress and everything else ready before I go to speak. I also want to avoid any kind of large human crowd."

"All right. Take Beatrice with you. Athelstan and I will be coming a few hours later,," Victoria said.

Both of them had decided to reach the venue earlier than they otherwise would have. Both of them were with someone: Liliana with Beatrice, and Raphael with Vincent.

The reason they wanted to go early, however, was to see if they could sneak another moment without the supervision of their parents. If pressed on why they had thought of this, neither would have a good answer. They felt inexorably drawn to each other, like two magnets, and yet could not voice their feelings. Logic and reason dictated there was no reason for them to want to see each other again, aside from perhaps pure curiosity, but maybe that was enough.

Both of them were bound by their duties, bound to a mundane life with what were golden chains yes, but bound nonetheless. This was a small chance of a 'rebellion' of sorts, but a chance nonetheless.

Raphael, as planned, reached the City Square far earlier than he really needed to, with Vincent by his side.

"This place really is quite different from the docks, ain't it?" Vincent mused.

The City Square was originally the heart of the werewolf part of the city. Lycanthropes mainly concentrated here before they began to move their center of operations toward the docks and the wider city in general. This was where the great werewolf rebellions had started, where the werewolves had clashed with vampires several times in the past. It had been taken over by the humans in modern times, but there were still many werewolf families who lived here.

Unlike the vampires, werewolves did not have strict aristocratic lineages; at least not in the city. Many people claimed to be descended from Balthazar, but most people put very little stock in that. Those who had come to the city had arrived with essentially no name, their identities, and any rank or title they held within their packs was quickly washed away by the fact that they were all serving under one master. And city life was so different from the wilderness it must have been quite shocking to many of their ancestors.

Over time, the old traditions were largely forgotten despite being ingrained within their blood. Sometimes though they manifested in other, more subtle ways, as with Raphael and his friends.

Most of the high-end human shops were here. Most of the goods that his father's company sold ended up in one of these trafficked. There were also numerous parks for the humans to walk around. Werewolves could do so as well, though they were a bit too confined for most of their tastes. If they truly wished to enjoy nature, they would go somewhere near the outskirts of the city -

not at the periphery, such as where Athelstan had his estate but rather near the foothills of the mountains that surrounded the city, where they could roam the wilderness as they pleased. The scent of the sea was weak here, though both of their noses could still pick it up.

The sound of people moving was constant, but it lacked the noise you would hear near the docks - the constant shouting and shuffling were absent. This was a more exclusive part of the city, and so the number of humans was greatly reduced. The buildings were more brick and mortar with regular architecture rather than the wooden kind haphazardly built often seen near the docks.

While there were times when Raphael might have thought this could be an okay place to settle down, he disregarded these things; growing up near the ocean had many advantages one could not find here.

"Look at that, she's arrived," Vincent said, noticing the telltale carriage that belonged to Liliana. Raphael noticed it well before Vincent, but had pretended not to.

The City Square had a fountain with a statue of King Alistair. Although he was a vampire king, the werewolves had not done anything to topple this particular statue simply because of his legacy. The humans saw no real reason to throw it out either; to them, he was a figure who had long since passed into the sands of time. There was no need to do anything to this kind of ancient relic. Of note however, he was not depicted holding the severed head of a werewolf in one of his hands, like he would in other places, but was instead simply lifting a sword up into the sky.

Liliana disembarked from her carriage. Even though she also pretended not to notice Raphael, she had noticed him far before Beatrice pointed him out for her.

"Why on earth is he here?" Beatrice complained.

"Maybe he wanted to come here early, like us?"

Beatrice sighed, fidgeting with the silver ring on her hand. "And here I thought we could get some time alone, or maybe even get some shopping done. Do you want to do that? Do you want to go find a store away from them? We can come back later." She jerked her head toward the werewolves when she said "them."

"No, there's no need for that," Liliana said, racking her head for a way to make this work. "I actually wanted to speak with him for a moment."

"Speak with him for what?" Beatrice hissed.

"I just wanted to know how that child was doing." Liliana already knew the answer. But she feigned ignorance in that matter, and this seemed a fine excuse to approach.

"Are they coming here?" Vincent said, unable to believe his eyes. He put a hand on Raphael's shoulder and unconsciously squeezed it. "Hold on. They're wearing silver all over. We'll have tot to watch ourselves."

"Don't worry, they're not going to pick a fight with us in the middle of the street. She probably just wants to talk about something," Raphael said, his heart thumping despite his reassuring words though not from apprehension as with Vincent.

She was wearing another crimson red dress, which matched the color of her eyes, this time with amounts of black lace and ribbons decorating it, woven through the fabric and splitting the crimson like strikes of lightning on a cloudy night. She still wore a silver crown, the same one embedded with rubies. Her earrings this time contained sapphires, which accentuated her flawless pale skin and worked surprisingly well with the crimson attire. The same smell he had felt back at the party washed over him; the scent of crushed pine needles.

Ba-dump. Ba-dump.

It might have just been his imagination, but he thought he heard two thumps come from her chest as she approached. *Impossible*, he thought to himself. *Vampire hearts don't beat.* He was unaware of the fact that when they experienced high emotions, their hearts would sometimes start beating, and so he dismissed this as a trick of his mind.

"Well met, Mr. Raphael," Liliana said, giving him a social smile - not a true smile, but the kind of pretend one you would give to people at a party. One could glimpse her fangs easily enough even through this kind of smile, but then again, it was harder for vampires to hide them. Not to mention there was little point in trying when one's crimson eyes would give one's nature away.

Despite the fact that the smile was entirely for social circumstances and nothing more, Raphael's legs - legs that could run a thousand miles without stopping - suddenly felt like they were made of pudding. He struggled for a response. "Well met, Lady Liliana. I'm glad to see you here." *Why did I say that? I knew she was already going to be here anyway*, he thought to himself, realizing how dumb he sounded only after the words had left his mouth.

Unconsciously, out of a sense of practiced tradition, Liliana extended one of her hands - the hand on which she was not wearing a silver ring - towards him. Raphael realized what she was hinting at. Had it been any other vampire, he might have hesitated, but he found himself reaching out with his own hand, taking hers in his, and courteously kissing the back of it. Her skin felt smooth, though cold, and as soft as silk. He could see the individual bluish veins coursing beneath her translucent skin. Blood did not flow through them, but they still stood out, making her skin look a lot more blue than white on closer inspection. She really was a true 'blue blood' through and through.

Ba-dump. Ba-dump. Ba-dump. Ba-dump. Ba-dump.

Liliana felt her heart thump over five times - a personal record. As his lips brushed against her hand, she found that they were surprisingly soft, almost like flower petals. *How would they feel if they brushed against my lips?* she wondered before dismissing the thought.

It was a simple enough gesture, and common enough in high society that it shouldn't have been a big deal. However, the way Vincent and Beatrice stared at the two of them, mouths gaping, one might have thought they had begun stripping and fondling each other right in the middle of the square.

Why would Raphael do something like that? Vincent thought to himself. *Does*

75

he expect me to do the same thing as well? He cast a glance at Beatrice, who immediately withdrew both of her arms behind her back and shook her head vigorously, as if telling him he shouldn't ever dare to come near her or her hands. Liliana also didn't offer him her hand, so he decided to just forget about it.

But then, why on earth did she offer her hand to him and why would he do it? Is it because he is the son of the Cain family, or because of something their parents did, or just... I can't wrap my head around it, Vincent thought. He understood close to nothing about politics, let alone how high society folks tended to move and behave.

"Was there anything in particular that brought you here today?" Raphael asked, once again realizing how dumb the question sounded once the words left his mouth. "No, I mean, of course, I know why you're here today. I mean... why you're here rather early?"

"Well, I really wanted to see the scenery before I gave my big speech," Liliana answered. "But when I saw you, I remembered the reason why I even got to be here in the first place. Did the child in question survive? How is he doing right now?"

"Oh right, Chester. Yes, he's been doing fine," Raphael said. He had not personally gone to check up on him after being discharged, but one of his friends had, and they said that he was doing as well as could be expected. "He may not be running anywhere anytime soon, but... well enough."

"That's good to hear," Liliana said, shooting him another smile, which almost made him melt into the floor. Seriously, why was he behaving like this? Even if she made his heart race, he shouldn't be completely spiraling out of control like this!

The two of them continued to look at each other as an awkward silence crystallized between them. *Is this it?* Raphael thought to himself. He didn't want this moment to end, even though he was sure Vincent was eager to pull him away any minute now. *Wait, she probably came here with an excuse to see me, right? There's no way that she had come specifically only to ask me about Chester. She must have been able to find out from someone else, such as a human servant. So, then, should I also think of an excuse for us to continue talking?*

"Have you prepared anything to speak?" Raphael asked, finding his voice and shattering the wall of silence that had descended between them.

"Oh yes, I have a little speech prepared," Liliana said.

"Well, I was..." Raphael began, trying to find the words to correctly steer the conversation in the direction that he wanted. "I was wondering if the little speech that I'd prepared was appropriate or not. If you wouldn't mind, would you like to listen to it and tell me if there's anything you might think could use some improvement?"

Liliana considered it for a moment before shooting him a smile. This one was an actual smile even if it was slightly awkward, or at least Raphael felt so. She was showing far too many teeth for it to be a "socially acceptable" smile. But it was far more beautiful than the others. His heart skipped a few more beats.

76

"That sounds wonderful, but I think there's going to be too big of a crowd here soon to talk," Liliana said. "Do you want to go somewhere a bit more... well, where we could be away from prying ears to practice with each other?"

Good thinking, Raphael thought. If they were going to be talking to each other, they might as well do it someplace away from the City Square.

"I happen to know of a park here, which shouldn't have that much traffic during this time of day," Raphael suggested.

"That sounds splendid," Liliana responded. "Would the two of you like to take a ride in our carriage?"

"Um, thank you very much for offering," Raphael said. "But I fear we may be a bit too big for it." Most werewolves were extraordinarily tall by human standards, and with the two of them inside, even without considering the two ladies' relatively petite frames, it would be quite cramped. "But I can tell you that it's rather close by. We could walk there, not too far ahead."

"That seems all right," Liliana said, glancing upward as a ray of sunshine seemed to penetrate the density of clouds above. "Hopefully, it's a place with some shade."

"Oh yes, there's lots of shade there. There's a bunch of trees, and we can stand, ah, sit under them," Raphael said.

"Wonderful idea," Liliana said. Raphael and Vincent took the lead while Liliana and Beatrice followed about twenty feet behind them so that it wouldn't immediately be apparent that the two groups were together.

It was at this point that both Vincent and Beatrice had found their voices. Vincent turned his head ever so slightly towards Raphael.

"Raphael, tell me something straight up. Do you..." He couldn't believe the words that were about to come out of his mouth. "Are you in love with that girl?" Even saying it felt odd, as if those words could not be put together in a sentence like that without being grammatically incorrect.

Vincent spoke through the corner of his mouth and softly enough that the two girls behind them would not be able to hear or notice. Raphael turned his head ever so slightly to respond to him, trying to open his mouth, but found nothing came out. Up until now, he had felt like he had been walking on clouds at the thought of spending more time with Liliana, but Vincent's words had snapped him out of his stupor.

"Well um... could you repeat the question?" Raphael asked.

"By Balthalzar, you really have fallen for her!" Vincent said, realizing the truth from Raphael's expression alone.

"No, it's nothing like-"

"Yes, you have, you dog!" Vincent said, punching him on the shoulder. It was supposed to be a playful punch even if it could have torn through a wall easily. Vincent leaned closer to him. "Of all the women within all of Necropolis, you had to find her to suddenly fall head-over-heels for? Really man?"

"Is it really that obvious?" Raphael asked back.

"That obvious? The only way it could be more obvious is if you had a tail and it was wagging whenever she happened to drop by," Vincent said. Vincent's face then shifted. "You do realize that the two of you can't be together, right? There's a thousand reasons as to why this is a bad idea.."

"No, I know. I know," Raphael said, reality quickly catching up to him and tearing his dreams apart. "But is there really any harm in just talking with her, even if she doesn't feel the same way about me? Is it that bad if we come to some sort of agreement together, you know, like, some sort of peace treaty between the werewolves and the vampires?"

Vincent rolled his eyes. Such talk might have sounded high and noble, but he knew Raphael was just looking for an excuse to be with her.

Meanwhile, Beatrice's mouth opened and closed constantly, like a window being battered by a hurricane, before she finally managed to force the words out to Liliana.

"Liliana, do you happen… to fancy that werewolf?" The word 'fancy' sounded strange in her mouth, as if it were grammatically incorrect when paired with 'werewolf' without a word like 'killing' in between the two words.

"Why did he just punch him up?" Liliana asked, responding not to Beatrice's question but to what Vincent had just done to Raphael.

"Oh, they're probably just playing rough," Beatrice dismissed. "It doesn't look like they were fighting - more like they're just being... themselves. I've heard they do it all the time. But really tell me, Liliana, do you happen to fancy him?"

"I... uh, well, not really, I mean, I can't say that I like… despise him or anything…" Liliana said, struggling to find the words. "But, honestly, he is different, you know? Different from the others. I just wanted to talk with him. That's not a crime, is it?"

"You know exactly what I'm saying," Beatrice insisted. "It's okay to talk with him, but what if your mother finds out?"

"How will she find out? You're not going to tell her, are you?"

"Now, Liliana, don't ask me to start keeping secrets," Beatrice said, sighing.

Liliana had to admit it was an unwise tactic to try and keep something secret by asking Beatrice of all people not to tell anyone. As a matter of fact, if one wanted a piece of news to be spread throughout the vampire world as fast as possible, one could simply find and tell it to Beatrice and ask her to keep quiet about it and then find that it had reached every undead ear in the city by the next morning.

However, Liliana knew that while Beatrice might be a bit of a gossip, she would definitely keep this under wraps, because Beatrice knew how important it was. At least, Liliana certainly hoped so.

"But Liliana, I am serious," Beatrice insisted. "This relationship can't go any further. No vampire has ever married a werewolf before."

"I know that!" Liliana snapped. "And why are you talking about marriage of all things? I just wanted to speak with him!"

"As if I couldn't see you trying to charm him the entire time you were speaking with him," Beatrice retorted, flashing her a dark look. She then softened. "Just be careful, okay? I know you don't think of me as being more mature than you, but I don't want to see you hurt. And you're going to get hurt if you keep this up."

Beatrice was correct: she did not think of Beatrice as being much older or wiser than her. If anything, there were many times Liliana had bailed Beatrice out of trouble because she was the more mature of the two. In this case though she had to admit that Beatrice was correct.

"And if I'm not mistaken," Beatrice said, leaning in, "Did your heart start beating?" She had heard it, much like Raphael had. And much like Raphael she found it hard to believe her own ears.

Liliana looked downcast before nodding once.

"By Sanguinus, girl!" Beatrice said, looking like she might very well faint on the spot. "You really have fallen for him!"

"Don't worry, I know what I can and cannot do," Liliana said.

Raphael had been correct: the spot they were going to was indeed free of most foot traffic this time of the evening. A large number of trees grew close together, their canopy forming an almost seamless roof above them.

"Is this enough shade for the two of you, or should we go somewhere else?" Raphael asked.

"It's perfectly delightful," Liliana said.

They smiled at each other. Both Vincent and Beatrice rolled their eyes. Who did these two think they were fooling? They were going to be found out by tomorrow morning if they kept things up like this!

"Ahem. So, if you don't mind, may I go first?" Liliana asked.

It was only then that Raphael remembered that they had not walked over there simply to admire the weather and scenery. "Oh, yes, of course. I would love to hear your speech."

It seemed as if Liliana's words flowed like a gentle river. Her voice was so extraordinarily soothing, he thought to himself. Every delicate facial expression she made while speaking only further enchanted him. For that matter, he had barely heard half of her speech before realizing he was supposed to be paying attention to the individual words as well.

Her speech started off fine enough, talking about how the vampires had a long history within the city and had always been its protectors. Nothing too objectionable, although it could be said that she was injecting a bit too much "vampiric pride" into it.

She then went on to how she had helped rescue the human in question and how glad she was that he was safe, further solidifying Raphael's initial conjecture that she had known about what happened to Chester and had only been pretending so she had an excuse to talk with him this morning. She concluded by stating that the vampires would continue in their aristocratic duty toward the city.

It was all fine, Raphael thought to himself. *My father would probably hate it, but there's nothing in there that I could bring myself to hate.*

"I think that sounded perfect," Raphael said aloud.

Beatrice's face twisted. "Did it sound perfect? Because I think there were a few places where she could have changed things," she said, her voice practically egging him into an argument.

"No, I think he's right. I think this is fine as is," Liliana cut in, giving Beatrice a smug smile. "Anyway, my mother wrote most of it, so I think I will continue with it."

Beatrice rolled her eyes so hard she seemed in danger of being able to see the inside of her skull.

"And now, if you would, your turn?" Liliana said.

"Sure," Raphael said. Liliana had completely memorized her speech, which he had to give her credit for. He, on the other hand, had prepared a piece of paper and, while he'd memorized the general points, he would likely have to refer to it at certain times. His speech was longer than Liliana's and was essentially the werewolf's perspective on the same themes. He spoke a lot more about the unity between werewolves and humans and how much his father's company worked with both, and mentioned the little food distribution project he was in charge of.

"Oh, that's a curious thing," Liliana said. "How has that been going?"

"It's been going well enough," Raphael said before going into a spiel on some of the hurdles he had run into.

He described the challenges he was facing: they had managed to find a place near the poor areas of the docks where there would be less blowback from other shop owners, but they hadn't finished preparations for moving their line of people there, as well as other logistical details like ingredients. He still had quite a lot of work to do.

He didn't know why he was telling her these things, given that he wanted to keep many of them secret, as it was slightly embarrassing to admit that his plan had run into so many barriers. But somehow, his chest felt so much lighter now that he had gotten it all out.

"That sounds wonderful," Liliana said. Her eyes had glazed over slightly, and Beatrice wasn't even sure if she had listened to anything he had said or had simply been staring at his face the whole time. Liliana had to admit it truly was a beautiful face. Perhaps nothing within it was that striking, but once again, his features reminded her of freshly-turned earth shining in the evening sunlight. His eyes spoke of warmth, ready to take her in his arms, promising stability and... something else that her heart craved. His physique spoke of power, yet he once again seemed strangely restrained, more so than she would have expected from a werewolf.

"Raphael, I think it's time we should be going. Otherwise, they'll start wondering where we are," Vincent said.

"The same here, Liliana."

"All right. And thank you very much for your help," Raphael said.

"And thank you very much for yours," Liliana replied.

The two of them smiled at each other, and both their minds arrived at the same destination. Earlier, Raphael had simply kissed her hand out of a sense of obligation, as was tradition. Now, however, he was thinking how her cherry-red lips would feel against his own. And she, likewise, was wondering whether she would be able to see those soft brown eyes up close.

However, both Raphael and Liliana knew that such a thing would be taking things a step too far. With a final courtesy from each other, the two parties - Vincent and Raphael, and Liliana and Beatrice - left in different directions, ensuring it wouldn't look as though they had been together moments ago.

"If you don't mind me asking," Vincent said to Raphael, "what exactly do you see in her?" Vincent could never imagine himself falling for a 'leech', though he had the presence of mind not to say that word in front of Raphael.

"Well, she is beautiful-"

"So are poisonous flowers-"

"-but not just that, I got the feeling she was different, you know? I've been told what vampires are like my whole life - she just doesn't seem to fit the mold. And she shocked me quite a bit when she agreed to help me rescue that kid."

"Is... that it? I mean that's neat and all, but not massively so. You know that any of us would've helped you too," Vincent said. "Matter of fact, I think that most she-wolves would've done so too."

"What are you saying?"

"I mean, I don't think that's enough to, you know, fall in love with someone."

"Have you fallen in love with someone before?"

"No."

"Then how would you know?"

"I'm just saying - I can't wrap my head around it."

"I can't really explain it either," Raphael said, struggling for the right words to describe how he felt. "I'm not sure you would understand what I'm saying."

"You're right - I don't understand what you're saying," Vincent said, shaking his head. "I just thought that... well, I don't want you to get hurt, you know? And going after her is going to get you hurt, whether she feels the same way or not."

Raphael nodded wearily. The words rang true, but there was a part of him that just couldn't accept them.

Liliana and Beatrice were heading to the City Square from a different direction but their conversation also went in a similar direction.

"Remember what I told you earlier," Beatrice said. "You can't get involved with him, you just can't. I don't even know what you see in him."

"Oh, you don't think that he's quite handsome? That isn't everything, of course, but..."

"You don't think he's too muscular?" Beatrice asked. "Almost like a wild animal, in a way. I'm sorry, I don't mean to insult him."

81

"But... well, it's not just how he looks. It's how he behaves, I mean - or..." Liliana found it hard to put her thoughts into words. Was this why Beatrice wanted to learn how to play the violin - to put thoughts that could not be expressed through speech into notes? "Anyway, it doesn't matter. We won't be meeting each other after this," Liliana concluded. It was true; only by chance had the two of them been able to interact today. When would another opportunity arise? Perhaps that was why they had both been so eager to make the most of this one.

***

The first king of the city, King Alistair, had been succeeded by his son Hadrian. Hadrian in turn had two sons who succeeded him - Hector and Dmitri. Despite being twins they did not get along very well, and Hadrian, sensing an impending political schism if he chose one of them over the other, instead chose to appoint both of them as co-kings.

Hector and Dmitri thus jointly ruled Necropolis, and initially, things were cordial enough between them. It was the first and only time Necropolis had two ruling chief executives. Quickly enough, though, friction developed between the brothers, egged on by their supporters despite their father's wish for them to rule jointly and peacefully after he had entered the Shadowsleep. Unable to avoid petty arguments, they agreed to a compromise and to share the city, dividing it in half rather than ruling together.

But even this was not enough. The hatred between the twins reached the point that they refused to be in the same room, communicating only via messengers. Small skirmishes broke out between their factions, occasionally even turning violent. Soon enough there was two of almost everything - two main castles, two groups of royal guards, and two ceremonies where possible.

Historians disagreed on whose idea it was to first employ werewolves as mercenaries, but both of them eventually had their own Lycan legions.

Where this was not possible, like with the Walpurgisnacht, one would sit on one side of the room and the other on the opposite end.

This had been an incredibly difficult time for the governance of Necropolis, and their mismanagement and the mounting tensions within the city eventually led to the civil war in which the Montefalcos were wiped out alongside the twins. King Hadrian's worst fears had come true, with the measures that he had taken to prevent such a thing ultimately causing it. The monarchy had collapsed and an elected representative ruled over Necropolis from that time forth. Many vampiric historians pointed to this civil war as the start of the downfall of the vampires' dominant position within the city.

Victoria and Abraham may not have been twins or co-rulers, but much like Hector and Dmitri they too could not stand to be in the same room for too long. Both of them arrived to support their children, but they couldn't have two separate ceremonies. And so, in the bustling City Square, Abraham and Victoria stood on opposite sides, preferring to avoid contact as much as possible. This was why neither of them had accompanied their children earlier - to maintain some distance. A few werewolves, mainly Abraham's colleagues and Raphael's friends, had come to support him.

Victoria was there with Athelstan. Not many other vampires cared to come out for this event, especially since a few rays of sunlight were breaking through the cloudy skies. Although both Victoria and Athelstan wore their medallions, they were visibly annoyed by the sun's intrusion into the gloomy atmosphere of Necropolis they were accustomed to.

The short ceremony and introductory speeches were simple matters that were over within about half an hour. Mayor Corvin went to a large podium and introduced the two heroes, Liliana and Raphael.

Raphael then made his speech. Abraham nodded along with every word, though Raphael had to glance at his paper occasionally when he lost track of things. It was not a bad speech, considering it was his first time speaking in public. There was a round of applause as he stepped down. Liliana followed, delivering hers from memory.

Without a doubt, her words did not have the same positive effect on the humans as Raphael's did, as her speech was less about unity and more about the vampire's status within society as the natural ruler of Necropolis. While the human applause was minor afterward, Victoria and Athelstan cheered loudly as she left.

"Well then, I think that's it," Abraham said, glancing toward the vampire faction for but an instant. "I think it's time we wrap up and leave."

"Sure thing Dad," Raphael said.

Liliana similarly departed alongside her mother and uncle.

The two of them glanced at each other once more. Both Vincent and Beatrice noted this exchange of glances, though nothing as extreme as they feared occurred with no one else noticing. Liliana and Raphael departed, resigning themselves to more likely than not never seeing each other again, despite the ache in their hearts.

Sacrifices have to be made, Raphael thought. He really did want to make his father proud and by extension, the werewolves of the city as well. As such, he did not wish to succumb to some kind of selfish desire for self-indulgence, even if he believed his budding feelings to be true. Could he really throw away everything he had for her? He did not think so.

Liliana, likewise, although her heart yearned to see him one more time, could not bring herself to go against her family, especially her mother who had raised her. Beatrice's cautionary words echoed in her head.

And so, the two melancholic hearts parted.

***

Meanwhile, Dunn Sutherland had most of his freedoms restored, though the trial was still pending. He must have pulled some strings with the mayor to make such a thing happen.

Raphael wouldn't be surprised if Sutherland ended up fleeing the city eventually, though he seemed bound for the moment by the goods he had brought. It wasn't so easy to leave Necropolis and get back to Solaris, given the distance and the lack of safe ports in between. But he didn't doubt that someone like Dunn Sutherland would have a contingency plan. Of course, if Sutherland's company stopped doing business, it could lead to poor outcomes for the Cain Shipping Company as well.

They could always try to find other buyers, but that could take time. Necropolis by itself still purchased a large amount of goods from Solaris so it could be said to be a two-way street, but when push came to shove, Raphael knew that they needed Solaris more than Solaris needed them.

Raphael went on to continue his project of attempting to feed a portion of the city's poor. The new warehouse they had found was set up to handle a larger population and was located in a poorer district that didn't have much else going on for it, meaning they weren't getting in the way of any other kind of business. Things went well for the first couple of weeks. He supposed some of the novelty began to wear off; it just became something people took for granted now. He didn't mind, as this was supposed to function as a safety net for the city, after all.

But it really started to dawn on him just how little he seemed to be accomplishing. The line seemed never-ending, and he would see the same faces pass by every single day. He was helping these people, but he was just barely allowing them to survive, rather than making a meaningful difference. *No, it might not seem that much to me - but I'm sure for many of them this is a very helpful lifeline.* He counted about four hundred meals they were giving out now regularly, occasionally going as high as five hundred. Demands were increasing, but his father did not mind considering it to be a 'necessary expense.'

For now, though, everything was running smoothly.

Raphael even felt like he could hand over the running of this operation to someone else while he went to do other things for his father that other people could not do. This is precisely what he ended up doing, though the reason would not be because there was something else he needed to do, but rather because of Vincent.

Vincent came to him with a problem one day, and before the request had even completely left his mouth, Raphael was already walking with him outside, and telling him he would do everything he could to help. Vincent truly was like a brother to him. There was a reason Raphael had trusted him when he had gone to meet Liliana, and to his credit, Vincent had not breathed a single word of what he had witnessed to anyone else, even within their friend group. That secret was still under wraps and things were mostly fine in that regard, even if Raphael's heart continued to pine for Liliana.

"Hey - remember to add more salt, they were complaining about it earlier. Sorry, just needed to get a word with the chefs, Vincent, but what's going on?"

"So, there is a human family who lives near the Darkling Woods,"

Vincent began.

"Isn't that near the outskirts of the city?" Raphael asked. He had never had a chance to go there, but he had heard the name often enough.

"Yes, it's right there, just beyond the mountain range." Necropolis was bounded by mountains and hills which formed a U-shape around the bulk of the city, enclosing most of it with the sea creating another boundary. Just beyond the mountains, there were the wastelands, but there was an intermediate border zone that was outside the city walls but still not considered completely uninhabitable. Most of these areas functioned as a buffer zone for the city against any potential foreign invaders. The Darkling Woods were no longer inhabited by anyone, whether mortal or vampire, and it was said that wild werewolves occasionally roamed around the forest.

"So, the head of a village there says they've been running into some problems, and they think it's werewolf-related," Vincent said.

"Okay, but, how does this involve you?" Raphael asked.

"The thing is, the village head in question helped my family back during the old days when they had still lived there," Vincent continued. Raphael remembered that Vincent had mentioned living near the outskirts of the city before coming to the docks. "They really helped them out a lot during that time. Pa says it wouldn't be right for us to not do anything if they're having trouble."

"Shouldn't the lord of the area be doing something?" Raphael asked.

"He should, but the vampire in question, Athelstan, doesn't seem that eager to actually do anything," Vincent said.

"Athelstan… where have I heard that name before?" Raphael mused. It sounded familiar.

"I don't know, but it's the same with a lot of vampires. I guess he just doesn't care much for them," Vincent said.

"Seems that he should be concerned if it is this big of a problem," Raphael said

The vampires were well known for treating their human subjects mostly like cattle. The thing was, of course, that a cattle farmer would care if someone was going around killing his herd. Especially given the recent political changes which had greatly changed humanity's status. Or maybe Raphael simply wanted to see vampires in a more positive light because of his experiences with Liliana and was projecting this onto this vampire named Athelstan?

"So, this vampire Athelstan keeps saying that he'll do something about the events," Vincent explained. "But he hasn't actually done anything yet. Now, my parents owe the family quite a lot. But you know how things are right now given their business, so they wanted me to go check it out."

"And then I'll be coming with you," Raphael said immediately.

"Raphael, you don't have t-"

"I know I don't *have* to," Raphael said, "But I *want* to, and as a matter of fact, I'm sure Carlton and Ed would like to come too."

"But don't you have to take care of… well, this?" Vincent said, motioning toward the line of people gathered for a free meal.

85

"Oh, this? I can probably set someone else up to do it," Raphael said. "I mean, this is technically a partnership with a human noblewoman called Lady Cecilia. I'm sure if I speak with her, she'll have someone who can take over things for a while. Or maybe she can even come down herself."

"Doesn't your father need you, though?" Vincent asked.

"He'll understand if I explain it to him," Raphael said, pretty sure that Abraham would, though he would need to actually ask him before heading out.

"I originally came here to ask you how many of the crew I could take without inconveniencing you..."

"The answer is all of them, including me."

"But-"

"I won't hear another word about it," Raphael said. "After all, we are in this together."

He had said those words with extreme confidence, even if he wasn't entirely sure that his father would agree to it. He was, however, far more comfortable bringing this up to his father compared to anything regarding his feelings for Liliana.

"So, that's what's going on," Raphael said to Abraham that evening. "Do you mind if I step away from the business for a few weeks while I try to sort this out?"

Abraham looked at him. "I only have one question regarding what all of you boys are trying to do - let's say that you happen to find that there's a wild werewolf on the loose. What do you intend to do? Fight them? Get yourselves maimed - or worse, killed?"

"No, I mean, if there's danger, of course, we're going to run away," Raphael said.

"What's even the point of you going there, then?" Abraham asked.

"Well, the village folk are kind of uneasy about things, and they think a werewolf is involved. We just want to see if there is. And if there is, then we can go ahead and ask someone to come in to take care of it later on from the mayor. And if it's something like a wild panther or leopard that we can handle, we will."

Abraham considered it before agreeing. "Just promise me that you won't do anything reckless."

"I won't, Dad."

"And do let Lady Cecilia know about this as well before you move out," Abraham added.

The two of them continued their meal in peace afterwards until another topic was brought up.

"How are things going with Sutherland?" Raphael asked.

"He's trying to move his trial as far off into the future as possible," Abraham explained. "Probably hoping that the anger around his actions will die down later on, and it might be easier for him to get off."

"Will it?"

"Well, the public's memory can be rather short. If some other scandal happens, then he might end up getting off with a fine or very light sentence.

And worse comes to worse the man can just pack up and leave the city. His finances might be ruined in that case, but he would still be a free man back in his country."

Raphael nodded. Despite what many people told him growing up, the justice system was far from impartial. Those in power got away with things all the time. Back in the day, "those in power" meant the vampires, and in modern times, it meant people with money or influence.

"Not to mention, I don't think that the mayor wants a bad relationship with Solaris anyway," Abraham added. "If trade was cut off, it would be terrible for all of us. The humans were the ones most outraged by Sutherland's actions, but they would lose the most as well if he were convicted. I'd even wager that Mayor Corvin might end up helping the man abscond if it comes down to it. He knows how much we need Solaris."

As he had promised his father, Raphael went to see Lady Cecilia in person before heading out towards the outskirts of the city.

He had only been to her manor once before. It was at the end of a large, cobblestone-paved road and was about the size of the warehouse back in the docks. Considering that this was in one of the more affluent parts of the city, the land here was worth far more than the building back there.

Lady Cecilia was a woman in her late fifties. Her husband had passed away three years ago, and she had no children, so she spent most of her time organizing social events. Raphael had seen her in passing during some public events with the mayor in the past, but had never spoken with her prior to organizing the soup kitchen.

"So, you see, that's what's happening," Raphael explained to her. "I'm going to have to step away from our little base of operations for a while, and I need someone to fill in for me. So if you have anyone in mind, I'd be happy to hear about it."

"I can think of a few people," Lady Cecilia said. "As a matter of fact, I've been thinking of taking a visit down there myself and seeing what exactly is happening."

"I think you'll be quite proud to see what we've done," Raphael said, putting emphasis on the "we."

"Well, I'm glad to hear it," Cecilia said. "Allow me to get back to you this evening. I need to make sure, though, that they are actually willing to do this."

"Not a problem," Raphael said.

His eyes then landed upon something. They were both sitting in her tea room, which was usually where she received her guests. As such, it was decorated the most extravagantly of all the rooms in the house. There were several paintings, most depicting the landscapes around Necropolis, as well as a miniature statue of King Alistair along with his three queens.

There was one painting he hadn't seen during his last visit, however, which surprisingly depicted a scene that he recognized. "I'm sorry to ask, but is that a painting of... me?"

It showed someone who looked a lot like him near a building resembling the *Misty Marionette*, holding a child in his hands. His depiction in the painting wasn't completely accurate, but the way the scene was set up was more than enough for him to recognize what it was attempting to depict.

"Oh, yes, it is! I can't believe that I forgot to tell you about this," Lady Cecilia said. "There's an artist who was there who saw you rescue that boy, and he was so inspired that he's been making paintings and drawings like these. He's also made some regarding... what is she called... Lady Liliana of the Light as well."

Raphael had not expected to hear Liliana's name in this kind of scenario. "They're calling her 'Lady Liliana of the Light?' I mean, why?"

"Well, I guess they're just greatly touched by what she did, you know," Cecilia said, "though I think he may have been one of the first people to use that term. If you want, and you're interested in his work, you can go ahead and visit him in person."

"Are you sure he won't mind?"

"Raphael, you're one of the objects of his paintings. If anything, I think he would love to get a closer look at you," Lady Cecilia said.

Raphael got the man's address and found that he lived somewhere close to the docks. He and Lady Cecilia eventually decided upon a replacement to oversee the soup kitchen, and then he went to visit the artist before he and the rest of his gang headed out towards the village near the Darkling Woods.

Raphael wasn't even sure whether the man was in or not as he knocked on the front door. He got no response, though his ears could hear something going on inside meaning there was definitely someone home, so he knocked louder.

"Who is it?" came a gruff voice from inside.

"I'm sorry to bother you, but could I speak with you for a moment, if you could spare it?" Raphael requested.

After five minutes of strange noises coming from within the building, nobody had come to greet him. Raphael was almost ready to just walk away, deciding it was a waste of time when the door was then promptly thrown open as a short man glared at him. "What do you people want no-?" The words died in his mouth as he took a good look at Raphael.

At first there was anger, then irritation, then contemplation, and finally surprise written on his face. He had clearly been expecting someone other than Raphael.

"Um, yes, my name is Raphael. I was near the *Misty Marionette* when the fire broke out. People tell me that you were there as well."

"Why, yes, yes!" the man said, his expression finally settling down from a scowl to a wide smile. "I'm sorry about this. It's just that I get all of these strange people coming to visit me, you know. People who have nothing but free time on their hands, wanting to know what happened. I mean, I've been drawing stuff regarding the incident so now everyone and their mother thinks I'm some kind of expert. It's... it's funny, I'll tell you. I had gone there hoping to get some kind of inspiration, but I didn't think I'd get *that* kind of inspiration from there, you know? And then I started making all of these paintings and distributing them - they were very popular but that backfired in some way and… and… I'm sorry to be talking your ear off," he said. "Come on in!"

Raphael took a look around the man's studio. Most of the papers scattered around were sketches. Not all of them were depictions of the incident; some were of other things, like famous castles around the area, or certain people whom Raphael did not know.

However, a good portion of them particularly the ones which looked fresh were regarding the incident at the *Misty Marionette*. Some depicted rough drawings of the building. Some depicted the building itself after it had been burned down and was being repaired. The man had clearly gone to the area several times to be able to replicate it with such detail. Judging from the way his studio was arranged - although messy - it was clear to Raphael that the man was at least moderately successful if he was eking out a living from his art.

"And you know what? It's rather fortunate that you came, right. Because I was thinking of making another sketch of you," he said. "Wait, where was it?" He looked through the stack of papers before finding one. "Yes, here, this is it. I started making it out of charcoal, but…"

He looked from the drawing to Raphael; comparing the two. Raphael stared at the half-finished portrait. He had to say that if one covered the lower half of it, it did look quite like him, but the man had gotten his jaw and teeth wrong.

"Well, now I know what the real thing looks like. Oh wow, this really… this looks nothing like you. I'm sorry," he said.

"There's no need to apologize," Raphael said. "I mean, it isn't nearly as bad as what you're saying. It does kind of look like me."

"Right," the man said, staring at Raphael as if trying to memorize every single detail of his features before he vanished or something. "Oh, I'm so sorry for rushing into work! Can I get you something to eat or drink? What would it be? And please, take a seat."

"Um, no, no, please, there's no need to go out of your way for anything for me. I just came by because I had heard of your artwork and was interested."

"Oh, well, I'm glad to know that I'm famous not only among humans, but werewolves now," the man said.

It was then that Raphael's eyes fell upon the portrait of a woman. In an instant, he recognized it as Liliana. But it wasn't made in the way that most portraits depicting vampires were - lacking the eerie, uncanny feel most of them had. Instead, Liliana was drawn much like he would have imagined her, with warm rays enveloping her and every trace of her angelic face. Just taking a glance made it very clear that the man had seen Liliana at one point.

"Did she agree to model for a portrait? That looks very much like her," Raphael remarked.

"Oh, that? No, no," the artist responded. "However, I did happen to meet her near her castle recently. I was greatly moved by the incident, you know. So, I painted her, and then I don't know what came over me. It was probably a stupid idea, but I went up to where she lives and just handed it to her. Looking back on it, it probably wasn't my best work simply because I realize now that I had missed much of how she looked, but I had a better idea of her then and made this." The current one was still only half-finished.

"Was this commissioned by someone?"

"Commissioned? No. I do get a lot of commissions, though, from people wanting various things - usually portraits of their family members or of the incident. Two different newspapers have reached out to me to draw illustrations for news articles they were going to publish on the event. But no, this... this is the most important kind of artwork. The kind of artwork I do for myself out of true artistic passion."

"Can I ask you a favor?" Raphael then decided to phrase it differently. "No, not a favor. Sorry. Could I commission you to make something for me?"

"You want to commission something from me?" the artist asked, surprised.

"Yes, if you could make me a portrait of her," he said.

The artist scratched his chin before saying, "Well, I am rather busy with some other commissions, but I think I can make an exception for you, Mr. Raphael - if you just agree to sit there and let me make a rough sketch of you for fifteen minutes. I can draw very well from memory, but it's not the same as having someone actually sitting here, you know."

Raphael considered that to be a great bargain, in the sense that he was getting exactly what he wanted for relatively little.

"I think we have a deal then," Raphael said, sitting down. Still thinking about her portrait, he couldn't help but ask, "Do you know where the name 'Lady Liliana of the Light' comes from?"

"No, I don't happen to know."

"I spoke with Lady Cecilia, and she told me that you came up with it."

"Uh, well, I didn't exactly come up with it. I heard it from someone else. I guess it just rolls off the tongue very nicely, you know, with the alliteration. 'Lady Liliana of the Light' so it caught on."

"But it's weird that everyone is looking up to her so highly when they don't know anything about her other than this," Raphael said. He didn't mind, it was just an odd detail that she was getting so much spotlight from this single event. Far more than he was getting. His father had his own ideas - but Raphael wanted to get a human's perspective on why that might be.

"I suppose it's because people have always looked up to vampires, you know," the artist said. "So, to see one actually do good is... well, something we had all desired at some point, somewhere deep within our hearts."

"Why do people admire any vampires like that? I mean, coming from the point of view of a werewolf, it seems strange. There was a time not that long ago when they used to hunt your kind openly."

"I guess there are a bunch of reasons, a lot of which I don't understand," the artist answered while his pencil moved across his paper,

90

occasionally glancing up at Raphael. "I mean, in the old days, if you were an artist, the only real way that you could survive was to make something for the vampires. They held such a stranglehold on the city... if any human wanted to do anything economically, the best way was to appease the vampires."

It wasn't just about money, that was only one aspect of it. Humans tended to bend over backward to appease the vampire overlords. If you were useful to the vampires, then you and your family were less likely to be eaten. You were not just another face in the crowd. It was at the very least a thin banner of protection.

Perhaps that was why, but there was definitely something more to it, Raphael felt. Why else would cults like the Bloodborne exist? That was not done simply out of a sense of self-preservation. Not when some of its members willingly gave themselves up to be consumed by the vampires. Nor was this just limited to Necropolis - he had learned that Solaris had had certain people like that in the past, but vampires were nearly extinct now in that land so that group had also died out.

Perhaps there was something primal in the human heart when it saw those creatures—creatures who were timeless, immortal, and far beyond the power of an ordinary human. Something which drove them to revere them in a certain way.

"But anyway, that's just one of my theories," the artist. "But it is quite a compelling story, you know. The bards in nearly all of Necropolis are telling and retelling her tale to anyone who'll listen. It almost sounds like a fairy tail when you think about it - a vampire helping a human? But, because it's true, it has really caught on. I'm sorry that these stories are overshadowing you. You did most of the work as far as I can tell, but you ended up reaping far less fame than she did."

Raphael chuckled. "I didn't really do it for fame." That was not entirely true.

He did want to improve his father's standing with the humans. But the reason Liliana was talked about more was simply because it was far less expected that someone like her would do something like that, and also because she was more aloof than Raphael. A lot of people had seen Raphael and knew of the Cain Shipping Company. Liliana, though, was an enigmatic figure who isolated herself within a castle seemingly in a plane above that of mortal men. At least, that was how it felt, and maybe that was another reason why the humans revered their undead overlords more than the werewolves who were somehow more pedestrian, both now and back then.

Even considering that though, he was happy that Liliana was getting some recognition. If enough people talked about her that way, maybe, just maybe, it might be easier to talk to his father about her, provided the public perception of who she was continued to soar.

"Well, I think that's it. Thank you very much for sitting so patiently. How do you think it turned out?" the artist said, flipping the page.

Raphael had to say that he was very good with his pencil. It was nearly exactly like him.

"Do you want one of these as well?" the man asked.

"Um, no, just the one of Liliana is fine."

"If you don't mind me asking, why the portrait of her rather than of yourself?" the artist asked.

"Well, I can always see my own face in a mirror, and my father has already commissioned portraits of me and my family several times already. I don't have anything to remember her by."

He was pretty sure the artist caught on that there was something beyond that, but he did not say anything, simply saying, "All right then, Mr. Raphael. When would you want this then?"

"I'm leaving the city for a few weeks, so it's okay if you take your time."

"Well, in that case, I don't need to tell those stuck-up noble families asking for family portraits that they need to wait. Are you sure you don't want anything to eat? Drink? Nothing else I can do for you?"

"No, thank you. You've already done quite a lot for me," Raphael said. "And I wouldn't want to get in the way of your work anymore."

"You're not in the way of my work, Mr. Raphael. If anything, you were part of the inspiration for it," the artist said, smiling. "But alright then, if that's all, a good day to you."

"And a good day to you."

Chapter Seven

The Village of Lute

Raphael and the rest of his pack did not need any kind of carriage and simply made the journey to the village in question, named Lute, entirely on foot. The long trek over the mountains, which may have winded any human traveler and would have taken three or four days for them - was covered in a single night, reveling in the freedom they found near the mountains.

They could turn into their Lycanthrope forms at any time, though this transformation was more powerful when under the blessing of the full moon. However, right now, they were all in their human forms, and though this did feel slightly constricting, it was better that they remain that way while near this part of the city. They wouldn't want to suddenly be attacked by patrolling vampires or the like.

Although most of the territory around the mountains was claimed by the vampires and their castles, several of them had decayed or were broken down and had just simply not been repaired. Because of this, there were several areas that had essentially been ceded to the wilderness. These areas were often used as hunting grounds. The prey there was rather sparse, as was the vegetation, but it was as close to the wilderness as many of them could get without leaving the confines of the city entirely.

The wind tickled their ears as they flew past the trees. Thousands upon thousands of new scents greeted their noses. The crescent moon seemed to almost wink at them behind the clouds, as if egging them on to transform fully.

Even though they were still within their human forms, they let out yells which echoed for miles around with no one to answer to, yells that would ordinarily be confined by the city. This was the kind of freedom that Raphael had only felt before when he was plunging into the ocean's depth - free away from the restrictions of city life, away from the various noises and responsibilities that shackled. Here, out there in the wilderness, they were truly their own people.

This is how the ancient werewolves had lived. Not within the city, but roaming free in the wilderness that lay beyond.

"I saw a bear over there," Edward said. "Do you guys want to go ahead and try catching it?"

"We're trying to reach the place as soon as possible," Vincent responded. However, it was clear that he was also fine with the detour. Hunting ordinary prey like deer would be something they would do if they had been out hunting for food. But right now, the four of them wanted a challenge, and where would they find it other than with one of nature's most ferocious predators?

***

The bear ran as fast as it could. It was not an animal that was used to being challenged or chased. After all, it had lived most of its life as the dominant creature in its territory. Vampires rarely went out to hunt anymore like they used to. And so, the only other time it had ever eaten a loss and retreated was back when it was little and had been bitten by a snake.

Now, hearing the howls tearing into its ears and setting off a primeval, vicious fear within its heart, it felt like a young cub once more. Although it did not fully understand what it was that it was fleeing from, its survival instincts had kicked in. It had long since learned to trust them far more than the petty amount of intelligence it had.

"Should we let it run out a bit further?" They had caught sight of the bear and knew they were almost on it, but Carlton was suggesting letting it run out a bit further.

"Why? We can catch it right now."

"I mean, to give the hunt a little bit of a thrill."

"Well, just remember we want to get to Lute by sunrise," Vincent reminded them.

They waited fifteen minutes, which was not enough for the bear to make a meaningful lead. However, it did make the subsequent hunt more exciting. There was a reason that hunters did not hunt the fox while it was still in its den - because it was unsporting.

The bear did not let up even as its lungs burned for air. It had to keep running - it had run past the boundaries of what was its territory, but it was more concerned about what was behind than what might end up confronting it from the front.

It heard something on its right side. Before it could even turn its head, something flew out of the trees and knocked it completely off balance, breaking two of its ribs in the process. It rolled along the forest floor like a ragdoll. *That's a human, right?* it thought, catching a glimpse of the culprit as it rose back to its feet. It had seen humans before - but they usually ran when they saw it, rather than the other way around.

In a rage, and with no other option, it decided that it was time to retaliate as it charged at the strange creature.

Raphael ducked, striking it in the stomach before flipping it over. It weighed quite a lot more than the packages he was used to carrying around, and it put some strain upon him as he had not transformed. His arms burned as he threw the bear in an arc before pinning it. He wrestled with it, avoiding its large claws as he pinned its arms away, one of the first few challenges he had gotten in some time.

"All right, I think that's enough," he said as the others emerged. They had managed to find it and corner it, but none of them felt like killing it. As it was, they didn't have a good reason to. This was not the animal terrorizing the village of Lute, after all.

They departed. The bear, confused and in pain, got up, wondering where those strange creatures had gone. Their scent still lingered in the air, and it did its best to walk away from where they were. Its injuries might heal within a few weeks; however, the psychological scars would remain for life. .

They arrived at the village of Lute just a bit before sunrise as Vincent had originally intended. The people of the village were already up and about being early risers compared to their city-dwelling counterparts.

As they approached, they saw that the village was surrounded by a wooden fence - though it would be more accurate to call it a haphazard assortment of planks of wood. It would not really stop even a moderately motivated wild animal, but Raphael felt that most wild animals would avoid this area anyway. That gave the theory that a wild werewolf might be responsible more credibility.

The four of them entered through the front gate, with several eyes drawn towards them. The place had a distinct smell to it, as it was far away from the sea and instead carried the usual smells associated with a farm mainly being those of manure and farm animals. Most of the village's income came from selling medicinal herbs that grew near the edge of the Darkling Woods that were not easy to find elsewhere, but they also grew a few crops and reared a few animals.

"Uncle Thomas!" Vincent yelled out as an old man approached them, beaming with a wide smile that revealed a few broken teeth. He had a wrinkled and tanned face from exposure to sunlight for decades - no small feat in the gloomy environs surrounding Necropolis. He sported a bit of a pot belly, but that only added to his jovial appearance. As he hugged Vincent, he said, "Little Vicky! Look how big you've gotten. You're enormous!" he said with a chuckle. "I remember when you were only this high," he said, pointing to one of his knees. "How have you been?"

"I'm great, Uncle Thomas," Vincent said. He motioned towards the rest of the group. "These are some of my friends who have also come along when they heard of what was going around."

Thomas looked at them, his jovial expression wilting a bit and then nodded. "Glad to see all of you here. I can't thank you boys enough for being willing to give us all a hand." He gave them each a handshake - extremely firm, though to them it may as well have been as soft as a baby's. His hands were rough from years of farm work, almost like leather.

"So, we heard that there have been people disappearing around the village," Raphael began.

"But why don't you all come inside first before I talk about those kinds of matters? Maybe even get you boys something to drink and eat?" Thomas said.

He led them to a big building just outside the wall surrounding the village. "This here used to be an old barn. I've tried to make it so that it would fit y'all nicely enough," Thomas said, opening it up. The barn was mostly empty, save for some piles of hay that had been stacked in a way to allow people to somewhat comfortably sleep on them. Hardly a first-class hotel, but none of the four people there minded. If anything, out here in the wilderness and sleeping on a mat of straw, they were more in their element than they were back in Necropolis.

The only thing that bothered Raphael was the strong stench of manure, but that was likely something they would not be able to escape, no matter where they went in this village.

"So, what exactly has been going on?" Vincent asked.

"It all started 'bout six months ago," Thomas said. "People started disappearing in other villages, not here, you know, but it was still odd. And initially, it would just be someone like a small child or one of the elderly. And not that them disappearing is anything good, but we thought it was just people getting lost in the woods or being taken away by animals. You know, stuff that happens now and then around these parts. But there were too many of them. Instead of happening maybe once a year, these things started happening every other week, and then every single week. We thought there was some kind of predator around, which was hunting humans. Folks were scared to go out after that, but things haven't stopped no matter what we do."

"It got really scary when a family who was holed up in a cabin not too far away from this village was found dead the next morning, a lot of what was missing from 'em had been eaten by some kind of animal. Couldn't have been a bear, they wouldn't have gone that far towards the cabin. But beyond here, in the Darkling Woods..." He shook his head. "I mean, strange things live in these woods, you know? Vampires and the like, but their blood wasn't drained, so..." he trailed off. "The only other creature to attack like that would be a werewolf."

"Have you seen one, or heard odd howls lately?"

"No," he said, shaking his head. "Some of the villagers tried planting wolfsbane here and there, but I don't know how much good it would do."

"Wolfsbane is annoying but not much more than that," Carlton said. "It causes an allergic reaction if our skin comes in contact with it. However, unless we eat it, it's not really going to stop anyone. And you would have to plant it in a massive field all around the village for it to have any sort of real effect." That was impractical, and also, once again, would not stop someone if they were determined to grab one of the villagers.

"Do you happen to know where the latest victim was? Maybe we can find some tracks or the like?" Vincent suggested.

"Well, there was someone who vanished a few villages away. I think they were the most recent," Thomas said. "You could try looking there, but you boys be careful. I don't know how strong the wild werewolves are compared to y'all, but I'd hate for something to happen to you or your friends, Vicky."

"Oh, we'll definitely be careful," Vincent said. From what Thomas was describing, this did seem to be the work of a solitary rogue werewolf, which is why the victims were so few in number - only about one a week. Otherwise, there would be far more traces of whoever it was, and more likely than not, the mayor of Necropolis would have had to intervene far sooner.

"On that note," Raphael said, still having the same question in mind. "The local lord... what was his name - oh! Athelstan? He hasn't done anything about it?"

"Some people have gone to speak with him, and he always says the same thing - that he's trying to do something about it. But he hasn't done anything, and we're not too sure how much we can trust 'em," Thomas answered, shuddering slightly. The fact that they were so uncomfortable around vampires made any kind of petition difficult from the outset.

"All right, then we'll get on the chase," Vincent said.

"Yeah, if you boys need anything, just let me know."

"I don't think we will, but thank you," Raphael said. For food, they could hunt in the surrounding areas, even in places where the farmers wouldn't go, meaning that they had no problem in that regard even if the villagers couldn't provide for them. As it was, they didn't want to burden Thomas any more as they ate far more than ordinary humans. .

A werewolf who lived within Necropolis would never choose to eat humans, but one of the wild ones who lived outside might have. The main defenses of Necropolis against outside threats were the sea on one side and the ring of mountains on the other, combined with a large number of castles that sat at the mountain passes. There had once been a huge, almost thousand-mile-long wall which had surrounded the outskirts of the city. The issue was that such a large structure was impractical to maintain and to man with soldiers, on top of which it did little to actually deter supernatural threats like werewolves. Given that, many areas of the wall had collapsed and there was no plan to repair them. Some of the villagers also took advantage of this to venture out to scavenge despite the dangers lurking beyond. But whoever this werewolf was, it had wandered deep into the wall.

"Are you guys sure you don't need anything like food, tea, or-"

"Nah, we'd rather just hunt," Vincent said. "It's not often that we get away from the city like this. We may as well make the most of it." He talked about it almost like it was some kind of camping trip.

"And for going up against these werewolves or vampires, do you fellas need anything? I mean, we don't have a lot of silver, and I don't know if you'd be able to touch it without it also hurting you guys, but maybe a silver-tipped arrow?"

97

"Don't worry, I think our claws and numbers are far more than enough," Vincent said.

Since the recent attacks did not seem to be the action of a pack, it was more likely a single lone wolf. If a wild werewolf was kicked out of his pack, he would often view humans as easy prey. However, if it realized it was being targeted by four different hunters, it would realize it was not worth the risk to continue targeting the villagers. They might not even have to fight it.

After a quick nap, Raphael and his team began setting to work. They first went around interviewing the villagers in the village of Lute and then moved to the neighboring village and so on and so forth.

Unfortunately, it had rained about two days ago, making it difficult to find any tracks. The rain had also washed away the scent they would have normally relied upon. However, by plotting the number of victims and where they disappeared from, they were able to create a rough plot of the attacks.

"It looks like our culprit is operating here," Raphael said, pointing to an area in the dirt where he had drawn a rough-sketched map of the region.

Remnants of the great wall were still present in many areas, but had a large number of gaps. The current government of Necropolis could not be bothered to fix them, given the cost and futility of attempting to maintain it.

The cluster of attacks seemed to occur within a radius of about ten miles from one of these breaches. Although a few outliers were present, this was expected considering the speed and ferocity of a werewolf, and so was still within their reasonable estimates.

"All right, we should probably split up and try to search this area," Raphael suggested. If they were dealing with only one person, the four of them could communicate relatively easily, but it would still take time for one to reach another. None of them had ever faced a wild werewolf before; other than wrestling with each other, they hadn't seen much combat.

As such, after some discussion, they decided to go in pairs instead.

Chapter Eight
Vladimir Carpathia

Liliana spent the next few days within her estate, her mind often drifting to Raphael no matter how much she tried to distract herself from him.

Athelstan's plea for resources to deal with the werewolf problem was met with pushback. The Council of Elders seemed reluctant to devote any significant manpower to the issue. They could have tried to reach out to the mayor, but what could a large number of humans do against a supernatural threat like this? The lack of concrete evidence was the major hurdle to clear.

"It is rather disappointing," Athelstan said to her one night. "However, would you still be open to seeing my estate once more?"

"Did Mother agree to it?" Liliana asked.

"She did, indeed, after your little stunt managed to earn you a Medal of Valor," Athelstan said. "Did you know that your father also earned one? That makes you the second person in the family to have done so."

"Really? What for?" Liliana asked, unaware of this part of her family's history.

"What else but for creating the Blood Lilies!" Athelstan said, laughing. "A monumental invention, that thing. Your mother may not show it as much as she should, but she's quite proud of what you've done."

"Uncle, is it safe out there?" Liliana asked. She normally wouldn't have questioned such a thing, but being with Raphael, while tantalizing, had also reminded her of just how strong werewolves were. It was one thing to hear about it and another to see it in practice. It was the difference between seeing a tiger in a zoo and being presented with one in the wild.

"But of course, I'm not expecting you to hunt down that werewolf yourself. Just wearing silver will be more than fine. I certainly would not lead you anywhere you might get hurt."

"Understood," Liliana said.

"So, are you agreeable to the trip?" Athelstan asked. "If so, I'll speak to your mother again."

"Why yes, absolutely," Liliana said. She also wished Beatrice could have come along. However, Beatrice was not related to Athelstan directly, and her parents would likely have refused.

Victoria simply waved her hand when Liliana mentioned this to her and said, "I wouldn't extend an invitation to Beatrice. Let it be. Go ahead and have fun on your own. I'm sure you'll enjoy it. But do stay safe. And no more heroics, understood?"

"Understood!"

***

"So, basically, I'm going away with my uncle for a few weeks to his estate," Liliana finished telling Beatrice.

She was worried that Beatrice might be a bit miffed at being left out, but if anything, Beatrice looked quite relieved that she hadn't been invited or she might've been forced to tag along out of etiquette. "Oh, well, have fun there," Beatrice said. "I really couldn't imagine having to go out there, you know, way off from the city, practically next to the wilderness. And please, please Liliana, stay safe, all right? Just because you met one nice werewolf doesn't mean that the wolves living outside are nice," Beatrice added, the last part in an extremely low voice. Much to her credit, she had not spoken about Liliana's little… *escapade* with Raphael to anyone else.

"Don't worry, it's not like he'll be waiting for me there," Liliana said. "And I'm not going there looking for trouble."

"Are you done packing yet?"

"I'm almost done," Liliana said. She didn't have very much that she needed to take with her, the most important thing being her own personalized coffin, of course.

It was later on while she was making sure that her coffin could last for the journey, as it wouldn't be easy to get a replacement out there near her uncle's estate, that her mother approached her.

"Liliana, do you have a moment?" Victoria asked.

"Yes, what's going on?" Liliana asked. Her mother had a strange look. An ordinary person wouldn't have been able to tell, but Liliana could recognize the slight tremor in her mother's left hand, as well as the way her eyes were constantly darting forth and back. Something had happened. Something which was deeply bothering her. "Mother?"

"I just got word that Sir Vladimir has woken from the Shadowsleep," Victoria said.

It took Liliana a moment to remember both who that was and why he was important. Vladimir Carpathia was technically her great-uncle. He had been in the Shadowsleep along with her father during the Night of a Thousand Torches.

"So, you mean to say that we can ask him something?" Liliana asked, the importance of this dawning upon her. "About that night?"

100

Victoria nodded. Words seemed to be insufficient to express her emotions - much like how Liliana had felt when trying to describe why she liked Raphael to Beatrice. "He is in Castle Krakenberg. I'm going there immediately, if you'd like to come."

"Of course!" she replied immediately.

Liliana wasn't sure if Castle Krakenberg was where all of the vampires in the Shadowsleep were currently kept. That location had been changed after the Night of a Thousand Torches. Precious few knew where the current location was as a security precaution.

The laws on waking one from the Shadowsleep were extremely strict, to the point that even though Victoria had wanted to get to the bottom of her husband's murder, she had been unable to convince anyone to allow her to do so forcefully.

As it was, many people had told her, "He will wake up sooner or later. It does not appear that Vladimir has gone into the Shadowsleep permanently. Just wait until he wakes up. Those within the Shadowsleep should be allowed to rest undisturbed."

There was one thing that Victoria wanted far more than to further the political ambitions of the Carpathian family: to get to the root cause of what had happened to her husband.

Liliana had heard the story about how the two of them had fallen in love countless times when she had been little, oftentimes hoping that a similar love story would be waiting for her. Their marriage had been arranged, but the two of them had hit it off almost immediately.

Tragically, however, her father's life was cut short, depriving her of a father and her mother of a husband.

An old vigor that used to be within Victoria now flared up. Liliana thought that she might even be ready to just run all the way toward Castle Krakenberg rather than taking a carriage. But she was not that anxious, at least not yet.

"Do you think he really saw or heard anything?" Liliana asked. She did not know much about the events of that night and what had happened to her father firsthand. Both she and her mother had hidden deep within their castle when the mob had looked like it was about to swarm them.

"They said that he was awake among the survivors the morning after. He might have seen something," Victoria said. "As it is, this is our only clue."

Initially, Liliana had thought that her father had been killed by part of the human mob, but the destruction there did not fit that story. It was not as chaotic as one would expect from a mob. It looked like someone had methodically targeted her father and a few other vampires kept there on purpose. The killer was likely either a werewolf, vampire, or a human who really knew what they were doing. The possibility of the third scenario being true was almost zero. She couldn't think of a single human who would have had the foreknowledge and the guts to do something like that. There were lots of humans who held deep grudges against the vampires, but to possess the knowledge of what the Shadowsleep entailed and how to kill one during it was information that was not easy to obtain, and for good reason.

Ba-dump.

Liliana heard her mother's heart beat once in anticipation. Victoria's anxiety was almost infectious, and as it was, it wasn't like Liliana had been tranquil beforehand, anyway.

Castle Krakenberg was one of the few castles which did not overlook a mountain pass, but instead sat atop the crest of a massive hill. It was built on a limestone foundation, making it impossible to undermine one's way into the castle. Liliana had to admit that it would make perfect sense for this place to be chosen as the site for those in the Shadowsleep to be kept. It was very easy to defend.

The Volkovs owned the castle, lending credence to the theory that this is where the rest of the vampires were also kept, because naturally, one would assume that Vladimir would have been brought to their estate, or Beatrice's, rather than kept here being a part of their family.

Victoria almost tore down the doors of the castle with how swiftly she moved. "Mother, I know you're anxious, but we have to keep up appearances," Liliana whispered weakly. Victoria nodded, but Liliana had the feeling that if push came to shove, her mother would abandon all civility in order to get to the bottom of things. If that happened to involve tearing down this castle - she would do so without hesitation.

They spoke to Lady Camula Volkov, a pleasant enough four-thousand-year-old vampire lady who was close to entering the Shadowsleep herself, before they were allowed to see Vladimir Carpathia.

"He's right this way. I should warn you. He's kind of... well, how vampires tend to be when they're woken up from the Shadowsleep. I don't know if you'll be able to get much useful information out of him," Camula said.

Vladimir was seated in an empty, dark room. His coffin had been brought up here and lay open next to him. He looked like a desiccated mummy. Vampires were often described as being corpse-like, but he was devoid of many of the features that made them look animated. His eyes were a dull shade of red and lacked the brightness of Victoria's and Liliana's. He had lost most of the hair atop his head, and his skin had shrunk itself around his body. His eyes were sunken in their sockets, and he looked painfully thin. There was a certain lack of luster to his skin compared to theirs. His eyes also seemed to be only half alert, as if he was half asleep.

"Sir, Vladimir Carpathia, I am pleased to meet you," Victoria said, flashing a small smile as she and Liliana sat down. The room was extremely sparse when it came to furniture. There were only a few chairs and a table. Liliana could think of a few reasons why Camula might have arranged things like this. More likely than not, it was to minimize the amount of stimuli that Vladimir would be exposed to. He may very well end up going back into his coffin and deciding to return to the Shadowsleep once more. Excessive stimulation could hamper that process.

102

As vampires grew older - although they were timeless creatures and many humans viewed them as immortal - certain mental changes would start happening. As they endured for thousands of years, they would start entering periods of deep hibernation known as the Shadowsleep. Initially, these bursts would be short, and they would wake up and resume their everyday activities thereafter. But over time, the periods tended to become longer and longer until they eventually went into a near-permanent comatose state.

Liliana's father had entered the Shadowsleep for the first time, and she had fully expected him to wake up within a few months. But it had not been so. He was found in his coffin with a wooden stake driven through his heart once the mob had dissipated. As to who had done it, that had been a question that plagued the two of them for a very long time. Now, they might finally get some answers.

"Have we met before?" Vladimir asked. His voice was thin and raspy, like two pieces of sandpaper rubbing against each other. Liliana nearly winced.

"My name is Victoria Carpathia. I don't know if you remember me, but we met when I was quite little-" Victoria said.

"You..." Vladimir said. "You are... Lucian's wife, aren't you?"

"Yes, yes," Victoria said. "Or at least I was. I'm now Lucian's widow."

"He's dead? How unfortunate," Vladimir said without a single drop of emotion in his voice as he slowly turned his head to look at Liliana. "And you... his daughter? Or granddaughter?"

"Yes, my name is Liliana," she answered when she found her voice a moment later. "Sir Vladimir, we're sorry to have bothered you, but there was something we wanted to ask."

Ordinarily there would be quite a bit of formalities to go through when two vampires of a high rank met each other, but it didn't look like Vladimir could last that long. And so, Liliana jumped to the meat of the matter. Victoria did not reprimand her.

"Ask away," Vladimir said. Every word seemed to cause him a great deal of trouble to get out. Vampires tended to be like that after having just emerged from the Shadowsleep. He would either recover over the coming few days and regain most of his vitality, or go back into the Shadowsleep. If it was the latter case, he was probably going to go into it practically permanently. Were that the case, they would need to get their answer right then and there.

It was technically possible to forcibly awaken someone from the Shadowsleep, but it was a massive taboo and had questionable effectiveness.

"The night that Edward passed away," Victoria said. "They saw that you had partially awakened from the Shadowsleep the next morning. Did you happen to see who or what was responsible for killing him?"

"Let me think," Vladimir said, closing his eyes and furrowing his brow.

He was silent for over three minutes, and for a moment, both Victoria and Liliana thought that their trip was in vain and that he really had gone back into the Shadowsleep. Until he slowly opened his eyes that is.

"I remember now. I had heard footsteps and the door of a coffin being opened. But no breath, no heartbeat. It was a vampire, it must have been," Vladimir said.

"Is there anything else you can remember that might help us?" Victoria asked, her voice almost cracking from desperation. At the very least, they were somewhat closer to getting an answer, but there were several vampires who would have benefited from her husband's death.

"I remember shouting and screaming," Vladimir said, no doubt referring to the mob that had been moving through the city during that time. "But even closer to me, I heard... a soft bell. A bell. There was definitely a bell."

Vladimir nodded, each movement of his head being extremely stiff. "Yes, that is all that I remember."

Victoria tried probing him a bit more, but she couldn't get anything else that seemed to be useful. At one point, Vladimir really did fall asleep and did not respond to anything for over an hour.

"He might have gone back into the Shadowsleep once again. Perhaps permanently," Victoria said, sighing.

The two of them left, informing Camula on their way out about his condition. Liliana was a bit disappointed. She had been hoping that they might be able to get a name; that her father might finally get justice. But the only clue that they had gotten was about the sound of a bell, and that it had been a vampire who had done so.

"If only we had fresh blood," Victoria said on their way back to their estate. "One of the few things that can give them vitality once they've emerged from the Shadowsleep, even if it's just for a moment, is a large amount of fresh human blood..."

It was certainly not easy to obtain in this day and age. The last time that Liliana had tried fresh human blood, back during her younger days, was something Victoria had managed to obtain for her by securing the blood of a criminal scheduled for execution. That itself had been an uphill battle and was very difficult to arrange even during that time. Now, though, it would definitely be difficult to do openly.

Difficult to do openly, Liliana thought, *but not impossible to do secretly*.

For a moment, she thought of the bustling crowd on the docks. If she happened to take one of those humans - no, forget one, even two or three, would anyone notice? She shook her head as her thoughts then went to the boy she had rescued, and these former ideas scattered from her mind like autumn leaves in the breeze.

"Let me see if I can arrange for something," Victoria finally said after contemplating the matter, her voice filled with determination. Although Liliana had pushed the idea aside for now, it seemed that Victoria had her own machinations for trying to obtain what they needed. "It might take some time, but I think I should be able to get my hands on it."

Liliana and Victoria, despite trying their hardest over the next few days, were unable to uncover anything else of note. It turned out that Vladimir had, it seemed, returned to the Shadowsleep, potentially permanently.

104

"You mustn't allow yourself to get frustrated, dear," Victoria said to Liliana one night.

"I'm not really frustrate-" Liliana began before Victoria slammed the book she was carrying against the desk with such force it could've broken an ordinary table. Thankfully, like all other things within their household, the table in question was high-end and withstood the very unladylike blow.

"Just go ahead with your uncle and relax a while, I'll see what else I can find," Victoria added, apparently not having even heard what Liliana had said.

Athelstan and Liliana set out for his castle a few days later. The journey took them three days by carriage; if they ran, they could have covered the distance as fast as the werewolves, but they would not be seen like that and it wasn't like they were in any hurry regardless.

"Uncle, you've started keeping human servants in your castle?" she asked, noting the differences here compared to her home.

Athelstan sighed. "I know what your mother would say, but I have many things to attend to, and vampires alone won't be able to do it. Vampires don't want to live here, you know, not near the outskirts of the city."

Inequality existed among vampires - if anything, their long lives and strict adherence to tradition only amplified things compared to humans. Most of the vampire servants whom Victoria employed were from lesser families or from wild vampires who had accepted that role for the sake of protection.

It was extraordinarily difficult for this lower class of vampires to gain employment otherwise because of their nocturnal nature and how much the humans feared them. Given how expensive things like the talismans which kept the sunlight at bay were, and in order to procure enough Blood Lillies, they could only resign themselves to doing the bidding of the higher-ups. Still, there weren't enough of them to meet everyone's needs, and few would want to wander to a remote area like Athelstan's estate.

Liliana cast her gaze at the horizon. Her uncle's castle was located in a defensive position near a lake, and the moon and stars reflected over its smooth, glass-like surface.

"The lake is man-made, you know?" her uncle reminded her, something she had heard before but which he still liked to talk about. "And they say that at the very bottom, they put in silver spikes in case werewolves ever tried to swim across and breach its walls."

"Is that true?" Liliana asked. It would have been extremely expensive if they had tried it. People also said that Solaris paved the roads of its capital with gold, but much like this story, that seemed to be far too fanciful and impractical to be true.

"My father told me that story many times, but I never had the heart to actually dive in and see for myself," Athelstan remarked, laughing.

From the castle, one could see the mountains looming behind them, blocking out the sight of the rest of the city. In front of them was a region partially enclosed by the remnants of the great wall at various places, beyond which lay the wastelands. A section of the wastelands included a thicket of woods whose canopy was so dense that light rarely, if ever, reached the ground: the Darkling Woods which bordered close to Athelstan's territory. It was said that King Alistair had fought a powerful Lycan king there before establishing the city.

Her uncle told her various stories of successful skirmishes from the past. "They are usually limited to one or two Lycans, though there were sometimes groups as large as four or five. Anything bigger than that didn't happen in my time," he said. "They are not very smart, you see, and we always repelled them."

Whichever Lycan it was, it seemed to have the basic common sense not to come too close near her uncle's castle, as all the attacks were occurring at the fringes. However, she was not here to deal with that, as her uncle reminded her. "Take your time to wander the place and relax a little. No need to worry about the woes of mortal men, or your uncle's estate."

Liliana could spend days wandering through the halls, a nice change of pace from back home where she felt like she was constantly banging her head against a wall regarding her father's murder without reaching anywhere substantial.

She still remembered most of the portraits. She saw portraits of vampires from her mother's side of the family, as well as some tapestries depicting important battles that occurred near the frontier. The werewolves were always depicted as massive monsters thrice as tall as the vampires in these tapestries with massive fangs dripping with blood, while the vampires faced off against them wearing armor and silver-coated swords.

There was a small altar dedicated to Sanguinus, which had probably been made by one of the earlier owners of the castle given her uncle was never particularly religious.

What she had been most looking forward to seeing were the fields - which were as beautiful as she had always imagined them to be, even during the night. The moonlight sparkled off the soil and the grain waved in the wind.

It reminded her of Raphael once again - his hair and his soft eyes - waiting to embrace her. She felt her heart occasionally beat once or twice before she suppressed it. She knew that the more she indulged in these fantasies, the worse it would be when she had to return home and never see him again. After all, that was the harsh reality of the world even if her heart wouldn't accept it. Beatrice was right; they could not be together.

"Do you want to go to the villages and see if we can find any trace of the werewolves ourselves?" she asked her uncle one day.

Although she was still scared of them, she figured that if the two of them, along with some servants, went, they would stand an excellent chance against any threat they might run into.

"Oh, I don't very much fancy my chances with them," Athelstan said. "We might be just as strong, but you have to remember, Liliana, that these are *wild* werewolves we're dealing with. They're used to fighting for survival at every single point of their lives. As much as I hate to say it, being civilized has its disadvantages. Our main strength is in the fact that we can join together and use our wits against them, which we won't be able to do in such small numbers. Hopefully, the Council Elders will respond at some point, though." He tugged at his chin while considering things. "However, if you want, you can go and interview some of the villagers. That should be safe enough, but don't go too far or into any of the areas I'd warned you about."

Liliana found herself wandering too close to the villages during her nightly strolls. Ever since she had saved that human child, she had a strange curiosity regarding how the people there lived. Without her mother breathing down her neck and her uncle giving her far more leeway now that she was older, it felt extremely freeing. The only thing she lacked with this freedom was to meet with Raphael again, but she knew that she couldn't do that.

She would watch these villages - sleepy little places in the middle of the night - though occasionally they would burst into a flurry of activity before the sun rose. She made sure not to ever get too close; she had a feeling that her mere presence would cause a large amount of panic among the villagers. However, she could still admire them from afar.

Here in the villages, many people got up long before dawn to start their work. It was nothing like the city, where Liliana could roam until sunrise without seeing anyone. She often watched them - going into the fields and drawing up water for the day.

That night, she watched a family and their dog working in the early morning light, and almost forgot to slip back into the shadows by the time the sun was fully out. She thought one of the children might have seen her, but she vanished, unlikely to be remembered as anything more than a trick of the light.

They may not live as long as us, but they feel emotions just the same. The faces of that joyous family reminded her of her father and how happy they'd been when he was still alive. Had her mother found some more leads back home? She had thought about finding an *appropriate* target to exsanguinate, but these sights gave her hold. Not to mention they were impractical - there would be a massive number of hurdles in trying to forcefully wake Vladimir even if they got fresh blood. On top of which, Vladimir might've already told them all that he knew meaning such an endeavor might've been futile.

Still, she ventured out nonetheless. On these occasions, she wore a simpler dress more appropriate for movement, yet not so bare as to be immodest for a lady of her stature. She also wore sturdy boots rather than her usual delicate shoes. She had embellished herself with more silver than usual: a silver ring, the same silver tiara, a silver bracelet, and, of course, the silver dagger hidden within her bodice.

Her uncle had told her not to stray too far. However, she would occasionally disregard this advice, figuring that it couldn't be all that dangerous. She did not smell anything that resembled a werewolf trail, nor did she find any unusual tracks. If she had, she would have definitely turned and ran.

One early night while she was wandering around the area, the wind carried a strange, yet deeply familiar, scent. It had been slightly altered since she had last been in the city, but she felt that she vaguely recognized it.

"Raphael," she whispered to herself. It was impossible for him to be here. Why would he be here instead of at the docks? And yet, she didn't think that she was mistaken.

However, curiosity got the better of her. And if it truly was Raphael, as impossible as it seemed, her heart greatly yearned to meet him once more.

Chapter Nine
Forbidden Fruit

As Liliana got closer she felt a stronger certainty that she recognized the scent. She had wandered quite a distance from the area her uncle had deemed safe. As her eyes scanned the periphery, she detected nothing, even as she kept a hand on her silver bracelet - a special piece with a wooden section that could be modified to reveal a hidden silver spike within that made for an excellent makeshift weapon.

The wind shifted again, and the familiar scent washed over her one more time. She was downwind from where he was.

"Raphael, is that you?" she called out.

Footsteps rapidly approached. And there he was: the man she had been thinking about for months - the person she had been unable to expel from her mind. It was as if he had taken permanent refuge within the fortress of her heart, and no matter how much she attempted to besiege it, he would not yield.

He was wearing even more casual clothes than he would in the city, dressed almost like an ordinary farmhand. The simple attire revealed more of his tanned skin and burly muscles. There was some additional scent of his labor, such as manure and earth, yet he still carried that underlying smell of the warm freshly-ploughed soil that she recalled.

"Liliana, is that really you?" Raphael asked hesitantly, rubbing his eyes as if to make sure that he wasn't dreaming.

"Yes, it's me," she said, flashing him a smile as her heart gave a sudden, hard flutter for a few beats. "What are you doing here? This is quite a distance away from the docks."

"I should be asking what you are doing here," he countered. He took a step forward. "Is it alright if I approach you?"

"Why wouldn't it be?"

"It's just, you know, we're out here in the wilderness. Dangerous things can happen. I didn't want you to think I was attacking or anything," Raphael said. He then seemed to remember something. "You should be a bit more careful, though. I heard there's a rogue werewolf somewhere around these parts."

"I've heard that too," Liliana said, "which is why I was wondering, why are you here? Oh, and feel free to approach. I trust you."

He approached her slowly, still staring as if he couldn't believe she was real. It was as if she were a phantom or a ghost who had simply appeared to taunt him. He pinched his cheek for a moment. But it was only when he confirmed that she smelled just like he remembered that he was truly convinced that she wasn't some kind of mirage. A werewolf's nose was sharp enough to smell what you'd had for lunch yesterday by merely taking a whiff of your breath. And Raphael's nose had never let him down.

"Well, I came mainly to deal with the werewolf," Raphael explained. "A friend of mine - you've met Vincent, right? The werewolf who was with me?"

"Yes, I believe I remember him."

"He has some humans he's close with in one of the villages. They're being attacked."

"So you came to investigate? Alone?" Liliana asked, quite taken aback.

"No, four of us came," Raphael stated.

"Four?" Liliana asked, glancing around, but she didn't see any of his companions.

"Yes, initially we were going out in pairs to explore the area," Raphael said. "But then we didn't really find anything, so we decided to split up even further to cover more ground. I don't know if that was a smart decision or not, but we haven't caught sight of whoever is doing this as of yet. Then again, it's been about a week since the last attack, and we're sure they'll strike again about this time. So, we wanted to cover more ground to make sure we caught whoever it was."

"You seem to know quite a lot about this matter," Liliana observed.

"Well, we asked around the villages. I was able to find out..." Raphael began, filling her in on what his 'pack' had discovered. Liliana drank the information in; she knew next to nothing about the attacks as she had mostly been observing the villages from afar. She had to admit that he had done an excellent job investigating.

Why can't Uncle just ask him and his friends to deal with it rather than waiting for the Council of Elders? she thought to herself. *It seemed that would be the best idea.* A reluctance to seek help from werewolves couldn't explain it - one of their main occupations when they had first joined Necropolis was to serve as bodyguards for the vampires, mainly from other werewolves. In modern times they had better things to do especially as werewolf attacks were exceedingly rare, but it looked like Raphael and his small pack were quite willing to lend a hand.

Athelstan, however, was oblivious to their presence within his lands.

"Why are you here, though?" Raphael asked.

"I'm here visiting my uncle," Liliana explained. "He owns the castle nearby."

Raphael frowned. "Is your uncle's name Athelstan, by any chance?"

"Yes."

110

Now Raphael remembered where he had heard that name - during the ceremony where he had been given his Medal of Honor. He had been introduced to, and had seen, the vampire in question, and had connected him to Liliana. But he had never put Athelstan's name together with the events going on now, as he hadn't been focusing on the man at the time of the ceremony. *I let myself get distracted by her a bit too much, didn't I?*

"How much does Athelstan know about what's going on?"

"Oh, he knows about the issue," Liliana said. "He's tried to get help from the Council of Elders to deal with it, but they aren't really doing much. They are dragging their feet - saying they aren't sure that there's really a werewolf attacking. And it would take time to get a group ready anyway." That was news to Raphael; from what he had heard, the humans thought Athelstan had essentially done nothing whatsoever regarding their plight.

"The Council of Elders is a group of vampires, isn't it?" he asked, recalling their function.

"Yes," Liliana said.

The conversation trailed off then, as Raphael had nothing further to say regarding his mission. However, neither of them wanted to pull away. They were instead slowly stepping closer to each other, drinking in each other's presence; more intoxicating than the strongest of spirits.

"It's a beautiful night out," Liliana observed. The moon was almost half full above them. The silence and darkness surrounding them was beautiful in a way that she found hard to describe, as if the world had only been created moments before they walked there. It felt as if this place had been designed specifically for the two of them to meet and for nothing else. Here, where the two of them were alone.

Raphael's friends were nowhere close and Liliana didn't have anyone tailing her.

Raphael thought long and hard about what he was going to say next, and then figured he may as well say it. Did Liliana truly feel the same way about him as he suspected? "But not as beautiful as you," he murmured, his voice clear as day in the surrounding silence.

He didn't hear what he hoped to - a heartbeat from her chest. Instead, she gave him a wry smile. "That's a bit cliché to say. However, thank you." She then took a closer look at him. "The moonlight suits you as well."

She felt that his hair would be better suited to the morning sunrise however, where it would glow like a field of grain waving in a gentle breeze. But she couldn't deny that he looked amazing even under the gentle moonlight which brought out some of his sharper features.

To Raphael, her presence was extraordinarily striking. She was even more beautiful than he had remembered. He thought about the job the artist had done trying to capture her in that earlier portrait he had seen and concluded that the artist in question had done a terrible job. No, she was far more ethereal, far more delicate, far more exotic, with a smile that could break a million hearts. He didn't think there even was an artist who could capture all of that.

111

Before they knew it, they were standing so close to each other that they could have shaken hands. Liliana offered her hand to him, and he gently brushed his lips against it, carefully avoiding the silver ring.

"You may not look it," Liliana said with a demure smile, "but you are quite the gentleman."

"You don't exactly look like someone called Lady Liliana of the Light," Raphael said.

Liliana let out a laugh that was pure and unadulterated. "I'm sorry, I didn't mean to laugh at you, but that name... 'Lady Liliana of the Light.' It seems very silly."

"The humans have been calling you that for some time."

"What? Why?"

"I'm surprised you don't know. You're quite the celebrity outside your castle walls. Remember the incident at the *Misty Marionette*?"

"Because I saved a child? Simply because of that?" she said, giggling in a way she would have ordinarily never done, at least not in public. "That seems like such a small thing to be given that grand of a title for."

"Humans are weird, aren't they?"

"You're right about that," Liliana said. Despite all her efforts up until now, she felt like she still couldn't really understand the human psyche. Maybe the truth was that she could never fully understand them; nor they her. But did she really want to understand them? They were merely a passing curiosity compared to the man who stood before her. No, the person she really wanted to understand was Raphael.

The two gazed into each other's eyes for what felt like forever. Here, in this corner of the world isolated from everyone else, the darkness was their witness and accomplice. It was what separated and protected them from the rest of the cold, cruel world. In this small bubble they had created for themselves, they were truly free.

It was something neither of them could ever imagine lasting. Raphael was bound to his family and his responsibilities. Liliana was bound to her mother and her family's legacy. Neither of them particularly resented these bonds, because without bounds, how could one live in this world? Everything that came with benefits also came with drawbacks. But even if the chains that bound them were made of gold and studded with diamonds; they were chains nonetheless.

Raphael gazed into her deep, blood-red eyes, feeling their pull latch onto him, like the water beckoning him to dive into the ocean. A sea of crimson that had untold depth beneath.

She gazed into his golden-brown irises, which were like soft soil she could sink her hands into. "Tell me," Liliana asked. "You said the night was not as beautiful as I. Was that just flattery, or did you mean it?"

"I meant it with every breath, every fiber of my being," Raphael said, "and on my honor as a gentleman, if that means anything."

"It means quite a great deal, actually. Like I said, you seem to be a man of your word."

They moved closer to each other; held back by an infinitesimally small space. Both wanted to take the final step, the plunge that would dedicate their feelings for each other. The forbidden fruit was just a millimeter away from their teeth, yet both hesitated. Up until now, they had certainly entertained fanciful thoughts about being with each other, about what it would be like to embrace, to live their lives together. But these were all fantasies - fantasies that they had each told themselves they could not act upon because of the weight of their responsibilities.

Both of them were greatly conflicted. On one end was loyalty to who they were - loyalty to their political factions, to their families, to their friends. And on the other hand, was loyalty to their hearts. To accept one meant betraying the other. They could remain loyal to themselves, but that would be a betrayal of everyone else - or they could remain loyal to what society expected of them, and betray themselves in turn.

Both of them had told themselves they were fine with this betrayal of oneself. One couldn't have everything one wanted in life, after all. They would have to be content simply knowing each other existed. Only now, they questioned it.

"I thought that I would never be able to see you again," Raphael said, his breath warm on Liliana's face.

"And the same here," Liliana said.

Both of them wanted to do it, to lurch forward. However, this tiny distance, this insignificant amount of space between them, seemed to be an impenetrable chasm that neither could leap over. They had traveled many miles to get to this place. And yet, this small distance still separated them, because both of them knew that once they kissed, there would be no going back.

Up until now, there had just been fanciful dreams that both of them had entertained of being together. However, once they kissed, once they had whetted their appetites, they would be like a starving person brought to a feast who took a single crumb. It wouldn't be enough to satisfy them. They would throw themselves at the buffet until they could eat no more.

A thousand questions raced through each of their minds. They barely knew each other. And yet, even if the action would result in their destruction, they felt drawn to it like moths to a flame.

Like swimmers about to take a plunge into ice-cold water, they steeled themselves. And although their minds had a thousand questions, they were drawn forward by what they felt in their chests that could not think of anything else other than what it wanted.

After what felt like an eternity of waiting, their lips brushed against each other.

Their lips simply touched for about a second before both drew back.

Liliana's pupils dilated, her heart beating frantically - as fast as that of an ordinary human. Raphael felt the hair on the nape of his neck stand up. Every single one of his senses seemed to have been heightened, each of them focusing solely on her.

Neither could quite believe what had just happened. The brief moment had only deepened their hunger, rather than satisfying their curiosity. It felt like a jolt of lightning had erupted between them - something which was electrifying but at the same time explosive to the point that both immediately withdrew.

"Your heart's actually beating," Raphael said, surprised at the sound coming from her chest.

"It only beats like this because of you," Liliana said, as the pounding intensified.

Each of them wanted more. A mere brush of the lips could not possibly satiate what they felt. They approached each other once more. Now, there was no holding back - no doubts, and no second thoughts.

But before they could close the gap again, before they could surrender to the pull of each other's presence, the wind shifted.

And then Raphael was instantly on edge because of something else entirely.

Liliana noticed the smell too, but she did not react to it the way Raphael did. All she smelled was the distinct scent of another werewolf. To Raphael, however, it meant far more than that.

Vampires did not rely on their sense of smell as much as werewolves did, not to mention she didn't spend that much time around werewolves. To her, all of them probably smelled about the same.

Raphael knew that this was not one of his friends. Even though his packmates had left the city some time ago, they still carried the faint scent of the harbor and the streets. This new scent, however, was *raw*. It spoke of the wilderness, of the Darkling Woods, of a werewolf who had never known the touch of civilization.

Raphael had spent all this time searching for the culprit behind the murders - but it had found him instead.

Chapter Ten

Ambush

I've made a huge mistake, Raphael realized. If he hadn't been so focused on Liliana - no, if he had been paying the slightest bit of attention he wouldn't be in this situation. Ordinarily, there was no way someone could have snuck up on him.

But cursing himself for that was futile.

His mind moved from one thought to another at a lightning pace attempting to figure out what to do. Immediately, his priorities went to one thing: Liliana.

"Liliana, you should run," he said, scanning the dark bush in front of them. "As fast as you can." He knew that Liliana possessed supernatural strength and speed much like he did, but he seriously doubted that given the age she had grown up in that she was in any way used to or had trained to fight wild werewolves. For that matter, neither was he - all he had done at most was wrestled with his friends occasionally, nothing that even approached the lethality of a true werewolf fight.

Liliana understood what was happening simply from the tone of his voice and immediately reached for her silver bracelet, twisting it so the small spike contained within was revealed. Raphael sensed this as a shiver crept down his spine, but he knew that silver itself was useless unless they could use it properly. It might function as a slight deterrent, but wielded in the wrong hands it would be nothing more than an annoyance to a Lycan experienced with fighting.

Raphael still could not see who it was. At least, not directly.

The figure was remarkably good at disguising itself. However, it was that very lack of presence - the way it blended in too well, creating a dark void that contrasted even with the darkness itself, a spot that birds and animals seemed to avoid - was what finally gave it away to Raphael.

If the wind hadn't shifted like it did, he could've almost been on top of us, Raphael thought, cursing his lack of situational awareness yet again.

Should the two of them try to make a run for it together? Based on the distance between them and it, he gave up on that idea. It would be for the best if he try to hold it off in order to give Liliana an actual chance at getting away.

The biggest variable was how strong this wild werewolf was. If the legends were true, they were stronger than those who had lived in the city, whether from experience or simply the harsh dog-eat-dog world of the wastelands. Even among humans there was a considerable gap in the fighting prowess of a civilian and a trained soldier. Any werewolf who had grown up in the wastelands would've been through countless more fights than Raphael and would be used to fighting other werewolves.

There were other variables which he went through in his head one by one. First, what exactly did this werewolf want? If he was able to detect its presence, it was more than capable of detecting them. He was gazing at it, but it was also gazing back at him.

It must have realized that neither of them would be easy prey. Neither of them were one of the weak humans it was so used to preying on up until now. Which meant that it had approached them deliberately despite knowing that.

Did it intend to strike them? He could understand if the werewolf happened to stumble upon Liliana alone that it would want to get rid of her. But how would it view him? He didn't know how it would react to him, though if two werewolves from different packs crossed paths in the wild they would definitely fight.

From what he could tell, their only advantage right now was that it possibly had not realized they were aware of its existence. They might get a slight head start if both of them immediately bolted, as long as they weren't too conspicuous about it.

"Liliana," he whispered, turning toward her. "There is a wild werewolf in the bushes. Try to remain calm and don't react too suddenly."

Liliana slipped her bracelet back on, though she still kept the silver spike exposed. "What should we do?" she whispered back. Despite Raphael's repeated insistence that she flee, she had stayed with her feet rooted firmly to the ground.

"When I say go, you should run, as fast as you can, back to your uncle's manor," Raphael said. "I'm going to howl for my friends to come here and then run away as well later." His friends would take several minutes to find them at the very least, meaning until then, Raphael would be on his own.

Why had they split up like this? It seemed like such a dumb decision now, but he had to admit that none of his friends would have been caught off guard like he was. He had been too distracted by Liliana - otherwise he would've seen things coming far enough away that he could have made a run for it. Their plan to split up had not accounted for the fact that one of them would've decided to ignore all of his senses.

"You want me to run first... what about you?"

"I'm not its target. Probably. If it wants one of us, it's you," Raphael said. "And maybe, just maybe, I can talk him out of things." Raphael didn't have high hopes for that, but if he howled, it would also let the creature know that reinforcements were coming, and he had only detected one of them. In terms of numbers, they would then have the clear advantage. That might be more than enough to convince it to run away.

"I'm not going to abandon you like this," Liliana said, touching the tiara on her head. "I can fight too."

"I don't doubt that you can," Raphael said. In a fight, they would definitely have a better chance as a pair. However, if she happened to run away and then turn around to flank it   no, he realized, grinding his teeth in frustration. He wasn't sure how long he could hold the wolf off. Liliana didn't seem like someone who was used to a fight. That was the major issue here: neither of them had any true combat experience. Some vampires were old enough to still remember how to fight werewolves, but Liliana was not one of them. And whether in raw strength or experience, he was outclassed.

All of these thoughts were interrupted, however, as the shadow emerged from the darkness. It saw no more meaning in hiding itself.

"Liliana, go!" Raphael urged. But she stayed put, moving her bracelet to her palm once again.

A massive mountain of fur approached them. This werewolf was in his full Lycanthrope form, covered from head to toe in dark gray fur with matted areas that were either discolored or caked with mud.

Liliana's eyes went wide at the sight of the nine foot tall towering monstrosity as it approached them on its hind legs. It would have been even taller had it not been slightly crouched over. She could tell the difference between it and the city werewolves now; this thing smelled exactly like how many people described werewolves: a strange, unwashed, feral scent.

Its dark amber eyes shifted between the two of them, and its fetid breath escaped between a pair of long, dagger-like teeth. It may not have appeared much more than a larger wolf that could stand on its hind legs at first glance, but Raphael knew the kind of strength it could exhibit far surpassed what its physique indicated. To his dismay, it was slightly larger than his own Lycanthrope form.

It made no attempt to lunge at them, stopping in its tracks a spear's throw away from them as it turned toward Raphael. "Living in the city has neutered your survival instincts, boy. If my father had known that I had let another wolf come this close to me without noticing, he'd have kicked me out of the pack as a failure because there would've been no chance I could've lived to see another winter."

Its voice was deep and raspy, like humans who had smoked for too many years. Raphael did not respond, but he knew, without a doubt, that it was unmistakably a male werewolf. And it was correct in its assessment. Living in the city had indeed dulled many of his senses. There was constant background noise in the city, so one would learn to ignore many background noises he otherwise would've picked up in the wilderness. As for smell and sight - Liliana had been occupying those two domains.

Liliana picked up another scent now: the scent of human blood. Raphael noted this too. This wolf had eaten a person some time ago and was, without a doubt, the cause of the mysterious disappearances near her uncle's estate.

Liliana wanted to speak up, but the words caught in her mouth. She couldn't deny that his appearance was downright terrifying. This was nothing like meeting Raphael or his friends. There was a murderous intent in the air directed at both of them, suppressing both of their spirits.

"Who are you, and why are you here?" Raphael asked.

A guttural sound erupted from the wolf's throat, which Raphael recognized as laughter. "You are in no position to be asking questions, *boy*. But I suppose I may as well give you my name. Quickpaw, it is. And I was simply here for a small, succulent meal."

"You've been eating people."

"I've been eating *humans*, boy. I'm surprised you can't tell the difference. Or is that something that they don't teach you in the city?" Quickpaw sneered. He then glared at Liliana, whose free hand reached for the silver dagger hidden in the bodice of her dress. If there was ever a time to take it out, it was now.

Raphael glared at him, his fist tightening.

"Oh, relax, pup," Quickpaw said, now sitting down on his haunches and appearing to shrink a foot as a result. He let out a louder laugh. "Do I really have to say why I'm here, though? It's rather funny to see. I had heard stories about 'city wolves' and how they had been domesticated by the vampires, though I didn't think I would ever see a sight like this. Were you unable to find a Luna for yourself that you've decided to make do with something like her?" Luna, Alpha, Beta - those terms had lost any real meaning for the werewolves in Necropolis centuries ago. "I didn't know that these were the kinds of 'services' the vampires kept your spayed ancestors around for. Oh, don't mind me. Go back to rolling around your master's feet and licking her boots clean, like the dog you've been trained to be."

The words were clearly meant to rile up Raphael, though he did not pay attention to the taunt. Instead, he scanned the wilderness. Should he take the opportunity to howl for his comrades? That would draw them in, but Quickpaw would reach them far faster than they would arrive. If he chose to pursue them, they would be forced into a fight which Raphael did not want to invite upon them unnecessarily. There was a good chance that either he or Liliana could be severely injured, if not killed. He really wished she had left when he had asked her too.

"When I caught the scent of another wolf, I thought I might go ahead and see what it was all about. But to see a little pup like yourself being tamed by your master. Heh - she doesn't even require a leash," Quickpaw sneered further. "I may have considered fighting you earlier just to see what it might be like, but it looks like it would be nothing resembling a challenge. Pity, I thought that I might find a rival werewolf here, not some wet-behind-the-ears infant."

Raphael still did not respond. Quickpaw opened his mouth, but unlike, Raphael was on full alert and observing each and every twitch that the wild werewolf made. Just as it seemed that Quickpaw was going to unleash another tirade of insults, Raphael's instincts kicked in as he noticed Quickpaw's weight shift to his right side.

Quickpaw's talk of leaving them alone had been just that: only talk. Raphael transformed before Quickpaw could cover the distance between them. Transforming took nothing more than a thought. If Raphael had a proper silver weapon like a silver-coated sword with a normal hilt that would let him touch it, he could've fought while still in his human form. But without that kind of advantage there was no chance of him coming out of this situation alive if he didn't transform.

Raphael transformed into a mountain of gold-tinged fur that leapt out at Quickpaw, catching his blow head-on. Raphael felt the wind knocked out of him from the sheer momentum of the impact - this was nothing like wrestling that bear earlier.

Quickpaw quickly snapped back, and then swerved away rather than pouncing at him. At first Raphael thought that his sudden transformation had thrown the enemy off-balance, but he then saw a flash of silver fly past him and miss Quickpaw.

"Liliana, keep your silver - you might need it!" He then howled as loudly as he could, the noise traveling for miles around. His friends would've no doubt have heard it.

The only question was - could he survive long enough for them to come and rescue them?

As Quickpaw hopped back, avoiding the silver dagger thrown at him by Liliana, Raphael noticed something about his opponent. It looked like Quickpaw's left foot had been injured somehow, probably by a weapon imbued with silver or wolfsbane, because it had not healed completely. This caused Quickpaw to have a slight limp when running, though it did not seem to bother him that much.

Still, it was the only chink it Quickpaw's armor that he could detect. Most wild werewolves preferred to simply stay in their full form, only turning into humans occasionally for the purpose of hunting if they needed to get close to humans. They were only compelled to transform, and their transformation was also stronger, on nights with a full moon. In the city, during those nights, the werewolves would go to specified hunting grounds so that they didn't cause panic, but those in the wilderness were nearly always in their Lycanthrope form. Without a doubt, sans weapons, their full Lycanthrope forms were far better for any kind of fighting, especially in the harsh environment of the wastelands.

Quickpaw snarled. "Hiding behind your woman's skirt, boy? Can't fight one-on-one?"

Raphael did not respond to Quickpaw's taunts. Instead, he lunged directly at Quickpaw's left foot. He was right about it being slightly deformed.

There was some kind of injury there, as Quickpaw seemed to realize what he was doing and backed away, snarling. Raphael did not press the attack. Instead, he retreated as well. He knew he was likely going to be outmatched, even with the other wolf's weakness. As it was, time was on his side, so rushing into the fray was unwise.

The two of them continued to glare and snarl at each other, circling around each other like sharks, but keeping their distance.

Raphael did not turn his head, not wanting to take his eyes off Quickpaw for even a second, but he knew that Liliana was moving alongside him. He could hear her footsteps. If only she had run away. Then again, the reason that Quickpaw was so restrained up until now was because she was here backing him up.

And yet, even two-on-one, they were at a disadvantage.

"Do you consider this a fair fight?" Quickpaw asked. "Why don't you fight me one-on-one?"

"That's rich coming from someone who attacks defenseless humans," Raphael growled back.

"Defenseless humans? They are prey. Would you chastise a lion for hunting deer because the deer cannot fight back?" Quickpaw spat on the ground. "Living in a city truly has neutered you. Are all city wolves like this, tell me? Ashamed of what you are? Too fearful to taste what true freedom feels lik-" He then trailed off, his ears perking up, sensing something. "Careful, boy, I better not cross paths with you again, otherwise it truly will be your end."

Quickpaw turned tail and disappeared into the bushes.

Liliana and Raphael tensely stared at his retreating form for a minute before either of them relaxed.

"Should we go after him?" Liliana postured.

"I would love to," Raphael said, relaxing. He now sat down on his haunches, feeling exhausted. The fight had barely lasted a minute, and yet every single moment of it had dragged on for so long it felt like they had exchanged blows for hours. "But he already has a good head start on us," Raphael said, dismissing the idea. "If you had some kind of silver-tipped arrow maybe… but I don't know how good your aim is with that dagger."

"Not very good," Liliana admitted. It was really only something to be used as a deterrent. She had never actually tried to wield it in a fight before. Then again, she hadn't exactly spent her time training how to fight. She had had a few lessons here and there, but nothing that could prepare her for the intensity of facing off against an actual wild werewolf who was trying to kill her. She felt like no amount of training would've prepared her for something like that.

Did the vampires of old really have to deal with so many of them? No wonder they were said to be so hard to deal with. She had wondered why some of the Council Elders were so militant in their mindsets even now; but if they had had to deal with such stressors on a daily basis, she could now see why they were like that. She, like many other vampires, had taken it for granted that she would endure forever.

However, that only made the shock of losing one of their own ever more apparent. Humans may have died every day, but they were like flies who would repopulate and quickly forget about the deceased through the generations. Vampires, however, were limited in number; a death was a great and extremely atypical event.

"We have more of them coming."

"Those are my friends," Raphael said.

That was why Quickpaw had suddenly turned tail - because he had known that reinforcements were coming. It also meant that Quickpaw was almost certainly working alone, because were that not the case, he might have thought that the reinforcements could be his own. This once again demonstrated just how superior Quickpaw's senses were compared to his own since Raphael had just noticed his friends.

"Oh, that's good," Liliana said, retrieving her dagger. "Aren't you going to transform back?" she asked, noting that Raphael was still in his Lycanthrope form.

"Well, my clothes are torn," he explained. "So if I go back without a change of clothes handy... well, you know."

Liliana's cheeks flushed slightly. There was a limit to how much she could blush, given her undead nature, but for a moment, parts of her cheek had turned a light shade of cherry-red. Were it not for the gravity of their situation, Raphael would have found it absolutely adorable.

His friends burst into the clearing, all of them having transformed, sniffing the air, and looking for what the danger might be. Their eyes fell upon Liliana.

"Relax everyone, it's not her," Raphael said.

His friends began sniffing the air. They found the lingering traces of Quickpaw's scent soon enough.

"We found the wild werewolf," Raphael explained. "He nearly ended up jumping us - I didn't notice him in time."

"Did you end up fighting him?" Vincent asked, concerned.

"I did have a bout with him," Raphael answered. There were strange noises from his friends. Liliana couldn't make them out, but Raphaeal recognized them as sounds of amazement. They were quite impressed. Wrestling with pack members was one thing, but going up against a wild werewolf was completely different. Their respect for Raphael grew, even if the actual fight was not as nail-biting as they might have imagined. He had only lasted for a few blows and had been rescued once by Liliana's silver, after all.

"What is she doing here?" Vincent asked.

"You're... Vincent, aren't you?" Liliana found herself asking. In their Lycanthrope forms, the four of them were nearly indistinguishable from each other. Raphael's fur had a slight golden tinge, and Carlton's fur was black, but other than these blatantly obvious features an ordinary person would've had difficulty telling them apart.

"Yes, it's me," Vincent answered.

"She's here because her uncle is Athelstan," Raphael explained.

"Oh, is that so? Small world," Vincent said. "If we had known, maybe we could have talked to you first before coming here." That was certainly not feasible; even if they had known, there was no way either of them could have approached her.

"Should we go after him?" came Carlton's voice.

By now, Quickpaw had quite a lead on them, but his scent and trail were still fresh. If they intended to go after him, this was one of their best opportunities to do so. Even without Liliana, they had a massive advantage. They were relatively confident in winning a four-on-one fight. On the other hand, though, neither of them were used to this area. It was a place where Quickpaw would have stayed for some time, though.

They would be fighting on his turf, not within the city where they were more familiar with things. The odds of an ambush or the thought that Quickpaw might have reinforcements farther from the city limits gave them pause.

"If we don't get him, though," Raphael said, "he's going to keep killing the people here."

"Not necessarily," Vincent said. "We could report this and say that there's a werewolf here. I think back in the city they might want to do something."

"Would they? This is a paltry village, remember, not exactly an economic powerhouse. Even if they agree to do something, it might take them months to send someone."

"I'll speak with my uncle," Liliana interrupted them. "If the other vampires know for certain that there is a werewolf roaming around, they'll definitely intervene. I've seen it now, after all." She then added, "If you are not fully confident in chasing him, I would advise you against going unnecessarily. There are vampires who are trained for these kinds of things, you know."

She felt a little odd stating that there were vampires who dedicated much of their lives to killing werewolves to Raphael and his pack. However, these people must have known that already. She was mainly concerned for Raphael's safety. She still did not fully grasp how much stronger a wild werewolf was than one raised in the city. Maybe there wasn't that much of a difference, but battle instinct and experience counted for quite a lot, and Quickpaw could inflict heavy damage upon them if he were so threatened. What if Quickpaw took down one of them when confronted? What if that one casualty was Raphael?

Raphael looked towards his friends. " We're not going to accomplish anything by getting ourselves potentially killed, and I would hate to be the one to tell any of your family members that you didn't make it back."

"The humans who died until now also had families," Edward pointed out.

"That they did," Raphael said. "But we're not doing them any favors if we end up getting ourselves killed."

On the one hand, all four of them felt blood rushing through their hearts, the thrill of the hunt tantalizing in the air, and their minds hungry for glory, much like all young men were.

The rational parts of their brains had to speak up in response to this surging adrenaline and tell them that they were quite out of their league. They did not come here to fight someone. They had come to investigate what was going on. All of them had promised their families that they would come back home safely, and chasing a wild werewolf was not something that could be considered in line with that directive.

"I wish we could do something," Carlton snarled, sounding helpless. "Maybe if we just run after him, it'll at least give him the illusion that we're chasing him. We could do it for a few minutes and then turn back. If anything, it might scare him off so that he won't come back to harm the humans."

That seemed like a relatively easy compromise.

"All right, then, let's go," Liliana said.

Four pairs of wolf eyes turned toward her. "Liliana, you should just stay back," Raphael said.

"Why? I can fight well enough," Liliana said. She then brandished her dagger, the silver edge sparkling in the moonlight causing several of them to flinch. "And unlike all of you, I have a weapon that might be good against him. Can any of you use silver? Additionally, five heads are better than four if we're going hunting, isn't it?"

"I know," Raphael said, "but I'd hate for something to happen to you. It's one thing to explain to the other werewolves if one of us got hurt, but what would your mother think if we had allowed you to get hurt?"

"Can you keep up with us wearing that?" another one of them piped up. Liliana was dressed in something which definitely allowed for more movement compared to her regular outfit. But it would still hamper her, especially now that the others were in their Lycanthrope forms.

"Liliana," Raphael began, not sure how to phrase things without offending her. "We are… much faster in our full Lycanthrope forms, especially running through a forest."

"Why, I thought you weren't actually chasing him?" Liliana responded, folding her arms. "You're just trying to scare him off. He'll be more scared if he thinks that there's a pack of vampires *and* werewolves after him, won't he? And you're forgetting," she then added something else, "the humans here and this territory fall under the protection of my uncle. I have every right to chase him as much as you do."

"No one's saying you don't have the right," Raphael said. "We're just saying that…" He sighed. "You know what, all right. Sure, if you want to come with us, you can," he said, changing his mind.

He figured that if the four of them went to chase Quickpaw, he might feel a little uneasy if they left Liliana here. There might even be a slight chance that Quickpaw would circle around and try to get Liliana if she was alone. He probably hated her far more than he hated the four of them. Between werewolves, they could come to some kind of compromise after fighting.

However, when it came to a werewolf and a vampire in the wild, they would fight to the death. Given this, he would feel a bit more at ease if she was with them.

"Really? You want to let her come with us?" Vincent asked, surprised.

"She doesn't seem to be taking 'no' for an answer, and if she decides to run after us, what are you going to do?" Raphael asked.

His friends didn't entirely agree with the idea, but if they were going to make a move, they needed to make one soon. The longer they continued to dither, the more time Quickpaw had to run away.

"Remember - no heroics," Raphael said as they headed out.

The five of them then set out on Quickpaw's trail. His scent was still fresh, and although Liliana could not differentiate it from the scent of the other werewolves, she only had to follow the pack who followed their noses.

It turned out that they were right on one front: she really wasn't able to keep up with them, at least not easily. Not that they were able to keep up with Quickpaw either.

"He really ran like the wind," Vincent said as they had traveled for a mile and yet saw no trace of him. If they went any further, they would be going into the Darkling Woods proper, and none of them thought that was a good idea. Quickpaw might not be the only threat lurking there.

"I think we scared him off good though," Raphael said. "Hopefully, he's scared enough that he won't come back, and the humans will be safe."

"And if not," Liliana said, "I'll speak with my uncle, and I'll ensure that he sends someone to help them."

Vincent turned toward Liliana. Several people had already gone missing; several families bereft of their loved ones. "What exactly was your uncle waiting for all this time before deciding to do something?" he wanted to bark out at her.

Raphael could tell Vincent was thinking this. They had grown up together, and he knew exactly what was going through his friend's mind. Raphael gave Vincent a small shake of his head when Vincent glanced his way. No words were exchanged between them, but Vincent understood. Arguing with Liliana was not going to accomplish anything.

Chapter Eleven

Beneath A Pumpkin Moon

Having written off the hunt as a failed endeavor, they returned to where they had initially encountered Quickpaw. There were still two or three hours until daybreak, but their job was technically done. If the four werewolves wanted, they could go back home now.

Raphael's friends, however, wanted to take the opportunity to wander in their Lycanthrope forms as much as possible. They didn't always get such a chance near the city, but now that they were out here in the wilderness, they might as well take advantage of it. They had all transformed before taking their clothes off when they heard Raphael's howl for help, meaning they needed another pair of clothes regardless, so they thought to themselves, *We may as well enjoy it while we can.*

Raphael did not join up with them. Instead, he stayed with Liliana. Even if Vincent hadn't told the other two about what was going on between him and Liliana, it was clear enough to anyone with working eyes and ears.

He was sure that a good portion of Liliana's scent had intermingled with his own - far too close for them to have just been near each other. That by itself was more damning evidence than anything else. As his father would say, 'Appearances can be deceiving, and words are but air - but the nose knows.'

Raphael and Liliana sat under a tree as the moon glittered above them. His friends ran off, as free as wild wolves.

Raphael, however, felt free as well. A different kind of freedom - like his mind had been constricted within a cage up until now only for it to suddenly vanish. And now, possibilities that did not exist earlier were suddenly tangible.

The two of them sat under the shade of a tree as the moon glittered above them, just like the night at the mayor's party, which felt like it had happened an eternity ago.

"If you want, I can get you a spare pair of clothes," Liliana said. "My uncle's estate is not too far away, and I'm sure they have something that would fit you."

"No, no, that's okay," Raphael said. He already had a couple of spare pairs, and he was probably going to tear those as well anyway. "I don't want to damage one of your expensive suits. I do a lot of running around, and they'd get dirty if not torn to shreds."

"It's no problem at all even if you do shred them," Liliana said. She glanced at him. He was definitely far more intimidating now, just like one would expect of a werewolf. He was practically twice her size now and weighed several hundred pounds. Still, he was in no way like Quickpaw. There was still an air of gentleness about him.

If only I wasn't like this, Raphael thought. He really wanted to go back to his human form. Although being in a Lycanthrope form was freeing, it was not that powerful unless under a full moon, not to mention he was just far more used to his human form. He had grown up in the city, after all, unlike Quickpaw.

Additionally, what kind of woman would want to see him like this? He looked like a monster. He also could not do things like hold Liliana's hand without it being very awkward. All they could really do was talk as he continuously sampled the air in case Quickpaw happened to come back. It didn't seem so, though, and he knew his friends were running around nearby, but he would not allow himself to get complacent and be caught off-guard once more.

"Your sense of smell really is incredible," Liliana said. "I might not have noticed him until he was right next to me."

"I doubt that," Raphael said. "You would have noticed eventually, if only we weren't as, uh, I mean if we were not-"

"Distracted, yes," Liliana finished for him, flushing slightly, but nodding.

"As for a sense of smell," Raphael joked, "it can be more of a bane than a boon. Trust me, there are several smells at the docks you don't want to be exposed to."

"I could very well imagine that," Liliana said, smiling, her fangs revealing themselves.

Liliana looked different to Raphael now that he was in his Lycanthrope form. His eyes were more suited to the night and were positioned differently, the result of which being that she looked far smaller to him.

If anything, that made her look even more adorable than usual.

"So the Council of Elders, they'll send someone out to deal with Quickpaw, assuming he's still out there?" Raphael asked.

"Yes, they will," Liliana said. "They weren't sure of what was going on, but if I tell my uncle about this - that I saw one with my own eyes - then they'll be forced to act."

"Are witness testimonies that convincing to them?"

"They are. Coming from a vampire like me, that is."

"Okay, that's good," Raphael said, his muscles relaxing as Liliana traced a thin line over his forearm. He nearly flinched from the contact, but instead, he

126

just twitched slightly. "I'm sorry, I wasn't expecting that."

"Sorry," Liliana said. "It's just... you are quite muscular."

"Uh, yeah, I do get a lot of exercise," Raphael said. *What on earth am I saying, 'get a lot of exercise'? Think of something smarter to say!* He chastised himself inwardly.

"I can imagine," Liliana said, not skipping a beat. "There are not many people who would chase after a wild werewolf, or even survive a scuffle with one of them. You're not hurt, are you?"

"I'm pretty tough," Raphael said. "Even if he managed to get his fangs into me, it would have healed by now."

"That's good to hear. Do you... mind if I place my head against your arm?"

"What? Um, no, not at all," Raphael said, his heart skipping a beat as she gently laid her head of silver hair on his forearm, and he moved it slightly so that her head would more easily fit into a small depression naturally formed there, making a pillow for her. She had removed her tiara, the silver ornament safely sitting some distance away.

The two of them sat there like that for about ten minutes. It was a strange thing, Raphael thought. If it had been anyone other than Liliana, he was sure that he would have found the silence slightly awkward, and that he would have been compelled to try and interrupt it with some kind of small talk. However, with her, even the silence felt welcome, as if her presence was more than enough.

"What will you tell your parents about what you did today?" Liliana asked after a while. "They'll be impressed that you managed to fight off a wild werewolf, right?"

"I guess my father might be slightly impressed," Raphael said, "though mostly he'll think I'm an idiot for even getting myself into that situation in the first place."

"He gave you permission to come here, though?"

"Yes, but he didn't think I would be fighting someone," Raphael explained. "He would probably almost beat me over the head if I managed to come back injured. After I recovered, of course."

"You just told me that your injuries recover very quickly, though."

"Yes, most of our injuries recover pretty quickly, but you know, if we're hit with something like wolfsbane or silver, that can lead to some issues." Raphael explained. *Why am I telling a vampire our weaknesses?* He felt like he shouldn't have, but then again, he figured that if Liliana did have people or knew people who hunted werewolves for a living, they must have known this already. As it was, he was not scared of Liliana.

"And what would your mother say?" Liliana asked. "I can imagine she'd be quite worried about you."

"Oh, I suppose so if... well, about that," Raphael said, licking his teeth. "My mother's dead."

Liliana stiffened. "I'm so sorry, I didn't mean to probe into something that might be painful."

"No, no, it's been some time since it happened," Raphael said. "If anything, I guess if she saw how we were doing right now, she'd be quite happy that at least Dad was eventually successful. And that I was also doing nice things, you know. But yeah, she'd probably strangle me if she knew how careless I'd been, or demanded to go on this trip with me."

Liliana thought over what to say next. She was mildly curious as to how it happened; it was not easy to kill a werewolf. At the same time, she had a feeling that that would be diving into a topic that was deeply uncomfortable for Raphael, so she did not voice it. However, perhaps he had picked up on her intention, or maybe Raphael anticipated the next question would be about the circumstances of his mother's death, because he answered before she could ask.

"What happened was that she was out fishing. One of the fish she caught had something made of silver in its belly. Fish do that sometimes; they swallow junk. That's why you really should open them up and check before eating them, but I guess that day she was feeling confident and swallowed it whole. She was… careless. There was a piece of silver in there, some kind of jewelry I think that'd been lost at sea, and it ended up inside her. By the time she noticed, it was too late. The silver had already spread through her bloodstream, and there wasn't much we could do."

"I'm so sorry to hear that," Liliana said.

She had already removed her silver crown and other ornaments in the grass next to her so she could lie down more comfortably. She glanced towards them, wondering if he had ever been offended by her silver attire - a common fashion statement among vampires, but also useful in a sticky situation.

After hearing the tragic story though, she felt that it had been extremely distasteful to wear it. Much like she would find it offensive if a human came to her wearing a garlic garland.

"What about you," Raphael asked. "Did you get any trophies for fighting a werewolf?"

"Maybe if I'd actually managed to kill him," Liliana said. "But like this? No. I just think it would cause my mother to worry about what I'd done. She's probably going to go off on my uncle, too, for letting something like this happen to me. She's probably going to keep me locked away in our castle now that something like this happened, blowing what happened way out of proportion."

Anticipating his next question, much like Raphael had done earlier, she decided to address it directly. "As for my father, he's dead."

"I'm sorry to hear that."

"It happened during the Night of a Thousand Torches," she explained. The Night of a Thousand Torches was a night of infamous rioting that had occurred within Necropolis about ten years ago. It was an uprising by the humans directed mostly against the vampires, but also against the werewolves and the human aristocracy who had helped keep the vampires in power. There had been extensive fighting that night, and their castle had almost been

128

breached.

"Did a human kill him?" Raphael asked. That would explain Victoria's disdain for humanity.

"No," Liliana said. "My father had entered the Shadowsleep, and when he was found after the events of that night, someone had driven a wooden stake into his heart. We don't know who the culprit was. But I... it seems it was a vampire." She recalled all of what Vladimir had told her. She could only hope that her mother had found some way of wringing out more information from the aged vampire. If not, what could they do?

If Raphael happened to know that she had considered kidnapping one of the villagers to drain them of their blood, what would he think of her? She had not actually done it, but his evaluation of her would no doubt fall. She felt greatly ashamed by her earlier thoughts.

"What's the Shadowsleep?" Raphael asked. He had not heard that term before.

"Well, when vampires get a bit older, you see, although we don't die, we sometimes go into periods of extended sleep. I guess you could almost call it hibernation," Liliana said. "We wake up less frequently as we get older, and it can sometimes last for centuries and eventually millennia by which point it might as well be permanent. Once King Alistair realized he was entering the final stages of the Shadowsleep, he abdicated the throne to his son, Hadrian, and he did the same to his twin successors."

"Wait a moment," Raphael said, almost shifting his position but restraining himself at the last second, remembering Liliana was there. "Are you telling me that King Alistair is still alive, even after all of this time?"

Liliana looked at him, puzzled. "You didn't know? I thought that was common knowledge. Yes, he and a large number of other vampires who have entered an almost permanent Shadowsleep are kept somewhere under guard. We can technically wake them up, but tradition dictates they should be left alone while they rest. Someone managed to get to my father, and after that, they've all been moved to a new, more secure location. But yes, King Alistair is still 'alive'. I'm not sure why you'd think he was dead."

"Well, it's been seven thousand years since he's been last seen," Raphael said. "I think you can excuse people for coming to that conclusion... but he's really alive, huh? That's something." He had an odd expression, but it was hard for Liliana to read his wolf face.

"Thinking of something?"

"I was just thinking of what it would be like to meet him," Raphael said. This little factoid blew his mind. "I mean, I know that he would hate me just for what I am - but still, to be able to speak to someone like that, the first king of the city..." He trailed off. The werewolves didn't exactly love King Alistair, but his war against the werewolves had occurred long before their kind had been absorbed into the city. He was a revered figure among many of the werewolves who had grown up in Necropolis simply because of the long history attached to his name.

"I don't know what that would be like either."

"You've never met him? When he wakes up, I mean."

"No, it's been thousands of years since he last woke up," Liliana said. "I can't imagine he'd be very happy with how things are right now. Then again, he did abdicate all responsibility to the future generation, so he can't exactly complain…"

To Raphael, being in the Shadowsleep sounded almost like being dead - to sleep for centuries or even millennia, only to wake up once in a while for a few hours and then go right back to one's coffin. Sure, it wasn't death in the usual sense, but what real difference was there between that and living? He kept these thoughts to himself in case Liliana found them offensive. Instead, he said, "I never got to tell you this earlier, but you looked incredibly beautiful that night at the New Year's party."

"Do you think so?" Liliana said, smiling, her mind taken off the grim nature of their prior topic of conversation.

"Oh, absolutely," Raphael said.

"And as for you, I never saw you wear a tuxedo outside of that."

"What can I say? I'm not really used to wearing fancy clothes like that," Raphael admitted. When it came to clothes, he tended to prefer something loose-fitting and simple - more practical if you wanted to run around, and easy enough to replace if you tore them apart while transforming or put too much strain on them by accident.

"You smell really nice for a werewolf. I don't know if anyone's told you that."

"Well, I guess you can thank my mother," Raphael said. "She made me bathe daily. She also had this special kind of shampoo she used to make which I still use."

"I think I can smell it," Liliana said. "Almost like the earth." She reached over and kissed him once on the snout before giving him a small smile. "I think that's as far as we can go like this."

"I could always turn back," he teased.

"Don't you start…"

Silence reigned between the two of them, the morning sky gradually lightening. Soon, daybreak would come, and though the two of them wished that the night could last forever, reality would crash down upon them soon enough, much like the sun bathing the land in its unwelcome radiance.

"Do you think we'll meet again after this?" Raphael asked. It was the question weighing heavily on both of their minds.

The honest answer, if Liliana had to say it, would have been 'no.' However, the die had already been cast. She had crossed the Rubicon.

She had kissed him, and she knew there was no going back; there was no denying her feelings any further. Whatever fire would rain down upon them as a result of their romance, she could only endure it. "We'll find a way to meet, some way, somehow," she reassured him. "I would invite you into my uncle's castle, but-"

"-I guess he wouldn't appreciate that," Raphael said, finishing her sentence for her.

"Yes. And I would have loved to invite you into my home-" Raphael said.

"But your father would not appreciate that," Victoria finished his sentence for him.

"Yes, he wouldn't," Raphael said.

The weight of this pressed down upon Raphael's heart. They had managed to find the source of the disturbance that was bothering the village of Lute. More importantly for him, he had managed to take the first step with Liliana. He wasn't sure how seriously she took things, but he considered himself devoted to her now. As for Liliana, she wouldn't let go quickly either.

Yet, neither of them could find the right words to explain themselves. Words sometimes concealed more than they illuminated.

Love had bound them, but it had also freed them. The constraints they had placed upon themselves up until this point had been broken down now that they had resolved to find a way to be together.

So what if society looked down upon them?

So what if their families would not get along together?

So what of the thousands of problems this would bring?

Earlier, these obstacles had seemed like insurmountable boulders in their path to love. Now though, as they had finally made the decision to start pushing, the boulders began to budge. Solutions to each problem began to sprout instead of problem begetting endless problems in turn.

They spoke about many things after that: their upbringings, things they liked, how things were in the city, and ways they could still communicate with each other even after this was all done.

"The sun's coming up soon," Liliana said, getting up. The sky was dyed a light tinge of violet, the first sign that their time together was at an end. She performed a gentle curtsy. "I'm going to go back to my uncle's estate. I think your friends are also waiting for you."

She kissed him just above the snout before turning and walking away. Raphael gave a long, lingering look towards her retreating form before turning around to find the rest of his friends. This was not difficult as they had not exactly made an attempt to be stealthy; if anything they were being very noisy, something that was only amplified after Liliana left.

"Oh, look at this. It's lover boy," Vincent said once Raphael found them. Raucous laughter erupted from all of them.

"Was it that obvious?" Raphael asked.

"The only way for it to be more obvious is if you proposed to her on the spot."

His friends were having a good and hearty laugh at his expense, but to Raphael, this was certainly better than being scorned for his decision.

"And you guys aren't judging me for this?" Raphael asked. Getting their approval would be a welcome first step in the long journey that he would need to take.

"Oh, we all think you're dumb," Vincent said, rather bluntly. "With that said, even if you're being an idiot, you're *our* idiot. And I guess it's our secret now."

Raphael laughed alongside the rest of them. "You guys are the best friends a wolf could ask for."

Before the sunrise, they arrived at the barn where they were staying, transformed back, and found spare clothes. They went outside and spoke to Thomas, telling him they had dealt with the threat for the time being.

"We'll try to see if we can get someone back in the city to send someone who has a more permanent solution, but hopefully, we've scared him off well enough so he won't be back," Vincent explained.

"All right, so it really was a werewolf," Thomas said, letting out a deep breath. "Well, thank you, boys. I know it wasn't easy running around looking for him. Hopefully, he doesn't come back, or maybe Lord Athelstan will finally do something about it."

The werewolves chose to delay their departure for three days, just on the off chance that Quickpaw might return. This time, they all moved as a group, and now that they had his scent, they would be able to track him far easier than they could otherwise. They were vigilant, but Quickpaw did not make another appearance, even after all their days of waiting.

That wasn't to say that they did nothing, using that time to mark the place around the village of Lute with their scent. While a few weeks of rain would wash this away, it was good for other wild werewolves to know that this place was protected.

***

Liliana went back to Athelstan's castle, finding her uncle in his office. "Uncle, there's something I need to tell you..."

"Oh, what happened?" Athelstan asked. He was working on some paperwork, likely related to the finances of his domain.

"I happened to find out what's going on regarding the disappearances. You were right. There is a werewolf there who is attacking your villages."

"It's definitely a werewolf, my dear? How can you be so sure?" His eyes suddenly widened. "Wait, are you telling me that you actually ran into one?"

"I did. I saw him with my own two eyes," Liliana said.

Athelstan nearly fell out of his chair in his hurry to get up. "My child, are you alright? How did this happen?"

"No need to worry, Uncle," Liliana said. "He ran away, like I said. But if you want, I can tell the Council of Elders of what I witnessed if it will get them to do something about it."

"Tell me more about what happened," Athelstan demanded; not at all reassured by Liliana's words.

Liliana kept the details of Raphael and his group to a minimum. "It looks like the villagers asked them for help, and they also saw him when I did. Good thing too, or he might've come after me."

"Liliana, there's a high chance that they were working with the wild werewolf in question," Athelstan said once she was done.

"Uncle, what makes you think that? It doesn't seem like that."

"Yes, but it's easy to fake those sorts of things," Athelstan said.

"Why would they be working together with him?" Liliana asked, not understanding why her uncle had reached this seemingly bizarre conclusion.

"There could be several reasons. Perhaps they're sharing the human meat together? You don't know how werewolves tend to be. Some of them haven't exactly suppressed their thirst for human meat and put it aside."

Athelstan's words felt hypocritical to Liliana, given that he had insinuated that he took human blood at times but she didn't say so. "Uncle, I understand what you're saying, but I really don't think they were working together." She couldn't exactly explain why, as that might reveal what she felt for Raphael.

Athelstan seemed to take her words into consideration but then shook his head. "I'm sorry, dear. You're still very young, and you haven't seen much of the world. I'm afraid they've hoodwinked you more likely than not. But there is one good thing: we can definitely approach the Council of Elders and tell them about this. We may be able to find a suitable solution, assuming that the werewolf hasn't given up, knowing that his little scheme has been found out already," Athelstan said.

Despite Liliana's protests to the contrary, Athelstan was still dead set on the fact that he thought Raphael and his friends were in cahoots with the wild werewolf, and nothing Liliana said seemed to change it.

She was restricted to his estate after that, the guards now keeping a strict eye on her. He wasn't going to risk anything like that happening again. "What would your mother say? If you had gotten so much as a scratch, she would've had me impaled!"

Liliana sighed. She wanted to go out and explore the fields some more, but even that request was denied. She didn't push her luck, however, knowing that her uncle's mind was dead set on this. Not to mention she had betrayed his trust in a way - by wandering too far off.

If she hadn't been fortunate enough to meet Raphael there, and had still ran into Quickpaw, what would've happened to her? Even now, the thought of Quickpaw's fangs and murderous glare haunted her. Even if she had gilded herself with silver from head to toe, she still wouldn't have felt confident in meeting him in battle.

Speaking of Raphael, though her heart pined greatly for him, the issue as to how the two of them would continue to meet now reared its head.

I need to get Beatrice on my side, she thought to herself. That would be a good start to things, and from there on, she could work her way into introducing the concept to others that she knew.

However, a dark part of her heart knew that millennia could pass and the stars themselves could die out, but her mother would still not approve of this. But she was undeterred. Even if she had to wait for Victoria to enter the Shadowsleep herself in order to realize her heart's desire, she would do so.

She would wait for him for an eternity if that was what it took.

Chapter Twelve

Duplicity & Deceit

Quickpaw watched the outline of Necropolis from within the Darkling Woods. He was near a stream, the pain in his left paw pestering him just as much as it had for the last six months. He had not always been a solitary werewolf; he had been with a pack which lived deeper in the Wastelands.

However, he had been injured by some kind of silver implement while facing down a vampire. He had managed to get most of it out, but a small piece still remained deep within his left foot. His body had locked it away under scar tissue and it was not enough to kill him. Werewolves, particularly the wild ones, were not exactly expert surgeons, so his foot had simply slowly healed around it, but it still bothered him endlessly.

Were it not for that, he would not have felt the need to run away from Raphael and his friends. He may have even turned and charged them, but he knew he was not strong enough to fight outnumbered four to one with that kind of handicap.

The injury was the reason he had been kicked out of his pack in the first place. He was seen as too slow. Out there in the Wastelands, there was room neither for weakness nor for those who could not carry their own weight. Quickpaw was not related to anyone important within the pack's hierarchy and was thus thrown out. He had to survive on his own.

Living in isolation was an almost certain death sentence within the Wastelands, but he had managed to find something that helped him survive. Only, that something had now turned against him.

He howled in pain as he felt the sting of a whip across his back, striking like a flash of lightning.

"What kind of an idiot are you?" Athelstan asked, emerging from the edge of the Darkling Woods.

"I'm sorry, I'm sorry," Quickpaw pleaded.

After he had been chased out, Quickpaw had tried poaching from the villages at the outskirts of Necropolis. He had only eaten three humans before he was quickly caught and nearly killed by Athelstan. Athelstan had trained to fight werewolves nearly all of his life given how close he grew up to the border, and Quickpaw had a serious disadvantage with his foot injury.

Athelstan, however, spared his life. This was not out of pity or kindness. Quickpaw knew that the man would very eagerly kill him were it not for the fact that Athelstan had found a use for him to advance his own political motives.

"I asked one thing of you," Athelstan said, growling at Quickpaw. "I asked for you to remain hidden in the Darkling Woods and not draw too much attention to yourself. It was fine when you ate a few villagers. Why on earth did you challenge another werewolf? And not only that," he added, growling, "you nearly attacked my niece!"

"Your niece? That woman was... no, I would have never hurt her," Quickpaw said. "It was only the other wolf I fought."

When Quickpaw had seen the city werewolves, he immediately felt threatened, and like any large predator, he wanted to defend his territory. But more than that, Quickpaw had attacked Raphael because he was frustrated with his own condition.

Quickpaw's hatred of city werewolves and their devotion to vampires was projection more than anything else. He hated having to coordinate on behalf of this vampire, a creature he would normally have fought and killed outside of Necropolis - the same breed of creature responsible for his injured foot and banishment in the first place.

Quickpaw had challenged Raphael to prove to himself that he was actually strong.

He had thought that Raphael would be easy pickings, but that had not turned out to be the case, and he had been forced to retreat. It was not an extremely smart decision, but then again, if Quickpaw had possessed that kind of foresight, he would not have been in this situation in the first place.

"How could you let yourself be discovered?" Athelstan said. "The plan was for you to remain hidden so I could make good use of you. Now that the world knows about you - now that my niece has told me that you are here within my territory - I'm going to actually have to act. I won't be able to stall the Council of Elders any longer. They'll be coming for your head sooner or later"

Athelstan had been allowing Quickpaw to have his pick of the villagers because, like the vast majority of vampires, he did not care if a few humans were killed; especially so long as his aims could be realized. As a matter of fact, if the humans began to be more wary of the werewolves because of Quickpaw, it would only be to Athelstan's benefit.

Athelstan had tried to ignore the reports that his people were dying, but they soon began clamoring around his estate, and he could no longer sit down and do nothing, as people would naturally ask why he wasn't acting against a suspected werewolf. He had dragged his feet and delayed things so that he felt he would be able to accomplish his aim before he would have to throw Quickpaw to the wolves.

136

He did not intend to let Quickpaw live for very long; Quickpaw was a loose end that Athelstan would have to kill after his ends were accomplished. But now that Quickpaw had been seen by Liliana, Athelstan might need to accelerate those plans.

"Anything else that you have to say for yourself?" Athelstan asked. The whip he was carrying was coated with silver on one end and leather on the other. He had not used the silver end yet, but its mere presence was threat enough.

"Hold on a moment, hold on a moment. I have a piece of information that might be useful to you," Quickpaw pleaded.

"Information, really? What could you possibly have found out in this garbage dump that would be of interest to me?" Athelstan asked, his eyes filled with fury.

"I do know something… that girl. She is really your niece?" Quickpaw asked.

"Yes, she is. Don't you think about putting a single paw on her mutt, or I will tear you limb from limb before you can even breathe."

"Well, it's not me you need to worry about," Quickpaw pressed.

"And what is that supposed to mean?"

"Your niece… she's in love with that werewolf."

Athelstan paused. "What on earth are you blabbering about, you oaf?" he snarled, raising the whip above his head.

"No, no, believe me! I saw it with my own eyes," Quickpaw said. "She had locked lips with that werewolf. The two of them have a thing for each other."

Athelstan began laughing. "You really expect me to believe that?" The silver half of the whip now found Quickpaw's skin as he howled in pain. "Don't start filling my head with nonsense," Athelstan commanded. "Stay put. Do not draw further attention to yourself. I will attempt to fix this mistake that you've made, but if not, then I will lead a party to tear off your head myself."

Quickpaw whimpered as Athelstan melted back into the shadows and went back to his estate.

***

Victoria paced around the castle. She had no real destination in mind, it was just one of her old habits whenever she was mulling over things.

There were many issues that needed her attention, but the main conundrum that was vexing her was the issue of Lucian's death. Even now, the grief from his death gnawed at her heart. There were only two things that kept her going - one was the thought that she had to avenge him, and the other was that she had to keep Liliana safe.

Liliana was safe with her brother, so she was not concerned about such. As for the first issue, she had been looking for a way to speak with Vladimir once more. There were without a doubt vampires who still dealt in human blood. Not in the open, but she had heard whispers, rumors - rumors that she had to follow to see if she could find a legitimate seller.

That would only be the beginning, however. They were far more strict with handling those who had entered the Shadowsleep than before because of the Night of a Thousand Torches. She could only think of what to do ahead once she got that far though.

"Lady Victoria! A message from Lady Camula - she says that Sir Vladimir has awakened!"

Victoria was so engrossed in her thoughts that the words did not even register the words the first time around. "Hmm? Beg pardon?"

"Sir Vladimir has awakened from the Shadowsleep and-"

The following words did not register either, as a whirlwind erupted in her mind. She had been so engrossed in what she could do to achieve this outcome that it hadn't occurred to it that it might happen spontaneously.

"I have to go there immediately," she said, setting off for Castle Krankenberg. She had visited with Liliana by her side before, but she was away. Not that Liliana had known in advance that something like this was going to happen.

She practically knocked Lady Camula aside while trying to go see him - she had no desire to stand on ceremony. Not when Vladimir could very easily slip back into the Shadowsleep any minute.

Lady Camula was nonplussed but did not obstruct her further. Vladimir looked much the same and was even inside the same room.

"Lord Vladimir."

"Lady... you're..."

"I'm Lucian's wife, remember?"

"Ah yes," Vladimir said.

Victoria questioned him further, but got no better responses than the one she had during their prior encounter.

"The bell that you heard... what did it sound like?"

"Like all bells do..."

Victoria was frustrated, but she couldn't exactly get mad at Vladimir. He was not in his right senses having just emerged from the Shadowsleep. With no better option, she tried ringing various kinds of bells she had brought along with her. "Was it this? Or this?" The bells were made of various metals, some large, some small, but it was only a small silver bell that seemed to elicit a reaction from him.

"Yes - that's the one!" Vladimir said, eyes widening before he drifted off moments later.

Victoria took a look at the small bell in her hand. This was a bell her father had gifted her. It was helpful in signaling amongst vampires as it had a peculiar frequency that humans couldn't hear, and being made of silver made it useful against werewolves.

"It sounded... exactly like that..." Vladimir muttered when Victoria shook the bell once more.

138

The bell in question had been custom-made so the noise was quite specific. Only other members of her immediate family might've had a similar pair.

And so only one name came to mind.

Would... would he really do something like that? Victoria wondered.

She had not seen Athelstan during the Night of a Thousand Torches, assuming that he had been at his estate. But what if he had been in the city instead? With a vampire's speed, he could've made the journey in only a few hours so long as he chose to run the distance. *Wait, Liliana... she's under his care right now!*

Chapter Thirteen

By Proxy

Although Raphael left, Liliana remained near the outskirts of the city for a few more days. Raphael could not go too close to Athelstan's estate without revealing what was going on, and Liliana had been told to stay close to the castle after the recent incident. These were not just empty words from her uncle in this regard, no, she knew she was being tailed by the staff there. Not as close as back home, but the surveillance was quite annoying.

Still, it was not as if she was an outright prisoner. There were gaps in the watchful eyes trailing after her, gaps that she could exploit. And it was during one of these moments in which her uncle's surveillance failed that she would slip away to a predetermined spot.

She didn't know if Raphael was going to be there. He had spent quite a bit of time coming back from the docks to that area multiple times just to see if she might be there, but had been disappointed.

Up until now.

The bitterness of all the times when he had gone back to Lute disappointed only made the joy of their reunion all the sweeter. He was dressed far fancier than he normally would have been, just for their meeting.

"Any more troubles with Quickpaw?" Liliana asked.

"Someone disappeared the night that we found him, so he did get to one person before we could stop him," Raphael said, sounding defeated. But they had already known that. "After that, there hasn't been anything. Not even the slightest trace of his appearance. I think we did manage to scare him off for good."

"And if not, the Council of Elders will step in."

"How have you been?"

"I've been mostly fine, though I do think it'll be hard for us to meet up after this," Liliana confessed, with sadness in her eyes. "My uncle is keeping a close eye on me. We might have to end up talking through a proxy. I'll see what I can do. I have to go back soon, at most I can be away for five minutes before

140

they'll wonder where I am. And I'm going back home soon…"

"I would come by to you directly, but werewolves aren't exactly welcome in that part of town, are they?" Raphael laughed. Simply being a small distance from Victoria's castle would raise eyebrows.

"That may be, but I'm sure we'll find a way," Liliana said.

"Do you want me as a witness before the Council Elders?" Raphael asked. He didn't know how the council worked, but Liliana did, and she shook her head.

"No. You being there might actually discredit my testimony," Liliana said. "I'm sorry - I didn't mean it like that… but you know how some of my kind are."

"I know," Raphael said. He really couldn't call her out on it because it wasn't like his side was much better. It had been a tiny miracle that all of Raphael's friends had been so understanding. They had grown up together for a long time, and many didn't think it was their business to say anything. But the peace was only kept because it did not involve any of them directly. If there was the slightest hint of inconvenience to their lives or if they were pressed on the matter, Raphael wasn't sure how long they would remain silent.

"I wanted to bring something for you," Liliana said. "And for the first time, I wanted to get you something to eat. I have no idea what you like."

"I'll eat anything if it was made by your hands," he said. "That's my final answer."

Liliana sighed. It wasn't just the answer, but the fact that if she tried making something it would probably taste very odd indeed. "The kinds of flavors I'm used to might not line up with your palate."

"Once again, I'll eat anything you make," he replied.

"You haven't bathed in a while," Liliana said, poking him lightly in the ribs.

"Haven't had the chance out here in the boonies. I was waiting here for over a day. I'm sorry if I stink."

"You do so ever so slightly, to be honest," Liliana conceded, smiling.

"Oof, I really do need to do something," he laughed.

"Don't worry, I'll still give you this anyway."

Liliana leaned up to kiss him. Their lips locked this time; it was a true embrace, not just a gentle brush of the two against each other. Her lips, like rose petals, touched his. The air between them was hot - a fierce embrace under the moon that felt as if it would last forever.

"I'll find a way so that we'll see each other again," he said. "I promise it."

"And I will do the same for you," Liliana replied. Both of them had sworn a silent oath to each other the moment they had first kissed, yet neither felt sure they could actually fulfill it. But what did that matter? They had already committed themselves. Once they had accepted that fact, every other problem seemed simple enough; they would get over it. They would find some sort of solution.

Together.

***

In a dusty corner of Necropolis, near the bustling marketplace a few blocks away from the City Square, two figures met covertly. They approached an alley beside a nondescript shop under the shade of a tree. One of them was wearing a cloak with a hood, and the other a hat that covered most of his face.

After a quick glance around, noting that no one had followed them, they turned to speak to one another.

"I'm sorry, I'll have to be quick about this," Beatrice said, lowering her hood. She had made the excuse of coming here by saying there was something in the market that she wanted to buy. She had managed to dodge the people who escorted her, saying something had caught her eye which she wanted to check out, and would have to return soon if she didn't want to cause a commotion.

Vincent, on the other hand, was a bit more free to move. "Noted. All right, try and do this as quickly as possible."

The two of them were meeting in place of Liliana and Raphael, who could not do this by themselves. Liliana, much as expected, was practically locked up inside her castle by her mother after discovering her recent encounter with a werewolf. It was incredibly difficult for her to move anywhere.

Raphael, for his part, had become increasingly busy after returning to the city. He not only had to deal with his charity, but also with his father attempting to deal with the matter regarding Dunn Sutherland. Raphael had not come himself this time just so that his father wouldn't get too suspicious.

This was the closest Liliana and Raphael could be right now.

Liliana had told Beatrice that she had fallen for Raphael and everything they had done, and begged her not only not to tell anyone, but also to become her accomplice in hiding this romance. Beatrice had not agreed at first, dragging her feet and unwilling to go any further. But she was eventually dragged into it against her better judgment. She was quite soft-hearted when it came to her cousin, and found herself unable to say 'no' to Liliana.

"Well you may as well hurry up," Vincent said. "What message does she have?"

Beatrice cleared her throat before getting the words out. "She wanted to let him know that she thinks of him every day and all the time," she mumbled, blushing awkwardly. She had never been involved in a romantic relationship herself, and had grown up in a very conservative environment. The words felt extremely funny in her mouth. She had dreamed of maybe one day saying such things to someone she loved, not in this kind of alien context! It almost felt like Liliana was robbing her of something by asking her to do all of this. Beatrice's ears couldn't believe what her mouth was saying. And that too words that she didn't even make herself, to someone for whom they were not even intended for!

142

Why did Liliana have to talk through her? And why was Beatrice standing here, at a random street corner, saying these words to someone she didn't know? She forced herself to continue despite these awkward thoughts. "She says that she loves him, that her heart still pounds whenever she thinks of him, and she longs for the day that the two of them can finally be together."

Her odd behavior even threw Vincent off. Yes, he had also thought that this whole setup was quite awkward, but it wasn't until Beatrice's behavior had explicitly called it out that he was aware of just how odd it was.

Beatrice paused. "She also wanted me to give him a kiss. I suppose that would just be symbolic..."

"Did she honestly tell you to give him a kiss? How did she expect that to happen? She'd kiss you, then you'd kiss me, and then I'd kiss him? Even if he was actually here, that wouldn't work. This - this makes no sense!" Vincent said, rolling his eyes. It had only been three months since these 'meetings' had started, but both of them were quite frustrated by the whole thing. There were few things more exhausting than finding oneself between a pair of lovers, and unfortunately for these two, they were far too deep to find a way out now.

"Indeed, it doesn't make any sense whatsoever," Beatrice said. "Does he have anything for me to relay?"

"Well, he wrote a poem for her," Vincent said. "I tried to remember it, but I forgot most of it. Sorry, I probably should have written it down. It had something to do with roses and lilies and other flowers and talking about her - that kind of stuff. Also maybe something about spring."

"It's all right. I'll make something up for Liliana when I get back if she asks too much," Beatrice said dryly, only wanting to get this over with as quickly as possible. "So, other than the poem, do you have anything else you want to say? Or that he wants to say, I suppose."

"Well, he talked a lot about how much he thought she was beautiful, and all," Vincent said. "Honestly, I didn't catch half of it since it all melded together at one point. You know what? Why don't you go ahead and make that up as well? I sometimes wonder if they can even tell the difference."

"Same here," Beatrice agreed. The two of them glanced around, constantly worried that someone was going to catch them.

"He also wants to see her in person as soon as possible. That's the main thing that I remember, because he said it over twelve times," Vincent said.

"I don't really know when or how that could happen," Beatrice said, fiddling with her bonnet absentmindedly. "With how close of an eye they are keeping on her, and the fact that this is supposed to be something top secret, I don't know when that might happen. Maybe when there's a big public event they can finally meet again? But I don't know if her mother would even let her attend one of those now..."

"Oh well, then," Vincent said. He could not do anything about that, and after a point, this was all Raphael's problem, not his.

With that done, the two of them separated.

"So, what did he say?" Liliana asked Beatrice eagerly when she got back.

"Oh, he had a poem made for you, but... I think something got lost in transcribing it, because I didn't meet him - it was that other one, Vincent this time. He didn't have the presence of mind to write it down," Beatrice confessed.

"Why do I even bother sending you if you don't remember anything?!" Liliana cried out.

"Hey, stop glaring at me! I'm trying my best, okay?" Beatrice retorted. "It's pretty awkward trying to speak all of this romantic talk to someone who isn't even there! You should just write what you want down and exchange it via letters."

"We want to, but we're afraid that someone might find those letters and then catch onto this," Liliana sighed.

"Well, then, I don't know what you want me to tell you. He said that he thinks you're very lovely, and would love to meet with you as soon as possible," Beatrice said.

"I would want the same, Beatrice," Liliana said. "I just don't know when it might be possible."

"There were a few more things about how beautiful you are - you know, your crimson eyes, your cheeks, et cetera..."

"You're reading them like from a textbook!"

"Well, I don't know what you want me to say," Beatrice said. "I mean, it's mostly the same stuff over and over again. Just how much do you think I can possibly tell these things apart?"

"Well, at least I know that he's thinking of me," Liliana replied. "If only I had something like a locket with his picture in it, or even a lock of his hair. But if Mother happened to find out... ah! Beatrice, ask for a lock of his hair next time around."

"How am I supposed to carry that back here?" Beatrice nearly screamed.

"Why don't you keep your voice down? Someone might hear us!"

"Okay - sorry! I'll keep my voice down! But well, what do you want me to do? How am I supposed to get something like that and then bring it without them suspecting me?" Liliana persisted.

Vampires did not have as sharp a sense of smell as werewolves, or at least they did not hone theirs as much. The scent of a werewolf though would absolutely be a giveaway, being the one thing that they would be on guard for.

"Ah, well," Liliana said, taking a deep breath. "If only that I could see his face one more time..." She could not even keep a portrait or sketch of him without being discovered. In that regard, Raphael had a leg up on her.

***

144

Vincent went to go meet Raphael at their usual location - a warehouse. This warehouse was part of the supply chain for Raphael's soup kitchen operation as it had greatly expanded in terms of scope and scale. He had gotten much busier as a result, not to mention his 'illicit' activities on the side in trying to meet with Liliana without being found out. On top of which, his father had run into some problems with his shipping business which naturally trickled down to Raphael as well.

"No idea who it is," his father had mumbled one evening while storming into the house.

"What happened?"

Rather than reply, Abraham simply huffed and handed him a legal notice.

Raphael had to read it three times over before he fully understood the legalese it was written in. "So - they think that we're smuggling illegal goods? Why? How?"

"Anonymous tip," Abraham said.

"Who would do such a thing?"

"A rival company? The vampires? Some humans? Who knows - but this is going to be a massive tick in our fur," Abraham said.

Of course, the Cain Shipping Company was as clean as a whistle. However, in this case, the process seemed to be the punishment. The inspections, the questions, the blockades to their business - it was annoying even though Raphael knew it would pass eventually. It was still a massive headache that ate into his already packed schedule because he had to help his father with some of these dealings otherwise Abraham would be overwhelmed by them.

That wasn't to say that there weren't skeletons that the Cain family was trying desperately to keep in the closet. In the corner of Raphael's 'office', he had a dirty secret he was hiding from the rest of the world: the portrait of Liliana that he had commissioned. Once he saw the final product he was quite impressed by its quality even if he thought a few tiny details were off here and there - it was still something to remember her by. But he couldn't be caught dead possessing it. So, this is where he had stored it.

"All safe," Vincent said, knocking on the door.

Raphael stared at the portrait longingly before putting it away. The artist had painted her in an angelic light; the way that he would see her. He touched the canvas tenderly, as if it could turn into a window which would allow him to be transported through the painting and directly to his beloved. Alas, that was but a fantasy.

"So, what did she say?" Raphael asked as Vincent walked in. He hated having to use Vincent as an intermediary like this, but there were times when he just couldn't go out, not to mention people would get very suspicious if he was going to meet up with Beatrice.

Which is why he sometimes had to send Vincent and do things in such a roundabout way. He would have much rather heard her words directly, or in this case directly from Beatrice's mouth, rather than having Vincent in the chain of communication but it could not be helped sometimes.

"Well, you know, the usual," Vincent said, shrugging. "She misses you dearly and hopes that the two of you can be together. That's basically the gist of it."

"Vincent, can't you give me something more detailed than that? What did she think of my poem?"

"I told your poem to Beatrice, not Liliana, right? Remember?" Vincent said, rolling his eyes impatiently. "So you won't get a response for some time…"

"You're right, I'll get a response next time," Raphael said.

"You know, it's honestly quite sad to see you like this." That was one of the main reasons why Vincent was agreeing to help Raphael; he felt too sorry for him to actually say no. The same went for Beatrice. She often told herself that she would say 'no' to Liliana one day but once she saw her cousin's face she found that she couldn't.

Both Vincent and Beatrice had heard that to be in love was sometimes indistinguishable from insanity - yet to witness it for themselves was something else. *I sure hope I don't start behaving like this one day*, Vincent thought.

Raphael and his friends had not been 'punished' so to speak for running into Quickpaw like Liliana had. When Raphael told his father about what had happened, Abraham looked like he wanted to punch him for getting himself in a situation like that in the first place. He had simply told Raphael to stay within the city and not go out to the outskirts anymore, and thankfully it had been limited to that. "Let some other people handle the situation. You boys don't need to think about it any more. Don't try and be a hero," he had instructed.

The parents of the others had also reacted much the same, though they had also gotten off relatively lightly. If anything, the four friends' reputation had somewhat increased among the werewolves within the city. Most people had never even seen a wild werewolf, so the fact that they had actually gone up to one - with Raphael having fought one - greatly improved their 'street cred.'

The younger lycanthropes looked up to them, and some of the older ones acknowledged them with newfound respect. The story had morphed quite a bit from when it was initially told, the story being twisted by every mouth that repeated it. Now some people thought that Raphael had beaten Quickpaw to a pulp singlehandedly and that only his friend's arrival stopped him from dealing the killing blow - Raphael attempted to correct this rumor but in the end people believed whatever they wanted to. One only needed to note 'Lady Liliana of the Light' in order to figure that out.

"Has anything else happened near Lute?" Raphael asked Vincent.

"No, nothing has happened. So, I guess we really did scare him off. Mission accomplished," Vincent said, smiling. "I don't want to be a bee in your bonnet, but what do you plan to do about this in the future? I don't have a problem keeping a secret, you know, but sooner or later, this is going to get out."

"To be honest," Raphael said, "I don't know. I wanted to tell my father several times, but things have been busy. It doesn't seem to be the right time to say so… ever. I guess she's also in the same boat. Her mother is probably far worse actually."

"I get it," Vincent said. "I'm just saying that sooner or later, things are going to get ugly, you know?"

Raphael had a strand of Liliana's hair - a gift from her - which he kept hidden behind the painting, and he made sure to cover it up before the two of them left. It was a good thing that they stored a large number of vegetables and other ingredients in this warehouse, their pungent aroma filling the air. It masked the light scent present on her hair - else all it would take was his father wandering in for a visit to let the cat out of the bag.

Raphael went home, his thoughts still dwelling upon Liliana, the soup kitchen, and the smuggling allegations. When he entered, one of the servants told him that his father was waiting for him in his office. He knocked on the door. "Dad, you wanted to see me?"

"Yes, come in."

Raphael walked in to see that his father, Abraham, was sitting across from Dunn Sutherland. "Hello, how have you been?" Raphael asked.

It was more of a rhetorical question than anything because it was clear from a glance that Dunn Sutherland was not doing very well. His cheeks looked sunken, his clothes which used to fit him perfectly now hung over his thin frame. One could say that the stress of the trial, the poor conditions of jail, and everything else had done quite a number on him. He smelled like he hadn't cleansed himself properly for days.

Despite all of this going on, Dunn simply smiled and sighed. "Things seem to be going as well as they could be. Please take a seat."

"Good to hear."

This was clearly some kind of business matter, and for whatever reason, his father wanted him to sit at the table. Maybe he had finally acknowledged the fact that Raphael was ready to sit at these kinds of 'big table discussions?' Raphael was certain that this meant his little activity with the soup kitchen had indeed been quite successful. He kept a demure expression but would've been pumping his fist in the air if allowed to - finally, he was truly being acknowledged by his father!

"Mr. Sutherland's trial is in the next two months," Abraham explained. "As you can imagine, he is trying to obtain as much goodwill as possible before such a thing happens. It would be in his best interest to maintain a good relationship with the people of Necropolis."

Abraham did not say it, but Raphael knew that it would also be in the Cain Shipping Company's best interest that Solaris continue to trade with them. The Sutherland Shipping Company was not the only one in Solaris that they could trade with, but they had spent several years building up this relationship

147

and would have to start from square one if another enterprise came along. Not to mention with Sutherland taking up such a large portion of the exports to Necropolis, it would take time for another major competitor to emerge. Ships that were capable of sailing such vast distances could not be built overnight, after all.

"Regarding that aspect, I would like to lend a hand with your food sustenance program," Dunn Sutherland said. "I've heard that it's been quite successful."

"I have no problem either way, but this is your project," Abraham said. "What do you think, Raphael?"

"I don't have an issue with it, in theory," Raphael said. "Most of the people whom we have to serve are so poor off, they don't really care who's filling their stomachs. But..."

The contribution could have negative consequences for their company. Sutherland was basically trying to borrow their credibility by contributing to their cause.

Actually, given what Liliana had done for that child during the incident, it would have been even better if Liliana endorsed Sutherland as well given the fact that the general crowd thought more highly of her than they did of Raphael for the most part. Lilian, however, would not be able to help him, even if he asked and Sutherland had no real hope of reaching out to her. He lacked a connection to the Carpathians as he did with the Cains, and reaching out to her might very well worsen his relationship with Abraham.

"The whole thing was an accident. I hope you understand that," Dunn Sutherland said. "But there will only be a tangential relationship. I doubt anyone can seriously fault you for accepting money for a charitable cause, would they?"

"I guess," Raphael said. He weighed things in his mind. "Sure, we can go ahead with it, but I'm not sure how much of a difference it will make for you..." Raphael felt that he had to agree to this in order to help his father. The only real question was just how much Dunn Sutherland wanted to influence the running of the soup kitchen. Money rarely came without strings attached.

"Splendid," Dunn Sutherland said, giving him a warm smile. "I look forward to doing business with you." They shook hands, sealing the deal.

Chapter Fourteen

The Fragrance of Flowers

Life within Necropolis continued to march forward. Dunn Sutherland, as it turns out, had little to contribute when it came to actually running Raphael's soup kitchen, only passing by once or twice in person. Raphael was perfectly fine with that, even quite relieved to some extent.

But that wasn't all that Dunn Sutherland was doing to try and rebuild his image.

Part of the campaign to rebuild his image in the eyes of the public was contributing to Necropolis Day. It was the day upon which the city had been founded by King Alistair ten thousand three hundred and twelve years ago. Originally, it was something only celebrated by the vampires, but was now celebrated by all.

Raphael still found it odd to wrap his head around that the city's founder was still alive somewhere, being guarded by the vampires as he slept, having left the management of the city to his descendants. He only woke for certain bursts of time before falling back into the Shadowsleep from what Liliana had heard. In all probability even if he did fully wake up, given the way the city was right now, he would be unable to comprehend his offspring's "weakness" and the fact that they had actually lost the city to the werewolves and humans. If he knew of that, he probably would choose to go back to the Shadowsleep immediately after. Even if he revived at full strength during this day and age, he still could not turn the tide of what the city had become.

In the old days, a military parade would be carried out and several sacrifices, some of them human, would be given up to Sanguinus much like with the Walpurgisnacht. Over time the festivities had been modified. There was still a parade, although it was a short one, involving the City Guard who put up various stunts, arranging their chariots in formation down the street. Chariots were not actually used in a serious sense in military combat even back in the old days, but were kept for such ceremonial purposes.

Every medal was polished, every sword glinting in its scabbard, and every green uniform immaculate as the guardsmen marched down the street past the central City Square.

There were several guests who had a front-row seat to watch the goings-on. These were the main political heavyweights of the city. Raphael and his father would not have usually been considered among these, but they had supported the current mayor quite a lot, and as a sign of appreciation, they had been invited there.

From the vampire side, they had been expecting Victoria to come, but in her stead was her brother Athelstan. Raphael kept glancing in his direction, wondering if this meant that Liliana would also be here. She had not sent word to him, but the last time they had been able to exchange any kind of communication with each other was two weeks ago. And so, they had not been able to relay any plans to meet up. If she was going to be here, it would perhaps be later, along with her mother.

Raphael would only get to know for certain about Liliana coming or not if she arrived, as it really wasn't possible for him to ask discreetly whether Victoria was going to be coming without lots of people wondering why he cared so much. His father did not seem to be in any better mood even though Victoria wasn't there. Once again, the rivalry was entirely political and not on a personal level, so Abraham viewed Athelstan simply as an extension of his sister in that he was still representative of everything that Abraham fought against.

Athelstan was there with two other vampires whom Raphael did not recognize, either by face or name. They were both male and dressed in long coats with silver buttons and silver embroidery; looking like the very image of old, aristocratic vampires. Their amulets were the only pieces of jewelry they wore; the sky was cloudy and gray like usual, but that could shift at a moment's notice. Both of them were carrying swords at their hips. Swords were not very useful to either vampires or werewolves simply because they chipped and broke extraordinarily easily during combat given their strength.

"Made of silver," Abraham said, noting where Raphael was looking. "Mmm.. the entire blade probably isn't made of silver, too many problems with that, but it could be an alloy with silver or coated in some kind of silver liquid." Abraham had clearly seen weapons like that before.

Raphael had never seen vampires armed like that in public. Most of them did wear a large amount of silver whenever they happened to be near werewolves or anticipated being near werewolves as a precaution. If it was simply a fashion choice to show off their considerable wealth, they would've just gone with gold. The silver definitely carried a message - Lycans beware! But these tended to be ornaments that could be transformed into somewhat viable weapons in a pinch like Liliana's bracelet, not actual weapons.

He was sure that Liliana would not bring them around as much if it was just the two of them in the future. It was definitely a declaration of silent hostility, but Raphael didn't mind. Because it wasn't like Raphael hadn't come there prepared either. Keeping a vial of garlic oil in his pocket was rather easy and would not stink up the place like carrying an actual clove of garlic, and this also meant that the vampires were unaware that he was carrying something like that unlike their silver weapons which they displayed proudly.

The parade continued, but Raphael's eyes were not focused on it. He had watched the parade several times already, and this held very little interest for him. Being a werewolf, it was easy enough to climb onto a roof where he would get a good look at what was going on, seeing over the heads of the crowd even when he had been a child.

But he was more interested in catching a glimpse of Liliana. The fact that he had not expected to meet her here today only made him all the more anxious. Could he finally get to see her again? Maybe she was only going to come later on in the evening along with her mother?

Dunn Sutherland had contributed to the parade, not just in financial terms. After the original military parade was over, which was a serious and somber event, he had arranged for other festivities. In modern times, the proper military parade would be followed by things such as jugglers and other performers.

Dunn had decided to contribute to these events in his own way. The activities were far more extravagant than usual. There were wild animals which looked like they had been transported from Solaris. Raphael watched strange striped horse-like creatures, which he was told were called 'zebras' with some curiosity. It must have cost a tremendous amount to bring them here, likely to be sent to someone's private zoo but used in this parade instead. There were jugglers who tossed flaming torches into the air instead of ordinary balls, and musicians playing an array of instruments, ranging from flutes to violins. Ceremonial chariots and carts rolled past. Some of them bore the emblem of the Sutherland Shipping Company, drawing a mixed response from the crowd.

"Look at him trying to buy our sympathy after what he did."

"Damned Solaris people, thinking they can get away with anything so long as their pockets are deep enough!"

"Are you sure something isn't going to catch on fire again?"

Dunn Sutherland wanted to avoid a negative outcome. He was rich, but not an official ambassador or noble in that he might be granted diplomatic immunity. He had reached out to the Solaris Embassy within Necropolis, but had not gotten much help on that front.

Dunn Sutherland had joined the parade himself, sitting in a chariot, dressed from head to toe in armor like some kind of conquering hero while brandishing a sword above his head. It looked extremely gaudy to Raphael, though he was unsure how the larger crowd thought of it.

Raphael glanced toward the side. "Where are Athelstan and his people?" He, and the two vampires who had been with him had vanished.

"Good riddance to them," Abraham said, noticing their absence as well. "Maybe we can finally enjoy things now that they're gone."

Raphael felt differently. It seemed odd that they would suddenly disappear in the middle of this. For a moment, he considered whether Liliana and her mother were arriving and so they had gone to greet them, but his eyes could see no trace of another carriage around the City Square, nor could his trustworthy nose pick up the trace of her scent once more.

Speaking of his nose, it was soon overwhelmed by one of the attractions.

A float passed by, consisting of a massive arrangement of flowers in nearly every color of the rainbow. Many of them were from Solaris and were not native to the nearby area. Raphael wondered how they had managed to keep them alive for so long.

"That smell is so strong," Abraham said, wrinkling his nose. "And it's not just the smell of flowers."

The parade organizers had apparently saturated the float with every perfume known to man on top of the flower's own scent, likely to mimic the freshness of new blossoms and to hide the fact that they were somewhat old. Raphael even thought some of the flowers were artificial now that he got a closer look at them.

The smell was overwhelming to both Raphael and Abraham, even from this distance. The humans next to the float also recoiled, pinching their noses. It wasn't bad per se, but it drowned out everything else. Werewolves, regardless of what form they were in, relied extensively on their sense of smell. To fill the air with such a pungent and overwhelming odor - it was like someone pulling a piece of wool over their eyes.

The scent bothered Raphael. It triggered the same uneasy feeling he'd had back in the woods when he'd tracked Quickpaw - the sense that he was missing something. He sniffed the air again, ignoring the desire to pinch his nose, and detected a faint, familiar whiff.

"Father, do you also smell that?"

"Of course, I smell it. I don't think there's a Lycan within a mile's radius who can't! What were they thinking?"

"No, I mean..." A sudden realization dawned on Raphael. "There's a werewolf inside that cart!"

It would be easy enough for someone to hide within the layers of flowers piled on top. The overwhelming smell was meant to mask that specific odor.

Abraham stopped pinching his nose and reluctantly took a deep breath, realizing what Raphael was talking about. "Why would there be a werewolf in there?" Abraham questioned. Raphael didn't answer, sensing that something was about to go horribly wrong. "Raphael, what are you doing?" Abraham asked as Raphael launched himself past the barricade separating the VIP lounge from the rest of the crowd with ease and began sprinting toward the cart.

It was too late.

Dunn Sutherland had his back turned when a shadow launched out of the flowers, a creature of dark, matted fur.

"Quickpaw!" Raphael yelled. The noise distracted the werewolf for an instant. Quickpaw looked back at Raphael, seeming to hesitate slightly, but only for an instant.

152

And that was not long enough to change the outcome of what was about to happen.

Sutherland was too slow to react. Quickpaw lunged forward and tore out his throat, killing him instantly.

Quickpaw howled as he felt a sharp pain in his left foot. Raphael had morphed into his Lycan form and bit down upon the werewolf's left ankle.

Quickpaw turned around, snarling at Raphael, who backed off after releasing the injured ankle. Quickpaw looked like a wild beast, blood dripping from his fangs, looking every bit like a demon spawn from the deepest depths of Hell. Raphael felt awe and terror that seemed to paralyze his heart. How could he possibly fight such a creature?

However, Quickpaw's left foot was injured and badly swollen. Every time slight pressure went onto that leg, the werewolf winced and it was not healing as fast as it should've. *He is not at full strength*, Raphael thought.

That was all his brain could process before Quickpaw lunged. The two of them wrestled - a tornado of fur and claws rolling around the streets threatening to tear anything that got too close to shreds. Raphael was almost overwhelmed by Quickpaw's strength even with his injury. He had quickly put Raphael into a disadvantageous position. They had made the correct choice not to pursue him too deeply into the woods back near the village of Lute.

As Raphael struggled to keep Quickpaw's fangs from closing in on his neck for the kill, Quickpaw suddenly howled as someone else bit into his left leg and then threw him off Raphael.

It was another transformed Lycan, nearly the size of Quickpaw, snarling at the wild werewolf. "Are you alright?"

"Yes, I am. Thanks Dad," Raphael said. By now, the crowd was in complete panic. Every human who could had run off, but given the size of the crowd, this turned into an all-out stampede. The weak and the children were trampled underfoot by people shoving each other, trying to get away from the scene as quickly as possible.

Abraham had never fought a wild werewolf, but he was more experienced than Raphael when it came to fighting simply because of his age. His eyes burned with a fury at Quickpaw; the fury of a father willing to put everything on the line for his child's sake!

Quickpaw wisely chose to avoid them. He instead leapt into the VIP box towards Mayor Corvin, who was trying to back away quickly but only got five paces before Quickpaw was nearly upon him.

The sharp crack of a whip echoed through the air, knocking Quickpaw off course, but not before one claw raked across the mayor's stomach. Mayor Corvin collapsed, bleeding profusely.

The whip's wielder was Athelstan, standing with the other two vampires who had drawn their blades. Neither Raphael nor Abraham had seen vampires in full battle stance before.

The two werewolves quickly realized there was a reason vampires had survived against werewolves for so long. They might have lacked the primal strength of the Lycanthrope form, but they made up for it in their speed, precision, and ability to use weapons.

Their silver swords flashed as they opened wounds on Quickpaw that did not heal, unlike the many ones Raphael and Abraham had inflicted. The wounds remained open, weeping profusely and coloring the stands a bright shade of crimson.

The whip cracked again, and Quickpaw rolled over, trying to make a hasty retreat. His eyes scanned his surroundings, landing upon Raphael and Abraham once more. The thought of fighting them crossed his mind, but he realized it would be a costly delay. He instead scampered in another direction, only to be stopped by a flash of silver erupting from one of the vampires. A silver dagger embedded itself in Quickpaw's right shoulder. He howled in agony. The silver would poison his bloodstream and eventually kill him even if he got away if he didn't get it out soon.

But there would be no need for Quickpaw to be worried about 'eventually.'

Athelstan and the other two vampires carved him up with their blades and whip, dancing around him in a storm of silver and steel. Quickpaw made the best use of his strength, fighting with the ferocity of a cornered animal, but it was all for naught. He eventually bled out onto the streets, and Athelstan cleanly separated his head from his shoulders putting an end to everything.

Raphael and Abraham somewhat relaxed, believing the fight was over. But it was not. The three vampires turned to them now. Athelstan pointed a finger. "Get those werewolves! They're in cahoots with this one!"

"No, we're not!" Raphael snarled back.

He glanced around. There were hardly any human witnesses. Mayor Corvin was still bleeding out from his abdomen. Abraham went to check on him.

"Stop him! He's going to kill the mayor!" Athelstan said next, with the other vampires drawing their silver blades. Abraham backed away toward Raphael, both of them snarling, wary of the silver the vampires wielded.

"What do we do?" Raphael asked.

"We're going to have to make a run for it," Abraham began to say before howls joined the fray from the other end of the square. Five other Lycans, three of them Raphael's friends, approached and morphed right in the middle of the street. To their credit, they did not hesitate in the slightest before backing them up even if they didn't fully understand the situation and what was going on. They may have not been a pack like out in the wilds, but werewolves still stuck together, particularly against their mortal enemies.

Athelstan and his two associates froze. The werewolves now numbered seven, outnumbering them greatly.

Raphael took the opportunity to take out a vial of garlic oil from his torn clothes.

"I will get you for this," Athelstan said. "Do you think you can conspire to murder Dunn Sutherland, an important man from Solaris, as well as the rightfully elected mayor of this city and get away with it? You will undoubtedly pay for your crimes, fiends."

With that, the three vampires scurried away.

"What's going on?"

"Isn't that Sutherland? He's dead?"

"No time to talk about that. Let's get to the mayor," Raphael said.

The mayor had been badly injured. Blood was oozing out of the wound as he winced in pain. The telltale odor of intestines was absent, so it looked like the injury was mercifully limited to the superficial walls of the stomach, rather than deeper inside involving the organs. As far as Raphael understood, most wounds to the abdomen that involved the internal organs in the case of humans were ultimately going to be fatal, whether immediately or later due to infection.

"Press on his stomach. No, not that hard. Just press on it enough to stop the bleeding. It's the best we can do before getting him to a hospital."

"Mayor Corvin, Mayor Corvin, can you hear me?" Abraham asked.

Mayor Corvin's face was pale and coated in sweat, but he nodded weakly.

"Where… is Agatha.. and.. Cynthia…"

Raphael frowned for a moment before figuring those must be his wife and daughter. He had seen them before, but hadn't paid that much attention to their names given they were usually in the background.

"Did they come here with you today?" Raphael asked. If they were here, he figured they would've stayed with him and not run away.

Corvin's eyes were unfocused, not able to come up with an answer.

"Alright, let's take him to a hospital."

"Like this?"

"The alternative is we let him bleed out here. Come on, let's go. Down there in the parade, I think we can make a small stretcher for him."

Their makeshift stretcher was just two planks of wood with some cloth in the middle, hardly anything fit for transport, even considering the circumstances. Still, what further could they do other than put some cloth near the wound and press on it, hoping to stop the bleeding and get him to get real medical attention as soon as possible?

Even as the mayor grew ever more pale with each passing moment, they managed to get him to a hospital. One of them went to go fetch his family from their estate, who arrived two hours later. By that point, the mayor had almost completely lost consciousness, his face turning an unhealthy shade of green.

The surgeons explained that given his age and the nature of the wound, which, as it turned out, had ended up rupturing his bladder, he was unlikely to survive.

They were correct. Fourteen hours later, Mayor Corvin passed away.

***

Victoria had been the one who had ordered the emergency meeting of the Council of Elders at Athelstan's request. A group of Lycans had killed not only Dunn Sutherland, an important trading partner and citizen of Solaris, but also the mayor of Necropolis. None of them truly cared for human lives; however, Solaris was an important trading partner, even for the vampires and had been so for several millennia. Tradition was something they valued highly. And to kill the city's elected representative - a process they were involved in - was unacceptable.

"Why did the werewolf in question do so?" one of the members asked.

"I didn't exactly have time to conduct a full interview before we had to put him down," Athelstan said dryly. "I had brought along Sir Septimus and Sir Gaius with me at the time. Both of them can attest and be my witnesses to the events that unfolded."

The two others recounted what had happened at the square making it seem as if Raphael and Abraham had also been involved in the plot.

"This is unacceptable," a council member said. "We always knew the Lycans were little more than uncivilized dogs at heart, yet to think that they resort to such things!"

"The question is, how shall we answer it?" Athelstan said. "I think the time is upon us where we can no longer ignore the threat that the Lycanthropes pose to this city. If we have your permission, we should go ahead and form a large party in order to hunt down and kill those who were responsible. Just the three of us will not be enough."

There was chatter throughout the council. Athelstan was essentially calling for violence without any intermediate step. Ordinarily, they would hold a trial, but how would they restrain creatures as powerful as werewolves?

That was the crux of Athelstan's argument. "They are too dangerous to be left alive, and we cannot easily hold them to trial."

The Council of Elders muttered among themselves before deciding they wanted more time before coming to a final decision.

"Allow me to echo my sentiments once more," Athelstan urged. "I know the council wishes to deliberate. However, this is a serious incident which requires our immediate response. I'm afraid we do not have time for doubt or delay when it comes to dealing with such creatures."

Despite his urging, the council still wanted to take more time before coming to a decision - something Athelstan had expected but disgusted him nonetheless. *These ancient statues... they may as well be inanimate given how slow they move*, he thought. *The incessant need to emphasize tradition and the like is going to be our undoing one day.*

As the council broke, Victoria and Athelstan went into a sitting room to discuss the coming developments before they were interrupted by someone walking in.

"Liliana," Victoria said. "Ah, is something the matter?" Liliana was not present at the meeting in question as she had gone somewhere else at the behest of her mother and was still absent when the emergency meeting was called, but she had figured out what was going on through the chatter that echoed through the halls the moment that she arrived.

Liliana shut the door behind her, walking in with a grim expression.

"What's wrong, child?" Victoria asked, noting her odd behavior.

Liliana glanced between the two of them before stating, "Uncle was the one who staged the werewolf attack in the square."

Athelstan's expression froze for a moment, as Victoria gave her a confused look. "I'm sorry, child. What are you talking about?"

"The werewolf that Uncle killed was the same one I ran into," Liliana said. "How did he manage to get so deep within Necropolis? It would be impossible without help from someone in the city."

"Well, clearly he had some werewolf friends who happened to help sneak him in," Athelstan began.

Liliana shook her head. "No. He's been staying near the border of your territory for so long, and no one was able to catch him. Some villagers said the killings began months before you took notice, *Uncle.*" The last word was laced with frostiness.

"Humans die all the time, my dear. You can't possibly expect me to-"

"Why did you and your friends go there armed in the first place? Were you expecting a fight?"

"I just went there armed in case something happened, that's all - and a good thing as it turned out," Athelstan replied.

"But Liliana, what you're suggesting is preposterous," Victoria interjected once she found her voice. "Of course he took silver with him when he was around werewolves. How can we possibly trust those animals? That was simply a natural precaution to take."

Liliana shook her head. "I happened to know those werewolves in question. They wouldn't be helping him. Otherwise, they wouldn't have fought with him, nor would they have helped the mayor reach the hospital if they were the ones who had attacked him in the first place. Anyone can tell they were not responsible if you just look at the facts. Why did you set them up like that?"

Victoria looked perplexed as this is not what she had sent Liliana out for, though understanding finally dawned upon Athelstan.

Athelstan had been told that Victoria and a werewolf were romantically involved, though he had refused to believe it. Who would trust the word of a werewolf? Certainly not him. However, he was not an idiot. After putting the pieces together, he could see the truth for what it was.

"I'm afraid, as hard as you may find it to believe, sister," he said, turning toward Victoria, "your precious little daughter over here has fallen for a werewolf."

Victoria somehow looked even more incredulous than before. She turned toward Athelstan. "Brother, what kind of nonsense are you saying?" She then turned her head to Liliana. "The two of you are speaking as if you've been possessed by madness!"

"He's right, Mother," Liliana said. She had not intended for the truth to come out this way, but now that it had, she may as well own it. "Uncle isn't lying about this thing, although he has lied about much else. It's true. Raphael and I are in love with each other."

"Raphael? Who's Raph-" Her mother stopped, realizing where she had heard the name before. "You mean Abraham's son? *That* Lycan's son? The two of you have...?" She stopped speaking as she glared at Liliana, getting up and advancing toward her daughter with menacing speed. "How? How could you? How long have you been - how could you have an-" She seemed too angry to form a coherent sentence.

"Mother, if you want to punish me for all of that, then you may do so later," Liliana said. "But first, think about what Uncle has done. He is going to try to egg on a war between us and the werewolves, and maybe even the humans as well."

"And what is the problem with that, if I may ask, Liliana?" Athelstan asked, walking between her Victoria. There was a dangerous aura about him, but his voice and expression were completely calm. "Whatever I've done, I've done for the good of the vampire race."

"Good? You're going to spark a war and-"

"New saplings cannot bloom without burning the old trees down," Athelstan said, widening his arms as he turned to his sister and Liliana. "Why would I work with a werewolf to kill the mayor and that foreign trader from Solaris?" His hand clenched into a tight fist before he continued.

"Because we have lost control of our city! What is our city called? Necropolis - literally, the City of the Dead. We are supposed to be its true rulers, its proud kings. And what has actually happened? We have ceded territory and political authority to those who were once little more than our cattle. It is time that we take our city back. Change is inevitable. We just had the first human mayor. How long will it be until the humans have complete and utter power over us? Soon! And they will have weapons that will truly even the playing field between us and them. Do you think that they will forget our earlier sins so easily? That they will forget how we ruled in the past? No, they will hunt us down like animals. You may look at it as murder, but this is merely self-defense."

"Brother, you're going to get us all killed," Victoria said after a minute of silence that followed his outburst. "We don't have the numbers to overpower the humans and the werewolves together."

"Ah, but you see, we don't have to fight both of them," Athelstan said. "Have the humans kill the werewolves for us. And once they are weakened, then we swoop in and execute them. What do you think is going to happen to the werewolves right now? When the humans realize they killed their mayor, the first human mayor in history - well, they're probably already forming squads with silver in order to slaughter them. Once the werewolves start taking care of the humans, the humans will be vulnerable. Then, once we've dealt with the majority of humans leaving only enough to satisfy our appetites, we will close the port to Solaris. Necropolis would finally truly be a city of the dead once more, isolated from the world, a true city of vampires for vampires."

Liliana had heard enough of his ramblings and turned to her mother. "I found it like you told me to…" She handed her a silver bell.

"Where did you find this?"

"Right where you thought it would be."

Victoria moved the bell slightly. It made a familiar sound.

"What is that? I've heard of it before," Athelstan said.

"Oh, Uncle, I must've accidentally taken your bell," Liliana said. "I was away at your estate while you attended the events in the City Square, I'm sorry - I forgot something of mine there, and it looks like I took something of yours by mistake."

Athelstan had still not understood the significance of this as Victoria placed the bell on the table. Liliana walked away.

"Where are you going, young lady?" Victoria demanded, placing a hand on her shoulder.

"Mother," she said, with an icy tone. "I've done what you wanted - but I have other places to be tonight."

Liliana heard the sharp crack before she felt the sting of her mother's hand across her right cheek. The blow didn't carry Victoria's full force, but it hurt nonetheless. Liliana staggered back two steps.

When was the last time her mother had struck her? It was so long ago that Liliana couldn't even remember.

"I'm sorry, Mother," she said. "But I'm no longer the child you can demand stay cooped up within your castle. I've already done what you asked, now, let me leave." Liliana didn't unlock the door as she left; she tore it off its hinges before walking away.

"Liliana! Liliana! Liliana!" Victoria yelled, but Liliana did not look back.

"It looks like she has a bit too much of her father within her. He was always a bit too free-spirited for my liking," Athelstan said absent-mindedly, sitting back down. "Shall I go fetch her?"

"Don't bother. I will deal with her soon enough," Victoria said, fixing the door back in place.

Victoria sighed, stroking her hair. "How do you think we should go ahead and convince the Council of Elders about going forward with this?"

Athelstan could not believe his ears. He even forgot the issue regarding the silver bell for a moment as he could barely contain his excitement. He did not expect Victoria to get on board with his plan so quickly, else he would've approached her far sooner. "I… are you serious?"

"Of course."

"I wished - I've been looking for those who shared my view for a long time, and there are a lot who agree with me. Trust me, sister. However, even if they agree with me, the problem is that they are too cowardly to act. They don't want to do what's necessary. They do not want to be the first ones to step up to the plate. You know how some of our kind can be," Athelstan said. "Don't worry, we will guide them, much like how shepherds guide sheep. But sister, we should try to catch up to Liliana first. What if she goes ahead and says something that derails our plans? What if she goes to stand with the werewolves and is hurt sometime during this crisis? I never wanted to see anything happen to her. She is my niece, after all, even if she's been misguided and seduced by one of those beasts."

"Don't worry, I know she'll be safe for now," Victoria said.

Athelstan frowned - this was quite unlike her. Liliana was the most precious thing in Victoria's life since Lucian had passed away. Victoria had received several marriage proposals since his death, but declined all of them, preferring to remain his widow and Liliana's mother. Victoria needed nothing else.

Needless to say, this sudden lack of concern for her daughter was rather strange.

Victoria went up to a drawer in the room and pulled out a document. "But first, I would like you to take a look at this, if you would."

"Naturally, naturally," Athelstan said. His mind still could not wrap around the idea that Victoria had agreed so easily. She had usually been averse to violence much of her life and had led the portion of the vampire faction that interacted with humans. That was why he had felt he could not have relied upon her earlier during his schemes, but if she had been on board from the start, things would have been so much easier. "So, what exactly would you like to show m-?"

The words barely left his throat as Victoria turned around, uncapped something, and then launched a jar full of liquid at his face.

Athelstan yelled out, backing away and rolling on the floor in intense pain. It felt like his face was being burned by acid.

Garlic oil! he realized as the putrid odor entered his nostrils.

Shortly after, a piercing pain pierced his chest. His eyes had been burned to the point that they would not open properly, but he could deduce what had happened. Victoria had snapped one of the legs of the wooden table and used it to impale him straight through the heart.

"Sister, what are you doing? Why?" he croaked out.

"Because, dear brother," Victoria said, her voice as cold and unforgiving as the north wind. "You killed my husband."

"I... I... I did not," Athelstan retorted with difficulty, his tongue already beginning to dissolve.

"Do you still lie, even up to this point?" Victoria asked. "I had long suspected you were the most likely culprit, but I lacked decisive evidence. Ever since we were children, Athelstan, you have always been a coward. That was what held me back from accusing you. You were the one who went to check on the coffins of those resting during the riots, weren't you? The person who could have most easily driven a stake through his heart while he slept. It was a cowardly act, but one I didn't think you were capable of... not until tonight. And when you remarked how Liliana's father was 'far too carefree for your liking,' I saw the look in your eyes -the same look you had when Mother caught you

160

stealing silver from the family coffers. But if it weren't for this silver bell, the one that Father had gifted us some time back, I would still be in the dark."

"I... I..." Athelstan stammered, attempting to deny it further, but Victoria twisted the stake in his heart. "He... the Blood Lilies... they ruined us..."

Victoria's memories of Lucian - of the centuries they had spent together, of how they had raised a daughter together, and the pain of separation burst forth from her heart. This was not revenge. This was justice.

Athelstan felt the pain reach a crescendo and then he felt... nothing.

Victoria sighed. There was knocking at the door, the guards had clearly noticed the shouting, and even if they hadn't, half the castle would have.

It was good that Liliana had left. She did not want that girl to be caught up in this kind of event. A murder that she would now have to justify to the council.

Victoria had asked Liliana to visit Athelstan's estate while he was away, and to act like she had innocently forgotten something before looking for the other bell. As for the other events that had happened, those were outside her expectations. She had planned for Liliana to leave for her cousin's after this, not wanting her involved, but it was clear that Liliana had another destination in mind.

Oh, Liliana, please be safe...

Chapter Fifteen

A Thousand Torches

Liliana raced through the streets of the city. She was not used to moving this fast on foot. But she had to find Raphael and warn him about what was going on. If things went correctly, Athelstan would be dead by the morning.

But that would not save Raphael.

That was why she had not been with her mother during the confrontation - the real reason, that is to say. She would've loved to put him down as well for killing her father, but she also wanted to save Raphael. And in the end, the latter desire triumphed.

She first went to the soup kitchen Raphael had established, only to find it burned to the ground. She sighed, watching the backs of the humans who were tossing torches into the conflagration. Word had gone around the city that a werewolf had slain Mayor Corvin, the first human mayor in all of the city's history. Even though it had been Raphael and Abraham who brought the mayor to the hospital, most people had not seen this happen. And as it was said, a lie can travel around the world before the truth can even get out the door.

There was a massive human mob roaming through the city, trying to get its hands on any werewolf it could find. Liliana had a sneaking suspicion that several of Athelstan's agents must have been the ones who had caused the rumors to spread in the first place, and a mob was a dangerous thing which did not heed either logic or reason.

She then turned towards their house. Although she had never been to the area, she knew its general location from what Raphael had told her, only to find a massive crowd there as well, far larger than the one gathered outside the burnt remnants of his soup kitchen.

None of them seemed to have entered the building yet, but the crowd was twenty thousand strong. Without a doubt, some of them had silver and were just looking for a chance to be able to hurt a werewolf - any werewolf.

Liliana scanned the nearby area, observing the scene while perched atop a rooftop. The sea of human heads and torches beneath her formed an amorphous dark blob, interspersed in the night like a starry sea mirroring the view above.

And then Liliana saw it. There was movement from within the building. Whether that was the Cain family itself or one of the servants, she did not care much. What should she do, though? Several ideas came to her, but the one that she felt was the most direct and the most likely to succeed was also the most dangerous. But as she thought of what might happen to Raphael, should she not act...

These were interspersed with memories of that night. The Night of a Thousand Torches. When she had been cowering in her castle, only to find her father murdered soon after.

No...

She wouldn't let that happen.

Not again.

"Wait! All of you, wait!" Liliana said, descending from the rooftop and revealing herself to the crowd.

A few faces turned, catching a sight of her crimson-red eyes and flinching, before someone recognized her. "It's Lady Liliana! Lady Liliana of the Light!"

"Is she here to save us?"

"Lady Liliana!" they cried out.

"The werewolves have attacked us!"

"Please, we need your help!"

"Humans can't fight werewolves on their own. If you offered your help, we could deal with them more easily."

"Please help us avenge Mayor Corvin."

She had no idea why she had been turned into such a saint-like figure in the eyes of the general public and neither did Raphael, but it was rather simple. The humans of Necropolis had always hoped to see a savior among the vampires one day. They had both feared and revered their undead overlords, and some part deep within them had been looking for a hero amongst the vampires whom they could put their faith in. And so, they had latched upon Liliana's small act of kindness."

"Of course. I will help you all. But please, allow me to speak to all of you."

Up until now, only about a few thousand people had recognized her but word of her existence spread. The crowd melted wherever she walked as she made her way toward the Cain Household. The chattering and angry shouts of the mob died down as they saw her, even as she continuously felt a growing sense of apprehension.

Ordinarily, the humans would be the ones terrified of a vampire.

However, right now, walking through what was basically an army who could have very easily killed her given its numbers; the roles had been reversed. It wasn't just numbers - the humans were not dumb, many of them must have been wandering around carrying garlic and silver in their pockets even on ordinary days given they lived in Necropolis, let alone during a night like this.

She would be helpless if they turned against her, and yet not one of them attempted so much as touch a hair upon her head. No, they seemed to be genuinely curious as to what she was going to say.

She had never asked for any fancy title like 'Lady Liliana of the Light.' Yet, it had been thrust upon her unwillingly.

Now though, she was grateful for it, because she could use it to her advantage. And if it could save Raphael and his family, she would gladly accept it.

She noted that the mob did not seem to have any specific leader in question. There were only those who seemed to be in charge of small factions within the mob. She asked them to come with her as she made her way to the front of the building in order to speak.

"Humans, hear me. For those of you who may not recognize me, my name is Liliana. Some of you have dubbed me as Lady Liliana of the Light. Though I have never thought of myself as a savior, simply someone who has once helped a human in need."

Her voice, of course, could not reach the entire crowd. However, there were people to relay her words to those where her voice could not reach.

"Many of you are here, I see, in order to take your vengeance against the Cain family or perhaps against werewolves in general for what they have done to your mayor. Perhaps you are even hoping that I would join you in your crusade against them. However, let me assure you that these werewolves had nothing to do with the mayor's death."

There were noises of disagreement from the crowd and several people shaking their heads.

"Indeed," she continued. "The person who was responsible was a werewolf, but not from within Necropolis. I know the werewolf in question. His name is Quickpaw. He comes from near the Darkling Woods. He is not one of them. He was brought into the city to sow discord between humans and werewolves and to plunge the city into chaos."

She glanced around quickly. In the distance, she could see other fires burning and crowds milling through the streets. Were they all here to riot? Some of them must have been people who were simply scared and looking for places to hide. Her memories took her to that terrifying night, but she kept them at bay.

Several things had happened since that night which she would never have imagined even in her wildest dreams.

She had not known that she would fall in love with Raphael, that he would end up with her, that Athelstan would do what he did, or that the two of them together would rescue a human child. And yet all of that had led them to this point - to a point where she could finally take action.

"I implore all of you to return to your houses. This is not a night for violence. The Cain family has done nothing but attempt to help the humans. I am sure many of you remember, and several of you would have benefited from his kindness as well. Justice will prevail," Liliana said. "But it will not be found at the hands of a mob. It will not be attained by hurting innocents, whether they be human or werewolf. I ask that you all disperse and wait for justice to finally be done, and this shall be done in the proper manner. Not in this kind of a way."

Her words, as they were relayed to the rest of the crowd, did seem to touch them. Many of them began returning to their homes. As far as she could tell, this was the largest mob which had assembled within the city, and so long as this could be diffused, it would likely have negative feedback upon any others which would also die out. The truth would spread throughout the city, and hopefully, things would calm down once the crowd was gone.

She knocked on the door of the building, asking to be let in. A very scared-looking teenage girl opened the door. She appeared to be one of the servants of the Cain household. She was pushed aside by Raphael.

The two of them looked at each other for a moment before embracing.

"Why did you do that? You could've gotten yourself killed," Raphael asked.

"And what if you'd died? Do you think I could've stood by while that happened."

"A-hem," a voice nearly snarled, breaking them apart. It was Abraham, glaring at Liliana.

"Dad I can explain-"

"No, I think I've figured things out well enough," Abraham said. "But for now, let's get out of here before another mob shows up."

They could've dived into the waves a long time ago to escape, but had stayed as the servants had been trapped as well. Now, the humans left for their houses as they traveled by the sea to a spot that Raphael and Abraham knew of.

The cold ocean water greeted them as they swam to an isolated grove twenty miles away. Liliana had gone swimming before, but only within the large baths of her castle. Despite having no experience, it was intuitive enough, and it wasn't like she could drown.

The grove in question seemed to be used as a hunting spot by the Lycans as there were several of them there already. They all turned towards Liliana with venomous gazes instinctively though Raphael and Abraham told them to stay their claws.

They had a few moments to catch their breath before Abraham noted that they were safe and it was finally time to address the elephant in the room.

"About the girl," Abraham said.

"Dad, I love her," Raphael blurted out. He had been thinking that the moment would be far more impressive, with him going on a long and impressive speech, not just uttering those words and being soaked to the bone.

"Do you truly want to be with her? Do you really love her?"

"Yes, Father," Raphael said.

"In such a case," Abraham said, walking ten paces away before turning around to glare at his son. "Fight me."

165

"W-what?"

"You heard me. Fight me. Back in the day in the wilderness, whenever there would be a dispute between werewolves, they wouldn't handle it like you would in the city, not through the law, not through rules or regulations, but through fighting," Abraham said. "Why don't we? We may try to stay within the city, Raphael, but deep down, we are far closer to that werewolf who was killed in the City Square than we might care to admit. You say you love her. You want to marry her? I forbid it, though, if you can defeat me. I will acknowledge you as being right and you may go ahead."

Abraham then transformed into his Lycanthrope form, glaring at Raphael, who withdrew ever so slightly.

"What are you waiting for?" Abraham asked. "You said you loved her, didn't you? Are you afraid to stand up for her?"

"Abraham, please. This does not need to get to this point-" Liliana was about to say before the werewolf growled at her.

"Girl, I'm going to need you to be quiet. This is between him and I. A werewolf tradition as old as time. There's no point in a *leech* interjecting between us."

"Father, you really don't need to use that kind of language especially when-"

"Oh, in that case, why don't you shut me up?"

Raphael sighed. He did not want to fight his father. However, it was clear that those last words were an attempt to rile him up. "Father, I don't want to fight you. But if this is what it comes to..."

He then transformed, bursting through his clothes as he turned into his Lycanthrope form, staring down his father.

"Fights between Lycanthropes like this are always one-on-one," Vincent said to Liliana as he approached from the crowd of spectators, pulling her away. None of the werewolves were doing anything about the situation, only watching. "If Raphael wants to earn his father's respect, he's going to have to do it the hard way."

Raphael and his father circled each other, eyes scanning each other from head to tail, watching to see if there was a weakness. It was clear from Raphael's behavior - the way his shoulders sagged, the way his eyes darted a bit too quickly - that he was not really into this entire fight. At the same time, though, he knew that his father was right. If he wanted to live life on his own terms, just like he had always dreamed, he would need to stand up for himself sooner or later.

The two of them circled each other for ten minutes. Ordinary wolves would also do this, looking for any kind of opening before they pounced. But this had already gone on for what was an eternity compared to ordinary werewolf fights, which would have been over by this point. Neither of them, however, seemed to want to strike first.

Finally, Abraham let out an ear-shattering growl. Raphael had thought that he had been loud when he had called to his teammates back when first

166

facing Quickpaw, but that was like a kitten's mewing compared to this lion's roar. Despite flinching, he continued to hold his ground.

"So, it's like that, then," his father said. He stopped glaring at Raphael, and the killing intent he was sending in his direction eased up as well. "Fine then. I concede."

There was silence all around. "I'm sorry, what?" Raphael said, confused.

"You're clearly willing to stake everything for her. I simply wanted to see how far the two of you had gotten along," Abraham said. "But if it's really reached this point, then there's nothing I can do. I think, short of killing you. You've earned my respect. Whatever you want to do regarding this girl, I don't agree with it, and you know what my feelings are regarding vampires. But if you truly do love her, I won't stand in your way."

Raphael was more shocked more by this than the preceding events that night. And this shock was followed by a burst of joy in his heart. There was nothing else that he would've loved to hear more than this!

"Thank you thank you thank you thank you!" he yelled out, tackling his father to the ground, both still in their werewolf forms, though they were no longer sizing each up to fight but rather rolling around like puppies playing with each other.

Liliana would've almost found it cute but then her eyes turned to the other werewolves. They did not seem to be as accepting of her as Abraham was, but neither did they challenge her.

"Liliana, how did you get here? I mean, your mother let you come find us?" Raphael asked once he had left his father's furry embrace.

"Well, it's a long story. See..."

***

By the next morning, things in the city had calmed down. Victoria had spoken to the Council of Elders when they had reconvened, and the potential force being assembled against the werewolves was called off. Athelstan's two co-conspirators broke down rather easily when questioned and were slated for execution by the rest of the Council of Elders.

As for Victoria herself, she framed her killing of Athelstan as a form of self-defense. No one doubted that he might be deranged enough to attack her, and the trial for that was still going on, though things were in her favor. Victoria felt no guilt for this subterfuge. If she ended up dead, or exiled, who would take care of Liliana? Nor did she feel any regret for what she had done to Athelstan.

With an outright war averted and the mob quieted, the humans elected a new mayor a month later. It was Corvin's daughter, who, after seeing how much her father had given to the city, had decided to run and won in a landslide victory. Clearly, people were quite sympathetic to her and her family. She helped put a portion of her own family's budget toward repairing parts of the city which had been damaged by the mob, including the Cain Soup Kitchen, which she had praised as being an excellent display of werewolf generosity.

Liliana's reputation had soared through the city once more, with Lady Liliana of the Light being a title she would not be able to shake off for the rest of her days. Before, people had been drawing cartoons or making paintings of her. Now, they were preparing to have statues erected in her honor. She found the prospect to be quite daunting. She had never intended to become some kind of public figure.

"Oh, but now that they look up to you, you'll just have to do it," Beatrice said at the new mayor's inauguration party. "You can't possibly let them down."

Many people of influence were there. It was quite similar to the first party that took place just a while back. However, now, when Victoria and Abraham happened to run into each other, they did not glare at each other with as much enmity as before.

There was still lingering tension between the two of them and it was far from cordial, but they weren't leaping at each other's throats either. As the two of them sat down in a corner away from the main body of the party, Victoria said, "We narrowly managed to avoid a war which could have possibly gotten all of us killed."

"Indeed," Abraham said. "And we can't go ahead and risk something like that happening again."

Several things had become quite clear. One was that the humans really were the new rulers of the city, capable of threatening either the vampires or the werewolves, depending on who they supported. Secondly, the werewolves and the vampires could absolutely not fight, given this, because regardless of who won, it would result in both of them being wiped out.

The Sutherland Shipping Company was not going to be very happy that one of their key executives had been killed on their soil, and future trade with Solaris was definitely going to suffer for the coming years. In such a situation, they all had to band together even more than otherwise would.

Yet how to do so? Tensions were naturally still high between both groups. The werewolves blamed the vampires for instigating all of this, while the vampires said they had already dealt with the responsible party and that it had been Athelstan and Athelstan alone who had been acting.

In such a situation, it was hard to come to a concord between the two parties.

Historically, one of the oldest ways to seal this kind of deal was through a marriage between two key individuals of each side.

Neither Abraham nor Victoria would've ever thought of 'sacrificing' their children just for the sake of peace by forcing them into such a marriage. But if they happened to want so willingly…

"A marriage alliance between us seems to be the only way to move things forward," Victoria said.

"I'm quite flattered," Abraham said. "But you're not exactly my type." He chuckled at his own joke, but Victoria simply narrowed her eyes.

"Please don't make such jokes at the actual wedding," Victoria said.

The two of them glanced toward the center of the room. There was a reason why no one was really paying attention to them, even as they talked - though the two of them speaking on such relatively friendly terms would have ordinarily been front-page news.

That was because everyone was instead focused on an even more peculiar sight: a vampire and a werewolf dancing together, locked in each other's embrace, their eyes staring at each other not with hatred or killing intent, but with admiration and adoration.

"Am I dreaming, or is that really happening?"

"I don't think I'm dreaming, but I can't believe it."

"Neither can I."

Whispers of disbelief echoed throughout the room.

"Well, then, if that's what they want," Abraham said. "I don't really think there's anything we can do to stop them."

Epilogue

One Year Later

As many people had feared, it turned out that trade with the Sutherland Shipping Company and Solaris in general had taken a hit after his death. As the events of what had happened surrounding Mayor Corvin's death were cleared up, sentiments towards the vampires had worsened (with the exception of Liliana) and those toward the werewolves had improved.

Liliana had now become something of a folk hero, not only for her actions in saving a child or for her actions during the mob, but also for the steps she had taken in order to establish peace between the vampires and werewolves; efforts which would finally bear fruit today.

Because today, Raphael and Liliana were going to marry each other.

An event historians would talk about for centuries. A romance that would be told and retold by the bards over and over. The symbolic end to the long-running feud between the werewolves and vampires.

Liliana wore a black dress dark as the night sky itself as was customary among vampire brides. She did not wear a single speck of silver out of respect for the werewolves but was instead adorned with golden earrings and a necklace of rubies that complimented her eyes.

"Are you sure you want to go through with this?" Abraham asked Raphael as the latter straightened his suit some distance from the venue. Raphael was wearing a traditional tuxedo, and although he still looked somewhat uncomfortable in it, when Liliana later saw him, she could not deny the sentiment that he was the most handsome man she had ever laid eyes upon.

"Yes, I'm sure about it."

"You know, you don't necessarily have to do this in order to maintain peace or anything," Abraham said. "Because there are other people who might be willing to bite the bullet by-"

"Thanks for your concern," Raphael said, slapping him on the shoulder. "But no."

As he walked into the venue, he saw Liliana standing at the altar, looking every bit as beautiful as the day he had first laid eyes upon her. No, that was wrong. She looked far more beautiful. Victoria and Beatrice clung closely to her.

Abraham and Victoria still glared at each other with suspicion. Undoubtedly, this relationship was only the first step in what would be a long-term effort to mend the relationship between the two factions. However, while that was a nice side bonus, it was not why the two of them were getting married.

No. That was just the icing on the cake.

They were getting married because they loved each other.

"I love you."

"And I love you."

The two of them intoned that as Raphael approached the altar, much to the cheers of the vampires, werewolves, and humans within the crowd. It was early in the night when the ceremony took place, the stars twinkling above them, countless diamonds showering blessings upon the two lovers, who were at long last, together.

Other Works by Drechenaux

The Vampire in the Mirror

I Buy People's Souls off the Dark Web & Other Stories: An Anthology of Horror Stories